Summer
Flings and
Dancing Dreams

Summer
Flings and
Dancing Dreams

Sue Watson

bookouture

Acknowledgements

This book wouldn't exist without the wonderful team at Book-outure. Thanks to Emily Ruston who provided the inspiration, added the spangles and tightened the bodice. Thanks also to Kim Nash for editorial olive oil, and sparkly marketing magic and Jade Craddock who pulled the choreography together brilliantly, and added the sequins! As always a special thank you to Oliver Rhodes, who guided me with his usual wisdom, brilliance and fabulous footwork.

Thank you and lots of cream cakes to Russel Minton, for his friendship, advice, expertise, afternoon teas - and for teaching me the Argentine Tango in New St Station. Thanks to Barbara McLaughlin whose amazing knowledge of Flamenco dancing and culture provided me with a wealth of material for Laura's Spanish adventure and Flamenco passion. Thanks also to Patricia Skeet of hebdenbridgeflamenco.org.uk who shared with me her wonderful experiences of living a Flamenco life both in Spain and the UK. Thank you to the Escuela Carmen de las Cuevas, for allowing me to use their beautiful Flamenco school as a setting for the book.

Big thanks to my blogger friends and a special thank you to Anne John-Ligali at booksandauthors.co.uk for her support and 'writer chats.' And hugs and high fives to online BFF and 'spectacular book homie' - Katherine Everett at bestcrimebooksandmore.co.uk

Thanks to friends and family especially Nick and Eve Watson for putting up with me and for always making me laugh – sometimes unintentionally!

Finally, a very special thank you to my Mum, Patricia Engert – a huge 'Strictly Come Dancing' fan who knows her Paso Doble from her Argentine Tango – and who was happy to demonstrate in the name of research!

For my Mum,

Dance like nobody's watching...

Prologue

'But Mum, why?' she asked, her face looking into mine, tears spilling down oyster satin, bridal bouquet flung to the four winds. No one was there to catch it.

'I don't know, love... ' What could I say? My heart was lying with hers on the cold church steps.

'He seemed fine yesterday, what happened in the last twenty-four hours?'

I looked into her eyes and shook my head. I had nothing to offer her, no plaster to cover the graze, no ice cream to sweeten the bitter taste left in her mouth. All I could think was – how will we ever get over this? And in the middle of my daughter's devastation came the unbidden thought – would I still have to pay for the fucking finger buffet?

I hugged her. This wasn't about the wedding, not even about the controversial buffet at £20 per head to be served at 10 p.m. (on the off-chance that some greedy sod would still be hungry after the £60 per head dinner at 5 p.m.). Nor was it about the silk dress costing three months' salary, the perfect cake covered in fresh roses to match the perfectly pale scented bouquets and table arrangements. Oh the table arrangements – it was March, so roses apparently had to be imported from Kenya – and though I insisted Sophie have everything she wanted, I couldn't help wonder if it would have been cheaper to fly there first class and collect them myself.

'What do we do now?' she asked.

I didn't mention the obvious – which was that we could make a start on eating that finger buffet for five-hundred. I didn't know what to say, I ripped off my powder blue fascinator and we gazed out at the church garden, like the answer lay somewhere among the vicar's host of golden daffodils. The magnolia was almost over, waxy white petals lay on the ground, huge, overblown blooms too beautiful to last longer than a week or two. Is that what happened to Sophie and Alex? Was it all too beautiful, to last? We'd certainly aimed for beauty and perfection with this wedding. As a single Mum I was determined to pay for the wedding with overtime at the supermarket where I worked and late shifts, constant saving and scrimping on everything had paid for the dress, the flowers, and the reception. Then, just when I'd thought it was safe – the vicar had wanted his cut – can you believe it? Even God was on the wedding bandwagon these days. My desire to give Sophie the best of everything apparently gave people the impression I was the wealthy mother of the bride sparing no expense at her only daughter's special day. This was all true – except the 'wealthy' bit.

Nothing was too much, no night shift too long, no sacrifice too great. Our Sophie's wedding would be the best day of her life – and probably mine too. After years of struggling as a single mum, watching her walk down that aisle into the arms of a doctor would be my proudest moment – and, until about twenty minutes before, she was the glowing, beautiful bride I'd always dreamed she'd be. The beautifully fitting gown in a delicate nude shade warmed her pale complexion, enhanced her lovely figure, and made her long blonde hair glow in the spring sunshine.

I looked at Sophie, my beautiful only child, now twenty four – she would have all the things I never had. Sophie my torchbearer, taking her life into a world I couldn't even contemplate with her law degree and junior doctor fiancé. Sophie would have the detached home in that leafy suburb and blonde, Boden-clad children. My daughter would enjoy holidays by a foreign sea and her own career, her own life, and even in all this, she'd enjoy financial freedom. I'd never believed the magazines of my youth that said you could 'have it all,' but perhaps the fairy tale was finally coming true for my daughter's generation. If both partners had a career the odds were good that they would achieve the freedom and independence that money brought with it. Money had always been a problem for me – it had never come easy – even as a child we'd lived on very little. My dad, the eternal optimist, had an unhealthy relationship with money and I'd vowed to live differently.

Nothing was too good for my daughter and I'd made sure she was never short of anything, even if that was sometimes difficult. But I knew education was the key and would bring her a life neither me nor my parents had and encouraged her to work hard at school. I was also keen to give motherly advice about boyfriends. There was a slight glitch around 2007 when she brought home an unemployed musician and declared her undying love, but to my relief it was just a phase – and like her 2004 Goth period, she moved on. Sitting in an empty churchyard now with my daughter sobbing on my shoulder, I almost smiled at the irony. When Sophie had introduced me to Alex, the medical student boyfriend from university I thought it was 'Mother's Day', and my work here was done. My daughter had a doctor and I could die happy.

Alex's parents (a house in Portugal, two cleaners and a Porsche) had offered to contribute to the wedding, but pride got the better of me.

'No, no, no the bride's family will pay, it's tradition,' I heard myself say, as my brain screamed 'help... the bride doesn't have a family, only me and my ageing mother who hasn't earned a penny in her life.'

'If I can't give my daughter the proper send-off I've failed as a mother,' I'd said to Sophie, who to her credit told me I was a good mother and I didn't need to prove it by going bankrupt.

'Vol-au-vents would have been fine,' she'd sighed when I told her they were too seventies and Alex's mother would be horrified.

'We could have said we were being ironic?' Sophie had offered, but I wasn't giving that smug mother of the groom anything to turn up her nose at. Besides, my own mother would have been repulsed at such lack of culinary taste.

There were moments when I wondered if I'd taken too much on. Alex's parents with their six-figure salary, weekly flower delivery, and home in Monte Carlo would have been able to pay for the lot in one go without even feeling it. But it was the thought of

Alex's mother Anastasia in her designer gear and pitying face that spurred me on during those endless shifts on the tills. Each 'hello' and 'do you have a loyalty card?' and 'pop your card in there please' took me closer to giving my daughter the best day of her life and showing Anastasia, and her snobby friends that I was just as good as they were.

The catering alone cost me several months' salary, and when Anastasia wondered aloud if the planned scallops and chorizo were 'a bit of a cliché?' I smiled through my teeth, resisted the desire to punch her on the nose and went back to the menu for something apparently less of a sodding cliché.

'I wonder if pork pies are considered a cliché?' I'd said in Anastasia's posh tones to my friend Carole as we stacked shelves and filled freezers at the supermarket.

'Ooh love – not just a cliché, a working-class cliché,' she said. I waved a bag of mini pasties and we laughed at the prospect of Alex's mother and her cronies chowing down on supermarket finger food and frozen pastries from our optimistically named 'party range'. So it was Anastasia's cuisine of choice that I was working extra shifts for – and my calloused hands and blistered feet equalled seared pole-caught tuna canapés drizzled with a virgin olive oil and balsamic infusion.

'How can you even prove it's pole caught?' Carole asked.

I shook my head; 'I've no idea, but I reckon they're charging me for the poles, the fishermen and the bloody boats.'

Even my mother, who was partial to a bit of food snobbery was overcome by the drizzling and the foam.

'I will never understand why Alex's mother has to have balsam-ic virgins on her tarts,' was her confused response when I showed her the wedding breakfast menu. Don't get me wrong, I appreciate the finer things in life, but in order for five hundred people I'd never met to enjoy those fine things, I had to work every hour God sent. And as we know, God was charging me too. So after menus, dresses, cakes and flowers pored over for months it finally felt like we were getting there and I arrived in the bridal car with Sophie a few minutes late as is usual for the bride. Keep him guessing until the very last moment. But as we'd waited by the car just yards from the church it soon became clear that despite forensic planning, and the backing of God and his balsamic virgins, something was missing – we were minus a groom.

There followed an awkward wait outside the church, and many frantic, unanswered phone calls to Alex and the local hospital to check if he'd been involved in an accident. When we finally got the news I couldn't speak to the groom's parents, who shuffled through the church grounds without making eye contact. I made a vague and embarrassed announcement and the guests left, mortified, muttering vague clichés and condolences. And here we were now, just Sophie and me both desperately trying to come to terms with what had happened. Black mascara tears ran down her lovely face, her world had, that afternoon in May simply shuddered to a halt.

A text. That was all he'd sent her. He'd been too much of a coward to call and say he couldn't go through with it. I stroked her hair in the same way I did when she was little and had fallen off her bike. This would need more than a sticking plaster and a mug of hot chocolate. I just kept saying over and over in my head that it was going to be okay and it was all meant to be – I believed in fate – it had helped me through so much in the past. But at this precise moment in time it was hard to see why Alex, the eligible groom with a career in medicine and a car that cost my annual wage, would do this. I knew one thing though – if I could get my hands on the bastard I would probably be up for murder.

'What about the honeymoon... and the wedding presents?' she was saying through sobs. She didn't really care about any of that, it was, I guessed, part of the grieving process she was beginning to go through, a checklist of everything that had been destroyed by him. All I could think was how many innovative and untraceable ways I could torture and kill my son-in-law-never-to-be.

'It will all make sense one day...' I offered, half-heartedly, while cradling my daughter's head in my arms. I wanted to say 'come home love, the world's cruel, you can't trust anyone – especially men, they leave you... they always leave you one way or another.'

'Perhaps it's meant to be?' I said instead, once more allowing fate to relieve us of any responsibility – it wasn't our fault, it was that bitch fate. But Sophie pulled away, her mascara-stained face looking straight at me.

'Meant to be? Being stood up at the altar?'

The look on her face was incredulity.

'Sorry darling, I wasn't trying to trivialise the situation...'

'You just did. How can you say that... even *think* it, Mum?' she was angry now, taking out her hurt on me. The man who'd caused it was elsewhere, I would be the punchbag – but that was okay, after all it was part of the job description of 'being mum'.

'I just wanted to point out that perhaps, in the future, you might think he did you a favour... I mean would you want a man who could do this to you on your wedding day?' I saw by her face I was making it so much worse.

'Yes... let's just fast forward this bit shall we? Oh we'll laugh about it this time next year – this time never,' she spat through her tears.

'Darling... I didn't mean...'

She pulled away, her head slowly shaking. I spotted the vicar peering from behind the door, he was taking pantomime steps across the gravel and making an 'o' shape with his mouth in a clumsy attempt to convey concern. I was torn between bursting into laughter or tears. Was that the best a vicar could do at a time like this? I smiled politely and looked away, resisting the urge to hurl something at him and shriek 'where is your God now?' If he thought he could squeeze some more money out of me now for a ceremony that never happened I planned to hit him with my £100 powder blue Phase Eight clutch bag. In fact the only reason I wasn't hurling it across the gravel now was because I was hoping to take it back to the shop.

I would be sending a very stiff email to 'God.com' when all this was over, telling him and his staff to sort their shit out. No wonder people were going to supermarkets on a Sunday instead of going to Jesus. Sophie and I would laugh about the vicar and his silly walk one day, wouldn't we? I didn't point it out then, I'd said enough, but like toothache I had to keep prodding it with my tongue and looked at Sophie while searching my brain for reasons why her life would be better without Alex. I was just about to say something quite nasty and probably unforgiveable about Alex's mother when Sophie spoke, '"I can't go through with it," he said in his text. 'He made marrying me sound like a visit to the electric chair. What did I do wrong Mum? Alex was supposed to save me, take me away from it all... from you...' she held her hands up in the air.

'Save you? From me...?' I said gently, my heart suddenly hurting, my head now to one side like a dog trying to make sense of a strange noise.

'No I don't mean... that he would save me from you... I meant save me from becoming you, here, in your little life in this little town. I love you Mum, but I don't want to be you... I don't want to be left behind here. I don't want to turn round in twenty years and find myself single, working on a checkout with no future in my forties. I don't want my life to exist only between series of Strictly Come Dancing on a Saturday night clutching a glass of Pinot and imagining it's me on the dance floor. I want a real life – a big life – and Alex was my chance... he would have choppered me right out of here.'

I was devastated. I felt the cold stone under my bum and the knife in my heart, the wind rustled through the trees and I pulled the hydrangea blue pashmina round my shoulders.

'That's a bit harsh love...' I started, trying hard not to let my hurt show but unable to leave this alone, she'd never said anything like it before. 'I'm happy after all... my life isn't that bad,'

I almost added that I didn't always clutch a glass of Pinot, some-times I pushed the boat out and bought a nice Merlot and a bag of Thorntons chocolate caramels. But I felt that might be proving her point... not about Strictly Come Dancing, but about me hav-ing a little life.

'No offence...' she started, which usually means one is about to be hit with a truck load of offence that hurts like hell, so I braced myself. 'But Mum... I just don't want that for me... I want so much more.' she said quietly.

We sat for a while in silence. This was Sophie's day to be hurt, distressed, it wasn't a time for me to be self-indulgent and all wounded and tearful. I was already feeling her own pain as keenly as if it were mine, first-hand, I was living through her devastation, but to now have more piled on top was almost more than I could bear. Who did Sophie think I was? Did my daughter think she was unique in wanting a bigger life? Had it never occurred to her that I might just have wanted more too, but that it isn't always a mat-ter of choice? This was the child to whom I'd devoted my life and given up so much for – I didn't want gratefulness, even acknowl-edgement, but I would have liked her respect, her understanding even. Then I thought about my life and realised she had nothing to respect me for. All she saw was a mother who worked on the checkout at Bilton's and nothing else, no future, no goals, noth-ing to look forward to – the only fun in my life was a Saturday evening dance show. I was nothing for her to be proud of. And as I watched the final waxy petals fall slowly to the ground I realised I wasn't very proud of me either.

Chapter One

Six Months Later

Frozen Faggots and Little Lives

'What's the weather like out there?' I asked, I had arrived in the dark and would leave in the dark. The world could have ended and I wouldn't have a clue, I'd just keep pushing groceries through that checkout and making small talk about the weather as we raged into the apocalypse.

'It's beautiful. The sun's blazing, it's too warm really,' the woman smiled, almost apologetically. I clutched at the box of frozen faggots sighing at the delicious prospect of sun on my face while my machine beeped on and on and on.

'Do you have a loyalty card?' I asked, for the millionth time that day. She shook her head as she filled plastic bags with shopping. Her life was clearly too full to be bothered with little bits of plastic that may one day reward her with a voucher for a dodgy pizza restaurant somewhere in Redditch. She thanked me politely and wandered off into the shimmering heat of the dusty car park. How I envied her.

'Would you like me to help you pack?' I asked the next customer, feigning enthusiasm for the task. He shook his head, too engrossed in the phone conversation he was having with someone on the outside world. He stabbed his finger at the chewing gum near my till, I reached to where he was pointing, but it clearly wasn't the one he wanted. His brow was now furrowed and he was wagging his finger more urgently, presumably expecting me to be fluent in finger-wagging-chewing-gum-selection.

I just sat there miming as the queue grew bigger. At no point did he even consider interrupting his phone conversation to communicate verbally with me. Eventually he shook his head like I was too stupid to understand and with a dismissive wave of the hand he indicated with his finger that he wanted me to ring up the total. How I longed to indicate with my own finger what I wanted him to do – but I just smiled – and did as his hand had requested. After all, the customer is always right.

'Do you have a loyalty card?' I asked the next shopper who was equally brusque and non-communicative. She shook her head vigorously and I had an almost uncontrollable urge to speak with an Italian accent. I found it sometimes helped to do this if I was stressed or bored, to pretend I was someone else, in another country. The compulsion to say inappropriate things in strange accents had become much stronger of late. My friend Big Carole said I was having a midlife and it didn't help being stuck behind a checkout all day at 'Bilton's – where budgets matter'.

I used to laugh about the customers – but they weren't funny anymore. I kept thinking about what Sophie had said about me having a little life and now I saw the pity in their eyes, sometimes even the contempt for someone stuck in a life like mine.

'You're in a middle-aged menopausal rut. You need to get out, do something different – get a boyfriend now Sophie's off your hands,' Carole had said, echoing my daughter's comments about me having no life.

'Oh well, why didn't you say? I'll get out from behind this checkout and spend time at my south of France apartment with one of my many rampant lovers instead,' I'd said. 'That way I won't know if it's a hot flush or the heat of the Mediterranean sun on my face.'

'Oh what's got into you Miss Sarcastic knickers,' she'd snapped. 'I was only giving advice – I'm six months older than you and I've been on that menopausal flight already.'

'Yes, well, I don't need your advice on how to fasten my safety belt, thank you. I might be forty four, but I'm not quite menopausal, just bored. Why is it that we blame our periods for our bad moods and down days? Even when they stop, they get the blame for why we're fed up with our mind-shrinking-job-hating-groundhog-day lives.'

'Oh, listen to you coming over all Mariella Frostrup with your long words and your high drama; "Oh darling…I'm going to die if I don't get out of here and read some Tolstoy."'

I'd laughed at that. Carole could always make me laugh, even when I was worried sick about my daughter or depressed about my life. Sophie was so precious, my biggest fear was losing her, and now she'd gone to the other side of the world to get over her heartbreak. Carole thought the answer was for me to get a man and take my mind off Sophie – but it was easier said than done.

'It's your time now, Laura,' she'd said.

But I'd never had much luck with men. I was scared of losing anyone I loved, so it wasn't easy for me to give my heart away. The other issue with Carole's 'get a boyfriend' plan was that I wasn't exactly drowning in suitors. Funnily enough my chunky body, bespectacled face and total lack of confidence had rarely enticed men into my bed or my life. But it wasn't just about looks, I'd had Sophie very young and was changing nappies and running from work to collect at nursery and school while my friends met the loves of their lives in pubs, on trains, at work...They had the time and the money as younger women to make the most of themselves but I'd never had time to worry about my appearance. The few boyfriends I had (including Sophie's dad) left me just after conception, without whisper of a wedding and I decided I was destined to live alone.

So I happily celebrated my friends' engagements, played Maid of Honour, organised the hen nights and went back to my little life when it was all over. I'd once dreamed of being a bride, living happily ever after, but having arranged as many divorce parties as I had hen nights by the time I was thirty five - I wasn't convinced a man was the answer. I'd been alone too long to let a man into my life, but I needed something in my life other than work and worrying about Sophie. She was in her twenties with a degree and a big career ahead, but she was still my little girl.

Apart from the fact it broke my heart for her to go, I had to admire my daughter who, after being left at the altar, had taken life by 'the testicles' (her words, the legacy of being engaged to a doctor who insisted on the correct anatomical terms for everything). I knew it would be good for Sophie to lick her wounds and see the world and I also knew I had let her go and live her life. This wasn't easy for me and I confess there was an undignified scene at the airport involving me climbing up a security man's legs demanding he let me on the plane for a last goodbye that I'd rather forget.

I always wanted our lives to be cosy and safe, but seeing 'cosy and safe' through my daughter's eyes now translated to 'small and risk-averse'. I couldn't shake the feeling I'd had that day when Sophie had pointed out how small my life was as we sat on the steps of the church - and I felt so pointless. I'd never stepped out of my comfort zone because for years I'd been tied down by lack of money and being a single parent, but I'd been happy enough. But after what Sophie said I was now asking myself, 'Is happy enough good enough?'

I don't blame Sophie for wanting more it's what I wanted for her too. What child hasn't looked at their parents at some point and thought 'I won't be doing that when I'm their age.' I just wish she hadn't told me.

We had spent six months mourning the death of her relationship and the terrible wedding day that didn't take place. In that time she'd taken a sabbatical from the law firm where she worked and channelled her anger and hurt into a new adventure.

When Alex's parents had insisted on covering the costs of the cancelled wedding, I said no. But Sophie had called and informed them it was the least they could do and when they put £20,000

into her bank account she handed it straight to me. I was horrified; but she insisted I have it. 'Do something for yourself with it,
Mum. Besides,' she said, 'I can't bear to have their guilt money in
my account.'

I'd put some of the money towards my mum's care home bill,
but when Sophie told me of her plans to go travelling I put what
was left into her account. I remember the day I paid it in thinking
'what would I do with this?' Having a lump of money like that in
the bank that wasn't earmarked for bills or essentials would be quite
a luxury. It wasn't life-changing, but it would be possible, and very
tempting, to take a very long holiday from work and do the stuff
I never had the time or money for. I decided I would spend time
reading, travelling, learning to speak a foreign language. I wouldn't
fritter it, I'd spend it on something I'd look back on when I was old
and say, 'Yeah, I did that.' It made me think about Mum and her
life of regrets, the hard times my parents went through and how a
little money like this could have transformed their lives.

Despite my parents having no money when I was growing up,
it never stopped them chasing their dream. I had such wonderful memories of the three of us on family road trips to ballroom
competitions chugging around the country on a shoestring in our
clapped-out van. Dad would play the music loud on the radio
and they'd sing as he drove along, both so happy to be back on
the road. Despite the money worries, they loved each other very
much. I remember feeling safe from my sanctuary on the back
seat, mum and dad in the front. In the summer the car window
would be wound down, a breeze wafting music from the car radio

onto my face, anticipation and contentment filling me up. On winter travels I'd lie under a coat just listening to their voices, thinking, 'That's what love is.' Growing up in the middle of this relationship, I'd always assumed I would one day enjoy the same kind of love, that it was my destiny to have what they'd had. As a teenager I'd waited for it – the real love that made people laugh and cry and dance and hold each other in the darkness. But it had never come for me – I was still waiting.

❀ ❀ ❀

On Saturday night I settled down to watch the first in the new series of Strictly Come Dancing. Despite what Sophie had said about it being the only thing I did other than work I still longed for it to start and I was as excited and nervous as the contestants. It might sound silly for a grown woman to be excited about a TV dance competition, but it was so much more for me – it was a link with my past, my parents and the way we'd lived our lives. The music started and I was back there, a child watching Mum and Dad swish across the dance floor.

I couldn't wait for that first glance of the glitterball, the first chords of music, followed by the sparkle of sequins, the swoosh of satin swinging around taut, tanned legs. I settled in my chair as the presenters appeared and we met the judges, like old friends, I smiled at the screen. Even Sophie's comments disappeared into a puff of dry ice and glitter while the dancing was on. I could see her point and, from her perspective, I must have seemed like such a weirdo sitting there on my own smiling at Len and giggling at

Bruno like a crazed stalker. But in my head I wasn't on my sofa watching, I was there under the glitterball. I was moving across that shiny floor heading for the unparalleled joy that only a ten from Len could bring.

I gasped as the celebrities came on screen one by one, each with a new dress, a new story, a new take on an old dance. I decided that this series my fantasy partner would be Pasha Kovalev. He'd been voted out on the last series when his American Smooth failed to wow the judges... but he'd wowed me. I liked his strength, calmness and patience – and the fact his speciality was International Latin. The Latin section was my favourite, always so hot and fiery, with sexual tension bubbling just underneath the surface. I crunched on a Malteser imposter from my bag of Revels and thought how the sheer thrill of Latin dancing couldn't be further from my own life.

Within seconds my mood was dramatically lifted, the music swept me up and took me over and I forgot for a little while about me. I started tapping my toes, moving my upper body on the sofa (Sophie had witnessed this when she'd been home and joked about how 'disturbing' she found it). But sometimes sofa dancing just wasn't enough, the music and the rhythm was so bloody good I had to get up and dance. Occasionally they played something Mum and Dad had danced to, perhaps a waltz to a slow Frank Sinatra song, or more vigorous Spanish tango music. Those first few strains would drift into the air and I was five years old sitting in a ballroom somewhere in England watching Mum and Dad dance. I didn't understand the feeling that welled up in my chest as my parents waltzed by, but now I know it was sheer pride and I'd catch my breath as they, deliberately stopped near me to hold a pose. My father would twirl my mum round so she was facing me and she'd give me her secret smile. Then they'd twirl again so I was face to face with dad who would wink at me... and my five-year-old tummy would fill with glitter.

Watching the opening dance on TV, I was reminded of a pale blue dress Mum wore for the waltz. Dad said she looked like Grace Kelly, with her blonde hair in a French pleat and a string of pearls around her neck. She was such a cool, elegant dancer – her Viennese waltz was sweeping and graceful. Yes I'm biased but they were both so talented and apparently, when she was younger mum was spotted by a West End impresario. He'd promised her a glittering future in musical dance, but her mother, my gran wouldn't let her move to 'that London,' which was, according to her 'a fleshpot.' Mum was devastated, but then she met my dad, who put the sequins and salsa back into her world. She and my father had always been so ambitious for their dancing and their lives – but I wonder now if they expected too much from life?

'I watched the dancing last night, did you see it?' I said the following day to my mother over tea and out of date Battenberg at the Old People's Home she optimistically referred to as her 'retirement apartment'. She'd moved in several months before and it had given her a new lease of life after living alone for years in our old family home. She'd always seemed so sad, but having new friends in a lovely setting had really picked her up.

'What, love?'

Mum was deaf, but refused to acknowledge this and I some-times wondered if she chose what she wanted to hear. And as usual she didn't want to talk about the dancing on TV or any reminder of the dancing life she had with my dad. I would have loved to have talked about it, but it was never something I'd felt comfort-able asking about. There was so much left unsaid between Mum and I because I was afraid bringing up the past might hurt her. So as I bit into my Battenberg I abandoned Strictly Come Dancing and wondered what else I could talk to her about.

I wanted to tell her what Sophie had said and ask her opinion... did Mum think I had a little life too? I suppose I wanted her ap-proval, for her to say I was okay and my life wasn't a failure, but I wasn't sure she'd be quite so forgiving. As much as I tried not to say anything to hurt my mother, she was always happy to provide a brutally honest opinion on all aspects of my life.

Mum was now smiling imperiously at a group of ladies across the room, like a queen peering at her courtiers. My mother always behaved like a film star, believing she'd just missed her chance and was meant for better things. She always maintained that her life would have been quite different had Diana Dors not beaten her to a film audition for 'a pretty blonde' in 1942. No one was allowed to mention Diana's name in our house while I was growing up because apparently she'd 'ruined' my mother's acting career. But I reckoned even if mum had got the role my gran would have stepped in and refused to allow her to go to 'that London.'

Even now, Mum's still behaving like a bloody film star, I thought affectionately as she sipped her tea and nodded to her 'fans' Or should I say minions. Mind you, she might well have behaved like Hollywood royalty, she was living in an old people's home costing as much as a Hollywood mansion.

After a young life of never quite reaching the dizzy heights, Mum had been left vulnerable. And when she met my dad and found out he could dance I think she poured all her hopes and dreams into him. She constantly reminded him of what she'd apparently 'given up' and what she hoped he would bring to her life. Looking back, the guilt trips and the constant need to keep her happy, not to disappoint her, must have weighed heavily on my dad, but he never showed it. He loved her so much he just wanted to make her happy and forgave her anything.

Now in her eighties, my Mum lived off her own hype, telling everyone in the care home that she'd lived 'in Hollywood'. This wasn't a lie, but it wasn't the Hollywood with the hills and the film studios, it was the Hollywood in Wythall, near Birmingham. Mum had never been out of the UK.

She was sitting opposite me, legs crossed, head to one side like a confused bird.

'It's warm in here,' I said, going for an easy life – I decided not to tell her what Sophie had said. I think I was scared that she'd simply agree and add to the list of things I'd failed at in life.

She was still looking at me quizzically, unable to hear what I said, but making like I was the one with the problem and wasn't speaking up. But I was positively shouting in her face.

'Just saying Mum... it's hot in here. I AM HOT,' I shouted.

'That's because you don't do any exercise.'

'Really?'

'Yes you're getting bigger and bigger and...' she shouted this because, being deaf, she shouted everything. Private, personal and often acutely embarrassing information about me was regularly delivered to anyone within a ten mile radius.

'HOT... I said, I'm really HOT Mum, not really fat,' I shouted.

Those around us who could actually hear were weighing me up, and some were actually nodding in agreement. 'Her mother's right,' I heard one of them say. 'She should listen to her and lose some weight... letting herself go she is.'

Is everyone over the age of 70 given permission to say what they like about who they like – to their face?

'Enormous great tummy...' mother continued on her own, her chorus behind her. I turned away in an attempt to block out my mother's never-ending soliloquy to my weight. '...you should go on that Oxford Diet.'

'Cambridge...'

'Whatever for?'

'The diet... it's called The Cambridge Diet.'

'Yes you need to go on a diet – that's what I'm saying.'

I'd only been there half an hour and I'd hoovered up three slices of cake and lost the will to live. Conversations with my mother usually centred on my weight, my inability to find a decent job or man and my questionable mothering skills. And after a day surrounded by rude customers at the checkout it was just what I didn't need.

I can't blame age or deafness for my mother's brutal honesty, particularly when it comes to criticising me and my 'unfortunate shape', as she constantly referred to my body while I was growing up – and ever since. Even when I dieted down to 9 stone after Sophie was born, Mum said I needed to exercise 'the wobbly bits'. Oh yes, in the realms of super critic my mother had achieved a certain enviable excellence over the years and was clearly aiming for a 'lifetime achievement award'. I have always held my breath after her often used opening; 'Do you know what I think?' because invariably I didn't, nor would I want to – for it invariably involved an unasked for critique of me, my life, or my weight – and on special occasions all three. But since my daughter had jumped on the bandwagon with her 'little life' comment and joined my mother to co-write 'Laura's failed life and body – the novel', I wasn't in the mood for mother's remarks.

'Exercise... that's what you need,' she was still banging on, 'you need to move some of that wobbly...'

'I said HOT... I'm HOT MUM!'

'Hot? Oh why didn't you say?'

'I DID,'

I was now yelling in her face and Mrs Brown, the woman who kept an eye on 'the ladies and gentlemen of 'Wisteria Lodge', was now trundling towards me.

'Enunciate Laura, let her read your lips,' Mrs Brown was saying.

'Yes... I've told her about her hips.'

Oh God, I thought to myself, will this visit ever end?

'No, Mum, Mrs Brown isn't talking about my hips...'

'Who love?'

'Mrs Brown...

'Oh her...do you want to know what I think about her?' She leaned forward, asking this in a stage whisper.

'No Mum, and neither does she,' I muttered, standing up and suggesting we go through to Mum's room and leave before Mum regaled the communal area with her thoughts on Mrs Brown's shortcomings and booked her ticket out of there. Most of the residents were now gazing over at my mother's 'enormous' offspring, only a handful continuing on with their own lives. I guided her through the lounge, thinking how very genteel it all was, like a David Niven film from the forties. It was right up Mum's street, with tea and cake each afternoon and Vera Lynne and Bing Crosby on a permanent loop.

As Mum and I walked through we had to negotiate the traffic as Mr Harding attempted to dance with Mrs Saunders. He had one arm on her back and the other holding her hand and all was going well until Mrs Saunders' arthritic hip began to give way and they both landed in a heap on the floor. What had started out as a gentle foxtrot was beginning to look like OAP porn.

'Can somebody sort that out?' yelled Mrs Brown, gesticulating to a staff member from behind Mr Roberts. His gnarled fingers were playing provocatively with his waistband and threatening much worse than a deconstructed fox trot.

'Do you want to know what I think?' Mum said, ignoring Mr Roberts and the prospect of indecent exposure over the tea and cakes.

'I think you both need a dance lesson,' she laughed, marching over to survey the crumpled human heap, now groaning and clinging to each other. I spotted the fire in Mum's eyes, she was suddenly animated, brought alive by the prospect of dancing, she couldn't stand still if she tried. Mrs Brown called for back-up and the 'dancing' couple were placed upright on the floor, still using each other for ballast. 'Now hold her more tightly here Bill. Not like *that*, she's a beautiful woman, she's not a sack of potatoes are you Doris?' she grabbed Mr Harding's arm and manoeuvred it around, then she put both hands on Mrs Saunders' hips and straightened her up. With just a tweak they now looked like they might even be able to actually foxtrot and Mum swayed along with them as they staggered. It was interesting to note that Mum was probably older than both Mr Harding and Mrs Saunders, but she still had that swing in her hips, that rhythm in her step, I smiled as Mum rejoined me, pleased with her tutoring.

'You've still got it Mum,' I said.

'Yes I have. But Doris never had it, she dances like a bloody truck driver,' she said, in a loud aside. I gently took her arm and guided her away before she caused any offence and before Mr Roberts dropped his trousers and did a gentleman's excuse me.

The couple danced around us as I continued to usher mum out of the room. As she opened the door to her apartment she stood gazing around. Mum had insisted on living at Wisteria Lodge because it once featured in 'Country Life,' but it was expensive and my pay alone couldn't cover the fees. So Mum and I had talked about it, and our old family home was about to go on the market. Fortunately Mum didn't seem to miss it as much as I'd thought she would and had seemed to move on as soon as she had stepped into her room at Wisteria Lodge with its pink Laura Ashley sofa and antique coffee table.

How wonderful it would be to just turn your back on everything that made you unhappy or sad, to cast it off like an old rucksack and move on. As a single mum I'd had to make my own life. Okay, so it may not be everyone's idea of a big successful life, but I'd managed to keep the wheels on. I had a demanding mother, a young daughter, a full-time job and no partner - so I didn't have a lot of choice.

I suppose deep down I'd hoped something would change along the way. I'd seen it happen for other people – why not me? And for years I waited for that special someone to come into my life and make everything whole. But it never happened. I couldn't just blame fate – I didn't go out, I had no intention of online dating and had such a busy time juggling everything I'd have been too exhausted to notice if Mr Right was standing next to me.

And now, in what my daughter had referred to as my 'little' life I had suddenly become more conscious of my future, and the prospect of another twenty odd years behind the checkout. I also had the task of selling Mum's house and was completely daunted by the prospect of clearing thirty odd years of clutter from it first. Mum had left the house as she'd lived there – with her life in over-flowing cupboards stuffed with several hundred years' worth of glossy magazines and unworn designer clothes.

I looked at Mum now perfectly made-up, well-groomed with manicured nails and blow-dried hair, all available at OAP rates at Wisteria Lodge. She was settled on her pink sofa, leafing through *Hello* and confusing soap stars with their characters.

'I thought she was dead,' she said, holding up a picture of someone from Coronation Street.

'Well, *she's* not dead. She's the actress – she didn't die in real life, she just left the programme.'

'I know... she died of cancer,' she said very sombrely.

'Only in the programme, Mum.'

'But how did they get those pictures?'

She held the magazine up close to her face to read more about this apparently resurrected actress and marvel at how 'amazing it is what they can do with computers these days.' I wasn't sure if she was referring to the photo-shopped face or the human resurrection.

I smiled to myself, 'I'm glad you're happy, Mum, I haven't seen you this happy for a long, long time.' I said loudly.

'Yes I am,' she smiled, looking around. 'I like this room, it reminds me of the ship's cabin your father and I stayed in when we went dancing...' She had a far away look in her eye and told me about a time before I was born when she and my father had taken work as dance teachers on a cruise ship. 'Your Dad charmed all the ladies with his Viennese Waltz,' she said. This was the first time she'd ever really spoken to me about the past, and I was surprised, but pleased –and I asked her what else they'd danced and how long the trip lasted. I thought the spell had finally been broken, that she was finally able to talk about the past, but then she changed the subject, so as always the past stayed hidden.

Through the veil of thick make-up, the layers of life and lipstick, I had seen a glimmer of the Mum that used to be many years ago, before that terrible night when we lost everything. The move away from the family home had taken her away from the heartache and the memories of past sadness. And I glimpsed the woman who had once danced in the kitchen, twirled around the living room and who was always laughing.

I wondered if perhaps I should be more like my mother. Should I try to make a change, be more ambitious and grab life like my parents had when they were younger? Perhaps I should have worn shocking pink instead of safe pale blue for Sophie's wedding? Should I have stood my ground and ordered vol-au-vents instead of some tuna truffle-dribbled nonsense no one would understand – let alone eat? Should I have applied for that Junior Manager's job with special responsibilities in Perishables? Should I leave Bilton's? Get a career? I'd always wanted to travel, but at forty four I wasn't exactly a 'trolley dolly'. Perhaps I should start a campaign to employ geriatric cabin crew? I could always try Virgin Airways, Richard Branson seemed kind and up for a laugh – always ready for a challenge. But was I really ready to try something new.

Here I was for the millionth time feeling out of sorts, at odds with my life and work and wondering what the hell to do about it. I had gone over and over all the possibilities in my head since the day of Sophie's wedding – and I still didn't quite understand what I had done so wrong with my life that my own daughter wanted to escape from it.

※ ※ ※

Later that evening, I sipped my wine and watched the 'Strictly' Double Bill on TV and an actress I vaguely recognised from a soap being led onto the dance floor clad in sequins and sparkly heels. I wondered if my mum was watching – if so she'd be very confused, as I was sure this was another character who'd recently been killed off in a soap – not real life.

I knew it was painful for Mum to talk about dancing and the life she'd had with my Dad, but not talking about what happened hadn't helped her all these years. I was guilty too, because after we lost my dad I didn't want to talk about the life we'd had before either. But perhaps I'd kept it that way not only for my own security, but Mum's too.

I tried not to think about that night. I'd been ten years old and Mum and Dad were smiling, at me, and each other and I had been so happy, contented, secure. Afterwards, I don't recall ever feeling that safe, that complete again. I certainly never found it in a man.

I ate another Revel and scolded myself for dwelling on the past, on stuff I couldn't change. And the judging was about to start, there was no way I was dampening all that glitter with darkness, so I turned up the TV and lost myself in the show.

I couldn't get enough, watching the celebrities begin those first, faltering steps the swishing fabric and clicking heels on the dance floor were my therapy. As much as I didn't want to dwell on the bad memories – there were great ones too and in those seconds of silent stillness before the music began I could feel it all again. I could almost taste the excitement and anticipation of that moment before my parents danced in a big competition. As a child I'd never realised how nervous Mum and Dad must have been because for me it was just another wonderful dancing adventure. All the preparation, the final sequins sewn on the dresses, the car filled with petrol and packed, the sandwiches in tin foil for the journey – expectation and probably a little fear sparkling in the air. Just like on the TV there was always a glitterball. I was transfixed by the one on the screen now, each facet a different dance, a single moment catching the light, illuminating all my memories as it spun.

When the dancing stopped, Mum abandoned everything – including me. The music was turned off, there were no more competitions and something that had filled every crevice of our lives was instantly gone. Sometimes I'd find a sequin on the floor and I would keep it in a tiny box in my bedside table – each one a happy memory – hiding them from Mum. I didn't want her to find a reminder of what we'd had and be hurt all over again.

I'll never forget that first ever episode of Strictly Come Dancing when news reader Natasha Kaplinsky was whirled onto the floor by dancer Brendan Cole. It was like an electric shock, the movements, the music, and the old world elegance dragging me back into a childhood spent watching impossible, magical steps my eyes could barely keep up with. Without Dad our whole world of dancing disappeared and here on my sofa thirty years later I was rediscovering it all. It was like yesterday had grabbed me by the throat and hauled me back to a world of taffeta, tulle and tight bodices. A world where no one hurt me, or let me down or left me – and whatever happened I was safe in the knowledge that when it was all over I'd be kissed and carried to the car in a warm blanket.

That first night watching Strictly Come Dancing I'd sat on the sofa alone, surrounded by the ghosts of people dancing, with tears running down my face. It was, for me pure nostalgia, a crystallised moment in time when life was innocent and safe – before our hearts were broken and the stars went out.

Chapter Two

Salsa, Sparkle and Sequin-covered Secrets

Pulling up outside my old family home on the Sunday morning, my heart did a little lurch. I'd last visited almost three months ago, but Mum had still been here then, so this was a difficult visit and opening the little front gate on the terraced row I felt guilt and the past weigh heavily on me. I was still looking for my dad as I walked through the empty house, and I swear I heard laughter, voices, the clicking of dad's shoes on the wooden floor. I stood in the hallway breathing in the heady aroma of lavender and bergamot – the ghost of Mum's perfume 'Blue Grass'. I was comforted by that smell as I walked into the dining room, the big fake mahogany dining table stood waiting, as always, never really used. Dad said it was rather baronial for the three of us and he and Mum should have had more kids to fill it. Mum would disagree, and the look on her face told me the very thought of another child horrified her. Even as a child I wanted to make Dad happy and asked Santa for a little sister, but I'd received a Tiny Tears doll instead.

Dad could never sit still and on the rare occasions we did sit at the table he would be up and down, his legs constantly moving, toes tapping. I could hear Mum chastising him, 'Sit down and eat your tea, Ken,' she'd snap from behind a piece of celery and an ounce of cottage cheese. He'd suddenly leap up – 'Margaret, quick,' he'd say, opening his arms to dance. 'Oh Ken, you silly bugger, I'm having my salad,' but her feigned grumpiness dissipated into thin air as soon as he put the music on. Delightedly she'd leap up from the table and join him in a waltz or a tango, dancing around the room, she'd smile indulgently over his shoulder to me and I'd giggle happily. He was our hero – he was like an excited little boy, but at the same time the best husband and father.

I smiled to myself as I wandered through the rooms of my past. Without us here it was as empty and alien to me as visiting a stately home.

This was the first time I'd been back to the house alone, and it felt like I was seeing it for the first time, through someone else's eyes. Looking at the photos, the shabby furniture, the peeling wallpaper – it seemed time had stopped somewhere around 1980. In some ways, for us it had.

I wandered into the kitchen and turned off a dripping tap, the place smelt damp, unlived in, and soon it would be up for sale and all the memories sold with it. But just being here, breathing in the past was enough to evoke a million yesterdays. I remembered Mum standing on the kitchen table, stomping flamenco style as Dad clapped along. I'd joined in the clapping and when I tried to climb up to take part, Dad had lifted me onto the table where

Mum and I stomped so hard we'd left marks in the wood. As I ran my hand along the table, I could feel the indentations from our dancing, an imprint of how we once were, a happy yesterday preserved forever.

Walking upstairs into my parents' bedroom was probably the hardest part. The photos were still on the wall, gathering dust, a grainy black and white print of mum and dad in dancing clothes holding a trophy – I remembered the night, I could almost hear the applause, a golden memory from childhood. I gazed for a long time at a photo of me and Dad on the carousel in Blackpool. We were there for the Dance Championships and in between we'd gone out to the pier, up the tower and my favourite – the Pleasure Beach. It was a magical place for a child, filled with rides and roundabouts, fruit machines, faces full of candy floss – but the best of all was the candy-coloured horses on the carousel. I'd wait by the side with Dad, shaking with excitement, and when the ride stopped I would run to get on the purple or the pink horse, Dad running after me, laughing and calling my name. He'd sit behind me, holding me round my waist and when the ride started it seemed to go so fast my stomach would lift into my mouth and I would scream, scared I'd fall, but knowing I was safe in Dad's arms.

I moved along the photos on the wall smiling to myself at the 1970s shots of flared jeans and long hair. Mum's hair was always lovely and thick and blonde, but looking at her now, through my middle-aged eyes, I saw a beautiful young woman with so much to live for – who'd have thought her life would turn out the way it did?

I turned on the ceiling light, a large fake chandelier, all glitter and grandiosity, so typical of my parents. 'Kippers and curtains!' I murmured to myself, gazing up at the twinkling drops of glass twisting in the light. Then I spotted the opening to the attic and my heart sank. I hadn't even started yet and I'd forgotten about the bloody attic, a whole extra room to clear out – and no one had been up there for years, God only knew what was up there. And knowing Mum's hoarding tendencies you could bet it would be packed to the rafters – literally. Come to think of it, she had hinted that I might find the family treasure up there, hidden away.

'If only,' I'd said, knowing there would be nothing of value, because we had never owned anything of value. But I was intrigued as to what I might find there.

I searched for a stepladder under the detritus of my mum's life optimistically called 'the spare room'. There is nothing 'spare' or 'roomy' about it, I thought as I heaved up dusty boxes and tore my way through a dense forest of bags and clothes. I finally discovered the ladder and torch and headed back to the master bedroom from where I entered the dreaded attic. Reluctantly pushing open the hatch that lead into the roof, I saw the amount of stuff and all I could think was 'room of pain' – and not in a sexual way. Just what was my mother hoarding up here? Random flashes of my torch revealed huge black bin liners were stacked against the walls, but as shocked as I was by the quantity, I have to confess to slight relief at the vague sense of order. Even in torchlight I could see the bags hadn't just been thrown or piled six feet high with stuff spilling out, which seemed to be my mother's signature storage solution.

Whatever was in these bags had been put away with care and I was vaguely optimistic that it would be fairly easy to see (once I'd found the light switch) what was inside each one before clearing the space.

God only knew what those bags contained, but it was going to take more than a day to sort that lot out. I clambered up into the attic it was dark and cramped and I could taste the thick dust at the back of my throat. I found the light and looked at the first of the bin liners. It was huge, so I grabbed it with both hands and pulled at it with all of my weight to bring it out into the tiny square of attic that was unoccupied. As soon as I tugged at it however I realised it was light as a feather, which was surprising and I almost lost my footing, but managed to steady myself and sit down with the bag. It crunched slightly as I manoeuvred it into a position where I could open it – Oh God, don't say mother was hoarding family bags of crisps? Mum was particular about her food and though she didn't eat much she overbought her favourites perhaps she'd once had a thing for crisps? I began to tug at the knotted plastic tied several times – whoever packed this bag wasn't planning to open it again... or let anyone else open it either. Was this Mum's 'family treasure?' I doubted that very much, but whatever was inside would at least be protected from all the dust now nestling in the folds of the black plastic. The more I tugged, the more hopeless it became. I decided to throw caution to the wind and rip open the damn thing. I tore at it, gasping as the plastic split open easily and the contents slowly burst into life. Like a beautiful sea urchin, the powder blue tulle frothed out as

I gently teased it out of its black plastic grave and within seconds transformed back into my mother's ballroom dress.

My heart lurched; this was the one she was wearing the night it happened and I slowly and carefully brought the dress out of the bag. Gently wafting the layers of netting, breathing life into the frills as a handful of sequins fell to the floor, I gasped as my life rewound like an old cassette tape. There it was again, Mum's familiar fragrance of bergamot, dry and floral still living in the heart of the dress, now coming back to life in my arms. Again I breathed in my mother's perfume and was taken back to that night, the taste of happiness, the smell of Blue Grass, then nothing.

I sat for a long time holding the fabric to me, as if I was holding my mum, the one I'd known as a little girl. The Mum who'd laughed and danced and took joy in simple things, the Mum who'd needed no excuse to put the record player on and sing along. But then there were the times she'd cry for days, followed by a visit from the doctor, Dad's worried face, his wringing hands. Then sometimes Mum would go away for a while – as a kid I didn't know how long, but it seemed like forever.

One of my earliest memories is dancing with Mum to Elvis singing 'The Wonder of You'. It was a fox trot and Dad said I was a natural, shouting 'bravo' and clapping loudly when we finished.

Perhaps there was treasure here after all? I continued to tear at the bags, finding dress after dress, and as each one unfurled, another yesterday came to life and I was back in the moment. The black and scarlet satin Mum wore when they danced the Salsa at the North West Championships; a fringed dress in citrus shades she'd trotted around in when they danced the Charleston for a competition somewhere in Kent. Then I found bags containing all their trophies and medals. Holding the Latin American Dance Championships trophy from Sheffield 1976, I'd felt like an Oscar winner. I remember the clapping, the whistling, Mum's flushed, happy face and how I'd clutched the huge trophy as the photographer from a local newspaper took pictures and Mum and Dad beamed. Then I smiled, remembering the best bit of that night – we ate chips out of paper on the way home in the car. I licked my lips at the memory as I opened another bag and discovered my favourite of Mum's dresses. It was a delicious fondant pink and always reminded me of the thick, sugary icing on a birthday cake. I'd loved this pink dress as a child and remembered quite clearly it was the one she'd worn for the waltz for a competition in Birmingham. I carefully stroked the fondant pink satin bodice, which was tiny - I had never realised how slim Mum had been.

I sat among the dresses for a while, running the soft satin and prickly tulle through my fingers and marvelled at the memories suspended in those frills and spangles.

I held the pink fondant up against me and moved slowly around the attic in an attempt at the foxtrot. Catching myself in a dusty old mirror, I was disappointed to see me waddle – it wasn't Mum's elegant glide, but then I'd never been as beautiful or graceful as my mum. Even as a child I was aware of the surprise on people's faces when my mum or dad would say, 'And this is our Laura.' 'Your daughter?' they'd ask with unconcealed amazement that two beautiful people could create this chunky, plain child. It didn't bother me, I'd come to expect the reaction, and apart from some painful times as a teenager I didn't let my looks shape my life. Or did I? Here in the colours, the sparkle and surprises of the past... my past, I realised how grey my life had gone on to be. As I'd grown up, my parents' firework display was over and I'd been left with the embers. I'd retreated into a life, where I could be in control and there were no surprises – but looking around me at all this, I realised, there hadn't been any sparkles either.

I eventually gathered myself together, and remembering it was Sunday and the 'Strictly Come Dancing' results show would be on later I was slightly lifted. I would have a glass of wine in front of the TV and come back to Mum's later in the week to sort through all the gowns and the rest of the house. I would have to store them at my house. Despite the fact that they would fill up my tiny spare room, I didn't want to sell them. I couldn't bear the thought of flogging my parents' past on Ebay for a few quid. To others they would just be sparkly dresses, but these were the fabric of my childhood, their layers and sequins told a story – my story. I put the gowns back into their bags. They'd been preserved for over thirty years, I didn't want to leave them exposed to the dust and elements now.

Frothing the tulle on the pink fondant gown and drinking it in one last time, I noticed something fluttering out from the folds. An envelope, like an escaping butterfly, preserved in pink satin landed on the floor. I bent down to pick it up, and when I pushed my fingers inside the ripped top, I could see there was folded paper inside. A letter. I held it for a few seconds, knowing it was probably private – but I couldn't help myself, I had to read it.

My Darling,

You said last night you might have to leave me and I'm sorry I was angry. I wanted to write to you because it seems we can't talk to each other anymore without hurting. I don't blame you for saying you want to go – I haven't been the most attentive of husbands. But I'm begging you not to.

I can see the effect he had on you, and how, he changed everything. But leaving me isn't the answer, and my heart bleeds when I see that faraway look in your eyes. I don't know what to do, I don't know how to make it better. I'm hurting too, I can't even bear to say his name.

I know you think after what happened that I don't love you. But I love you in spite of everything – nothing has or ever will change my love for you.

I want you to stay, Margaret. It won't be easy but let's try to put the past behind us and concentrate on the future. If you won't do this for me, think of Laura. Let's make the most of what we have – our beautiful daughter, the golden link between the two of us. Let's teach her to dance, to lose herself in movement, and to 'feel' the music that has given us both so much. We must share that gift with Laura – I want her to believe in herself, to shoot for the moon and dance under the stars. I don't know where we'd be now without our ambitious tangos and complicated waltzes. Our dancing is the life blood that flows through both of us. During that difficult time when we couldn't speak about what was happening, our touch on the dance floor meant more to me than anything else.

Darling, stay with me and we will win at Blackpool, then sell up and move away from the painful memories, and start a new life somewhere else. We've always wanted to dance flamenco – let's stop putting it off – we can open that little school in Southern Spain and feel sunshine on our faces instead of tears.

I'm told it's so warm in Granada they dance flamenco outside and the rhythm echoes through the streets. They live in the 'now,' like gypsies, free of all shackles, living only for the dance. And it's there waiting for us my darling – we just have to reach out and take it.

Let us not be pulled back by the past... let's move forward, I know it's the right thing to do.

Please stay?

Yours always

Ken x

Wow, I thought. I never knew my dad had such passion, it was like beautiful, sad poetry. There was so much to take in, so much said in such a few words, my world, the one I thought I knew was suddenly wobbling. My tears were cold, sliding down my cheeks and dripping onto the letter, blurring the words. I tried to wipe it with my hands but that made it worse and made me cry harder.

My dad was so passionate, so determined, what happened for him to change his mind about leaving everything behind to dance in Spain? And what happened in their marriage that Dad needed to send a letter like this? Who was Mum thinking about that made her unreachable to him? Was it another man? I couldn't imagine what could possibly come between them, but Mum's illness had never really been explained, so perhaps she'd had a breakdown. After an affair? I felt like I'd been kicked in the chest. My poor dad, betrayed by the woman he loved. All the dancing and the laughter and the love – the perfect couple – had it all been a lie? The letter sounded just like my dad, listing the things they'd do, planning a future they would never reach. He never made it to Spain, and Mum never went there either – neither of them danced the flamenco. He spoke of winning the waltz category in Blackpool, so the letter was written around 1980. I racked my brain to try and remember anything of significance between them that would give me a clue about what had happened. Mum had been ill on and off for a few years then, so if it was an affair it had happened years before. It must have put a great hole in their relationship, an unspoken rip, right through the middle of their marriage that they couldn't even talk about it. I went back over my childhood, clawing at the past, desperately trying to recall anything, like a detective searching for clues among the endless bloody sequins. I seemed to remember a time when Mum wasn't ill, when she laughed a lot. But then a curtain came down... when was that? She changed somewhere in my childhood – I remember the first time she went away because Dad bought me a Tiny Tears doll, so

I would be about four or five years old, what had happened? Dad told me she was poorly and had to spend time in hospital... why? He'd said in his letter he couldn't reach her, I understood that feeling and recalled the 'faraway look' he mentioned. What sequin-covered secrets had my mother kept hidden? Perhaps things weren't so wonderful between them after all, because the more I thought about it I realised the only time she was really happy, when she came alive, was when she was dancing. Ironically it was dancing at the place of their imagined Waterloo where all their dreams died – at the Blackpool International Dance Championships. How cruel life could be, I thought, picking up the letter and going over the words. I was a child when I knew my dad, but reading the letter I saw him through adult eyes. It was hard to equate the happy, spontaneous, loving father I remembered, with someone filled with such pain. Almost forty years later, I could hear his voice, feel his arms around me – and learning that he'd been so badly hurt made me want to hug him so much.

I looked over the letter again. It was yellowing with age and had obviously been read so much the folds were almost worn. How could she? How could my Mum betray my father? I read and re-read his words, looking for a clue, trying desperately to remember the past and discover what had happened. I sat amongst the bin bags and the tears and the taffeta – my world had tilted slightly.

On a third reading, I could see that in spite of whatever had happened, my dad's pain was tinged with hope. I knew about Dad's idea to live in Spain, to learn the flamenco, but I didn't realise it was such a serious proposition – he seemed to want that so much.

He'd also wanted me to dance, had seen me as his second chance; 'shoot for the moon,' he'd said wanting to pass on the baton.

Then I landed with a bump, I wasn't that baton-carrying dancing girl. Despite my father dreaming of a life of glitter on the dance floor for me I had never got round to dancing – the closest I'd ever got was watching my parents. I had never been taught the waltz, never glided elegantly across a floor in a beautiful dress or whipped up a storm in a frenzied tango. I was a Bilton's checkout girl who stopped dreaming at the age of ten when her world came crashing down in The Empress Ballroom, Blackpool.

Chapter Three

Detox Chocolate and Bilton's Babes

'I knew she had eleven items in that basket,' Carole said, 'I said – just admit to it and we will leave it at that. I won't take any further action.'

I nodded as she regaled me with the story of how she'd publicly humiliated some poor woman trying to sneak into the 'ten items or fewer' queue with – shock horror – eleven items. Carole had been rejected when she'd applied for the police – but it didn't stop her dishing out her own brand of police-supermarket brutality at Bilton's. A few months before I would have loved this story, completely overreacting to the deed and declaring the shopper 'a sneaky bitch'. This would be followed by my own sorry tales of outrageous customer behaviour in various aisles and unbidden rudeness at the checkout. But it all seemed so petty now, the daily tussles with customers had lost their drama and spark for me.

'You're not yourself, love,' Carole said. 'You okay, you seem a bit quiet?' We were having lunch in the staff canteen and she was pouring something hot and brown from her flask into a mug.

'Oh I'm fine, just missing Sophie and I'm worried about family stuff,' I said and told her about Dad's letter.

'I don't know what happened between them, and I can't ask Mum. But it made me think – there was Dad making all these plans and it was futile, he never got to Spain, he never danced flamenco. I don't want to suddenly be in my seventies and think, where did that go? I know my parents never did what they dreamed of, but at least they *had* dreams. I don't have anything to aim for, no goals except to get through the day without verbally or physically abusing an annoying customer.. Do you know I've spent my life going to work, coming home, making meals and watching TV.'

'Welcome to my world,' Carole sighed, sipping at the foul-smelling brew now steaming from her mug.

'Everyone needs something...' I sighed.

'Like what?'

'I don't know... I feel like I want to go to Spain... do all the stuff my parents never did. Maybe I'll do it for them... and for me... one day.'

'There you go... 'one day.' Do it. Do "Spain and stuff" now. Just ask your Sophie and I bet she'll tell you to get on the next plane.'

I wasn't asking Sophie anything, because I had to get used to the idea myself first and I wasn't trying it out for size during the precious ten minutes of FaceTime we managed each week.

'She's the one that told you to get a bigger life...'

'I know. I just wish it didn't bloody hurt so much.'

It was such a big thing, and had become even bigger in my mind since she'd gone, and now Dad's letter seemed to be warning me to make the most of life before it was too late. There was Sophie off on an adventure, telling me about amazing sunsets and scuba diving in Bali and I just sat there nodding into my phone from the sofa. No scuba diving or sunsets here. She'd been to hell and back on her 'not-wedding' day and I didn't want to bring her down with, glad you're happy – now what about me?

I didn't have to 'front her up', I'd thought a lot about what she'd said and now I knew exactly what she meant. I had a little life. I had no plans to do anything daring or different, and if I didn't do something now, nothing would change. In ten or twenty years' time I would look at a day in my life – and it would be exactly the same as it had been since I was about twenty years old. The only difference being that my baby girl had now grown up and I was alone.

I was back there on that cold stone step of the church, and Carole patted my hand, she knew what I was feeling and was letting me know I was there for her. She was a good friend and after Sophie's wedding then her travels and now the letter I felt she'd listened to me enough.

'So how are you? Still doing the detox?' I asked, trying to change the subject to something a little less heavy.

'Yeah, but this detox tea is vile,' she said through a mouthful of chocolate.

'Detox?' I looked at her chocolate questioningly.

'Oh not this...' she held the bar up and looked at it like someone else had put it there. 'It's okay, the tea cancels the chocolate out,' she said, in all seriousness.

'Oh. I could do with a gallon of that then,' I smiled, unwrapping a hefty tuna mayonnaise roll that contained my calorie allowance for the next fortnight. 'I can't seem to stop eating at the moment. I really should make some changes, eat better, look after myself you know? I'd like to be a better "me".'

I'd always let my weight and my confidence hold me back, I was sure there were things I would have done if only I'd had more faith in myself. Perhaps I could start now... with my weight? My mum may have hurt Dad and disappointed him but I could make it up to him by shooting for the moon in my own way... 'Are you going to Slimming Club next Monday? I thought I might join,' I said, attempting to take the first, faltering steps towards a new me.

'I'm not doing slimming clubs anymore,' Carole said. This was like Rihanna saying she wasn't going to sing anymore and I looked at her, surprised.

'Natalie from "World Cuisines" is doing Zumba, she goes with her mate Mandy, you know, the beauty therapist from "Curl up and Dye"?'

I nodded.

'Natalie's lost loads of weight, so I'm going to try it... do you fancy going?'

'Yeah. I spotted Natalie restocking the "Asian Express" aisle yesterday, I thought she looked different... thinner. Not easy to notice under these horrific overalls,' I added, plucking at the nasty green nylon we had to wear as what the boss Julie sarcastically referred to as 'Bilton's Babes'.

'Yep. She says the teacher is fab, used to be a yoga teacher. Apparently she's all about "female empowerment". She's bonkers and uses the word "vagina" in every sentence, but it's a small price to pay for a tight arse and a tough pelvic floor.'

I'd love to lose some weight, and I'm a great believer in fate. So when in his letter my dad said he'd wanted me to learn to dance, I felt it was more than just coincidence that Carole was now inviting me to Zumba classes. Life often gives you just what you need, even if you don't realise it at the time.

Carole was raving about Zumba; 'The poster says; *"Ditch the workout, join the party."* And I need me some of that.'

I was quite daunted, and if it hadn't been for Dad's letter I'd have gone back to Super Slinky Slimmers where you get weighed then sit down for an hour while someone talks to you about food until you're so hungry you head for the nearest chippy when you leave. But this was the beginning of a new Laura – this was a Laura that said 'yes!' No more wallflower hiding away in the corner, I would take to that Zumba floor like my Dad took to the ballroom, with gusto... or more likely in my case gutso?

Carole and I had wandered out of the canteen and were now grabbing the very precious last few seconds of our twenty-minute break standing by the vending machine. As we chatted, our eyes were drawn to the chunky chocolate bars, the decking of crisps and the fountain of fizzy drinks.

'So, Zumba... tomorrow night...?' she said, licking her lips and gazing longingly at the stack of Snickers. 'Mmmmm chocolate soldiers standing to attention,' she sighed.

I was trying not to be seduced by the soldiers or the salt and vinegar crisps lined up next to them. Apart from the taste and the crunch, the obsessive in me was really getting off on the way they hung neatly behind each other, like a row of designer suits.

'Yes, Zumba here we come,' I said, determined to ignore the delicious temptations and focus on shedding pounds – not adding more.

'What time?'

I was keen to try something new but quite self-conscious about throwing myself around in front of other people. I'd sometimes hear La Bamba on the radio and jerk around the living room floor pretending to be a professional Latin dancer but that was in the privacy of my own home. Vigorous Zumba in front of other, thinner, fitter humans was quite different!

Just thinking about dance steps reminded me of my parents and I wondered again what sad secret they shared. Perhaps 'he' whoever he was, was the reason Dad's dreams and plans never materialised? Looking back, I could see that Dad and Mum had always put things off. 'When we've got enough money', 'next year', 'tomorrow', they had money worries, which surely played a part – but I was beginning to wonder if they both made excuses for staying here in the same life? What had they been scared of?

'All for one and one for all,' my Dad would say as we set off for another dance competition. I'd be in the back of the car, safe and warm the sandwiches in Tupperware containers, a flask and blankets in the back because you never knew what time you'd be home with the traffic. 'This is going to be the one,' he'd say. 'With these winnings we'll buy that villa in Spain, senorita,' he'd nod to Mum. 'And I will teach the dancing alfresco,' Mum would say in a funny Spanish accent while clicking her fingers in the air flamenco-style, which always made me giggle.

Our lives and dreams were planned in that little Ford Cortina with the twisted front bumper (Dad had been overexcited one year on arrival at The Winter Gardens in Blackpool and banged it into a wall in his anticipation to get on that shiny floor). I was as excited as they were about competing, and I can see them now, laughing, the glitter ball twinkling in their eyes, numbers on their backs and hope in their hearts.

They usually won their competitions, but after a posh meal, a new dress for Mum and another doll for me, there was little left of the winnings to save up for that Spanish dance school. I remember once Mr Robinson, Dad's boss at the shop went on holiday to Spain and he and his wife sent us a postcard while they were there, it was a photo of a woman in frills dancing. Her dress was scarlet with polka dots and I would look at it for hours. I kept the postcard under my pillow and would take it out at night just imagining the music and the heat of the dancing.

When Mr Robinson came back from his holidays, he and his wife had bought me a flamenco dancer doll in a see-through plastic box. I was speechless with joy, and I remember holding the box carefully and just gazing at her like she was behind a window. I thought she was a beautiful Spanish princess and christened her Senorita because I thought that was a Spanish name. I played with her for hours, twirling and dancing her on the furniture, the sideboard was the shiny ballroom floor and Senorita would do everything from the waltz to the Charleston. I'd never seen the flamenco danced, so Dad tried to show me; 'It can take years to learn to dance the flamenco – one day we'll go to Spain and learn it properly and you can teach Senorita.'

The problem was my parents were both dreamers and now I realise they were never organised or disciplined enough to save up to buy a dance school in Spain. They could barely keep their lives afloat here because of their inability to deal with money. Consequently life was a struggle and the only time we all felt relaxed and happy was when they were dancing.

And always my thoughts returned there. Blackpool – The 1980 International Ballroom Championships. Mum sweeping past in satin and tulle covered in two thousand hand-sewn sequins, bouffant hair and a toothy smile. Dad, handsome, straight and proud, his steps light, his arms strong. The perfect couple dancing through dry ice and glittering lights. I was so proud to be their little girl, breathless with awe watching them silently from the side of the dance floor. And as they disappeared into a tide of sequins and hairspray no one could have predicted how horribly the night would end.

Chapter Four

Slut Dropping Zumba Queens and Someone Else's Leggings

Standing at the checkout, the following day I was so bored I kept checking the time and couldn't believe how early it still was. I was just wondering if my watch had stopped when a disembodied voice hissed, 'Don't forget tonight.'

I felt a slight chill go through me. Was someone playing games with my head?

'...Zumba tonight?' the voice hissed again from behind a pyramid of tinned beans. I knew I wasn't having hallucinations when I saw Carole's mop of blonde curls behind the tins, which meant Julie the Supervisor was about so Carole was being careful. At Bilton's no one was allowed to do any of what Julie referred to dismissively as 'chit-chatting' on the shop floor. In her first address she informed us through bright pink lips that none of us were allowed to 'chew, call, text, sext or chat', when we were on the floor. I should be so lucky, I didn't have anyone to sext to anyway, even if I knew how to.

'That's the rest of my working life wrecked,' Carole had whispered in my ear.

'Mmmm I wonder if we're allowed to breathe?' I sighed, my heart sinking at this twenty-something aggressive blonde who'd been appointed, she informed us 'to keep you lot in check'.

Julie treated us like five-year-olds and it was all the more galling that she continued throughout her employ to speak to us like she was our nursery nurse. You can probably imagine the level of humiliation involved when someone almost young enough to be your daughter asks you nicely to stop 'chit chatting – or god forbid, sexting.' As I pointed out to Carole after the event, I was expecting her to put us on the naughty step or suggest we develop a 'news circle' to share 'our news at the appropriate time', like Sophie did at school... when she was five.

Working for Bilton's was a soul-sucking, lonely existence stranded on a checkout all day making small talk with strangers. So when she was on shelf-stacking duties, Carole would stack tins and packets near my checkout so we could 'chit chat' undercover. And bossy Julie had not even sussed our ingenious plan.

'So... Zumba, tonight?' came the disembodied voice again from behind the beans.

'Oh sorry, yes... I was daydreaming. Can't wait,' I said, and to prove to Carole (and myself) how ready I was for this body punishment I made my hips do what I hoped was a Zumba-like move.

'Are you all right dear?' a nice old lady said as she was checking through her single potato and packet of tea.

'Fine... thank you,' I smiled. 'Just limbering up for tonight's Zumba class,' I said, making like I had a life.

'Oh thank goodness for that – I thought you were in pain.'

❊ ❊ ❊

I'd been so excited to get to Zumba and embrace the new, lithe and flexible 'me', I'd pushed shoppers through my till at top speed in the last half hour of the day so I could get away quickly.

'I think my dancing genes will come alive tonight,' I hissed to Carole as I put up my 'Till Closed' sign.

'Ew that sounds messy,' she laughed.

I laughed along, happy that I had made a decision to do something instead of saying no like I always did. Just the act of saying 'yes' had made me feel ten years younger... why couldn't I do Zumba? I'd checked on YouTube, and though it looked very 'physical', there were women older and fatter than me throwing those shapes. It might take a couple of weeks to get the hang of it, but as dancing was clearly in my blood I was bound to pick it up quickly. I just hoped Carole wouldn't feel too bad if she couldn't keep up when I was leaping around, and picking it up quickly and zumbaing like a pro.

Earlier, during our afternoon break, Carole and I wandered (waddled?) over to 'Baked Goods', and she bought a big pie and I treated myself to cake, telling myself there was nothing wrong in a little reward after a hard night zumbaing. I looked along the line of different flavoured sponges under the glass and selected a vanilla one filled with fresh cream and thick, red raspberry jam. I'd never baked a cake, it must be genetic, Mum never baked a cake either – she said she didn't have time with all the competitions. I suspect her real reason was she didn't want to eat cake and put on weight or break a nail, which in the words of Craig Revel Horwood would have been a 'disarrrster.' Instead, Dad sometimes bought a sponge cake for us on Fridays on his way home from work. Funny how as adults we still take comfort in the rituals of our parents and to this day I crave cake on a Friday night... well, I crave cake every night, but especially Fridays. Mum would play around with a little portion on her plate – but Dad and I would have a large slice each celebrating the end of another week and the start of the weekend. Leaving Baked Goods with my little box of heaven I knew the comfort of soft, dense sponge, sweet, fruity jam and cold fresh cream would eradicate anything – even Julie the supervisor.

As excited as I was about doing something new, arriving at the Dance Centre in a pair of Carole's leggings was probably one of the low points in my life. Because I'd been late cashing up my till I hadn't had chance to go home and change, but Carole had thought of everything and had brought a spare pair of leggings, a T shirt and a headband with her to work. We'd changed at work and the crotch on the leggings was round my knees (to Carole's surprise they'd shrunk in the wash). The T-shirt was fluorescent orange and tight, and along with the bloody headbands she insisted we wore, we looked like Edina and Patsy from Absolutely Fabulous.

'Please Carole,' I tried, standing outside the big wooden doors. 'Let's come back next week.'

'I'm sorry, hon, but you can't stand there in that too tight T-shirt telling me you're coming back next week. Your body is in the same state of emergency mine is – and we can't waste another day.'

She was right.

'Bitch,' I muttered as her bum went in front of me through the door, and I could see in tight leggings it had a life of its own. Walking into The Dance Centre, I realised I hadn't walked into a new place where there might be people I didn't know for years. And I was scared. I thought calming thoughts of the cream sponge in the boot of my car waiting just for me and followed Carole across the room. I didn't think I could feel any worse in Carole's version of the zumba outfit than I already did – but looking round I could see we were the only ones in headbands. I never was one for being different – I always followed the flock – and ripped my fluorescent pink towelling headband off.

'You'll regret that, when the sweat's pouring off your forehead,' Carole sniffed.

All around me women were arriving, huge and padded in their October layers, giving me false hope that I wasn't the fattest there, only to cast them off – from caterpillars to butterflies within seconds. Sadly my layers weren't detachable... well, not without surgical intervention and believe me – I'd considered it. The only layer I took off were my glasses, which made everything slightly blurry and didn't make me feel like a butterfly at all. I felt like a big caterpillar and wondering if I really should have said a big fat 'yes' to this – I moved with everyone else to the middle of the floor.

'Laydeez, laydeez,' came a loud and rather aggressive voice from the corner, as a warrior-like woman emerged, clapping loudly with a very serious look on her face. It was the teacher, who introduced herself as Martha, and after announcing that our vaginas were the home to 'deep shaman magic,' she asked us all to 'roar from our core.' I don't know what shocked me most, that my vagina was magic or I was expected to roar (I doubted I even had a core). My prevailing thought was that I couldn't possibly roar without laughing, so while everyone made like lions I pretended to tie my trainers. Once the roaring stopped, Martha went off on one about 'goddesses' and 'she-wolves'. She lifted her arms up and urged everyone to 'feel your femaleness', which I initially refused to do, shaking my head vigorously, until I realised it wasn't literal, just another way of saying 'be aware of your body.' I was only too aware of my body so didn't want to dwell too long on that one. So after she'd stopped roaring and bestowing super hero status on our vaginas, she went on to declare war on fat and pelvic floors throughout the region. This woman meant business, and this class wasn't the light-hearted Olivia Newton-John in spandex style leg-kicking low-impact jiggle I'd imagined it was. And we hadn't even begun yet. She told us to brace ourselves and be ready to Zumba in five... or else? It felt like a threat.

'Christ she will kill me,' I hissed to Carole who was waving to a couple of younger girls who had wandered over with Natalie from 'World Cuisines'. They were all in very tight spandex shorts and tops with leg warmers, their pelvic floors were probably perky and I doubt they'd ever even seen fat. They looked like something from the 70s, but they hadn't even been born then, I smiled at them while contemplating my escape from the zumba hell-hole. This wasn't for me – I wanted to be home on the sofa with my lovely cream sponge.

'This is Mandy and Toyah,' Natalie said, introducing me to them. 'You know Mandy don't you – she's the beauty therapist at Curl Up and Dye.'

I recalled a brutal waxing incident and smiled nervously. Sophie had insisted I have my legs waxed for the wedding, and what was optimistically labelled a 'pampering session for the mother of the bride', turned into something tortuous as Mandy ripped the wax strips from my flesh while giving a detailed rundown of her last holiday (drinking, sex, followed by more drinking... then more sex). I'd never been to a beauty salon in my life until then – and probably wouldn't again.

'Is this your first time at one of Martha's Zumbas?' Mandy asked, one of her perfectly-arched, but heavy eyebrows raised.

'Yes, I don't know what to expect really...but I'm worried it's going to be agony,' a bit like one of your treatments, I thought.

Her face opened up in delight and she leaned towards me to impart some pearls of Zumba wisdom.

'You don't know what to expect? Well...' she grabbed my left buttock, which surprised me. A lot. 'Expect your arse to feel like it's exploded!' she announced. 'Your legs will feel like you left 'em in a car park somewhere after a hard night dogging,' she added, nodding in all seriousness. I found it hard to imagine that particular scene – but she'd now left me in no doubt as to how I would feel in the morning. I really should have gone home with my sponge cake, because it didn't matter how much I ate it never made me feel like I'd been through 'a hard night dogging'.

Carole saw my face and looked worried.

'I might make a run for it. Well, a waddle for it at least,' I hissed.

'Ha ha, you should,' Mandy said. 'If you stay, I'm telling you, all that slut dropping will make you feel like crap tomorrow.' And she set off again. 'I drank a bottle of vodka and three Porn Star Martinis after an all-nighter with Kyle Thomas last Friday and next day I still felt better than I do the day after Zumba,' she roared laughing. Now I was really scared and just looking at Martha's abs in her midriff-baring outfit was making me feel tired and sore in the way a bag of chips and Silent Witness never had. And what the hell was 'slut dropping'?

Before I had a chance to escape, Martha was yelling something guttural about 'the power of the vagina' and the music started up. It was one of Rihanna's slower songs which was promising and hopefully meant the moves wouldn't be quite so aerobic. I'd insisted we stay at the back which meant I could hide and I didn't have to look at Martha with her flexible limbs. But being behind a blur of fluorescent tops and pert bums wasn't much better – everyone seemed to be moving like they'd been Zumbaing since birth and I was worried I may get left behind. I was able to rationalise my feelings with Rihanna gently singing in the background and reminded myself I was a woman of forty four and not a bloody teenager. I told myself not to be so stupid and self-conscious. So I might not know all the moves – no one did the first time. I straightened up and began copying what the woman in front of me was doing. You could tell she knew her stuff because she had a tiny bum and a swinging pony tail, which in my book said Zumba Queen. Everyone was slowly wiggling their hips, it was just like belly dancing, nice undulating movements that wouldn't put anyone's back out. I took it slow, as my belly often danced without any help from me and if I gave it too much wiggle it could gather speed and behave like a large pink blancmange. I glanced at Carole who gave me a reassuring wink and through the still slightly blurry rainbow of fluorescence I caught Mandy's eye. Perhaps it was my eyesight, but I'm sure she made an obscene (but friendly) gesture.

'Yeah,' I thought, moving my body with everyone else, 'this is going to be okay.' I was almost (and I stress 'almost') beginning to enjoy myself when suddenly a high-pitched wail emanated from the front. This was quickly followed by a heavy bass beat that filled the hall and my head (probably filled the town it was so bloody loud). Without warning, everyone put their arms in the air and started whooping – I felt like I was on a rollercoaster – going down, fast!

I clenched my buttocks in fear as everyone else began leaping to the music. They were all in unison, all seemed to know exactly what to do like they were tuned in to radio waves I wasn't privy to, even Carole was holding her own despite a difficult pelvic floor. There was much yelling coming from Martha's side of the room – what I could only presume were instructions but meant nothing to me. Then I heard, 'Drop it low,' over the music and everyone dipped. 'Way down low,' the words boomed out as bottoms almost touched the floor. This must be the slut dropping Mandy scared me with, and I panicked – since hitting 40 I'd found it hard to pick something up of the floor and get back up without calling for an ambulance. There was no way I was 'dipping' anything that low without medical assistance – my bum just wouldn't go all the way down there. I made a fist at it but opening my legs wasn't easy in tight leggings and a crotch somewhere around my knees. I tried hard, but no, the 'dipping low' just wasn't happening. Carole's tight leggings were acting like a lower body hammock and I just hung there mid 'drop' completely trussed up and unable to move. It was less 'slut' drop, and more 'OAP' collapse - just not pretty. I looked around from my prone position to see all the others back up, raising their arms and swaying their hips and pert breasts while I remained suspended mid-descent. Why did I ever think I could do this?

I looked around for help, but Carole had gained so much momentum during the hip swaying thing she'd propelled herself across the room and Mandy and her friend were now way down at the front. There was nothing else for it, I put all my weight behind me (there was plenty) and using the pony-tailed woman in front to steady me I tried to raise myself to my feet.) But just as I began to lift my body weight I felt the most awful ripping sensation between my legs. I couldn't imagine what I'd done and almost fainted. Had I ruptured something vital? Would I soon be starring in the next series of 'Embarrassing Fat Bodies,' hoisting my bare legs into stirrups and telling my shocking story? I tried not to think too much about what was actually going on down there because I might vomit on the spot, and I'd already made a spectacle of myself without adding that to my zumba repertoire. I stayed very, very still and tried to gather my thoughts, feelings - and trembling thighs – together, but as I slowly moved my legs I sensed an unwelcome draught between them. To my horror it appeared that Carole's leggings had completely ripped at the crotch. My inner thighs were now inelegantly displayed to the world as I squatted on my haunches still clawing at the tiny bottomed, pony-tailed blonde in front for counterbalance. God knows what she must have thought to have me coming up the rear in my crotchless leggings with a desperate look on my sweating face.

I'd hoped to make new friends here, I'd hoped to take on a new challenge by saying a big fat yes but it seemed the bloody universe (and my body) had responded with a big fat no. I thought it might be a laugh, it might be fun, but everyone was taking it seriously, including Carole who, still upright, was now 'dropping it like it's hot', along with the rest of them. What a traitor she'd turned out to be, I thought, now back on my feet but keeping my knees together and my arse high, aware that any sudden movement could lead to major exposure.

The music was louder and faster and Martha was now screaming something about '... left, to the left.' Suddenly, everyone lunged left and did complicated leg movements as they did so. In an effort to seriously injure myself and then be allowed to leave, I threw my whole body left, but as I couldn't part my legs due to my wardrobe malfunction I was like a giant pogo stick. It was all so horrific and uncomfortable and painful and sweaty – and just as I got 'to the left', Martha shouted 'to the right, to the right.' Now the whole class was going in the opposite direction to me and I had to do a quick about-turn and jump weirdly. Don't ask what happened, but somewhere in the midst of the madness I lost control and found myself pogo-ing full on into the crowd of women. It must have looked like a rugby scrum as I appeared to 'take on' the whole of the Zumba class – knocking over the skinny little things and winding the bigger ones. I desperately tried to stop but ended up sliding along the floor, as everyone screamed, then I started screaming and even Martha was screaming and suddenly the music stopped.

※ ※ ※

Shaken-up, and disappointed in myself, I sat by the side of the Zumba class with a paper cup of water. I hadn't wanted to give up, but Martha suggested I 'take five', which I think was the zumba equivalent of 'the naughty step' and would be followed by immediate expulsion.

As I watched them 'cooling down' (which looked like another full-on workout to me), I noticed people coming into the hall for the next class. God help them, I thought to myself, glad it wasn't me.

Then I spotted the most gorgeous hunk ever – classically tall dark and handsome, with skinny hips in tight black trousers. You don't see men like that every day – he looked like a male model as he walked confidently through the throng of women, who were all eyeing him up openly. I spotted a couple of other men too, and they were a lot older – dear god they weren't going to allow Martha to wage war on their pelvic floors too were they? Did men even have them? Not after a session with Martha.

I rested my head against the wall, put my glasses back on and was able to get a better look at the hunk. He was probably in his forties, he looked very physically fit and had a lovely smile... oh god he was smiling at me! This was so unexpected, no gorgeous men ever looked in my direction, in fact, no man ever looked in my direction, gorgeous or not. I didn't look back, he might think I fancied him and be horrified, so I went back to watching the Zumba. Oh the horror. I was just contemplating how I would get up from my position on the floor without showing everyone my thighs when I looked up to see him wandering towards me.

'Hi,' he smiled. 'Was it you in the Zumba class... lunging quite quickly across the floor?'

'Yes – that was me,' I sighed, crossing my legs casually in an attempt to keep my torn crotch out of his eyeline. He was being polite – I did a lot more than 'lunge quite quickly,' I was like a juggernaut mowing them all down. I had single-handedly devastated and destroyed Martha's zumba class.

'Well, Zumba's not for everyone,' he said, tactfully.

'It's certainly not for me,' I was embarrassed, I hadn't thought about the spectators dotted around the studio who must have witnessed the whole episode.

'I'm Tony...' he said, 'Tony Hernandez... well it's Griffiths really but no one wants a dance teacher called Tony Griffiths.' He was slowly kneeling down next to me.

'Ahhh... you're a dance teacher? Hi,' I smiled, my face burning up, my knees clamped together. One false move and all would be revealed and this sex God/male model dance teacher would be faced with the horror of unleashed, middle-aged cellulite. I doubted a man like that even knew it existed, his women were probably young, firm and cellulite-free.

'I just wondered... if you would be interested in coming along to my class?'

'You are joking? You saw what I just did over there?' I said, pointing vaguely in Martha's direction.

'Yes, it was bloody hilarious... would you mind if I put it on YouTube?'

I opened my mouth but before I could speak he put up both hands in a surrendering gesture; 'Ha, only joking...'

I rolled my eyes. 'Good, I hope you didn't film any of it.'

'No... it all happened too quick, I couldn't get my phone out in time,' he smiled.

I was humiliated and disappointed and not really in the mood for his 'joking'.

'Look,' he continued, clearly unable to take 'no' for an answer. 'I don't think you can come to much harm in my class, it's far more sedate. A bit too sedate really,' he smiled.

'I don't know, after all that I feel a bit stupid.'

'I did Zumba once, nearly killed me. The only dip it low, pick it up slow I do is dipping my knife in Nutella and spreading it all over a big crust of bread.'

'Did Mandy send you over?' I said, rudely, suddenly realising this must be a wind-up.

'No.'

'Carole?'

'I don't know a Carole,' he said, looking a little deflated.

'Sorry, I thought someone was playing a joke on me,' I smiled.

'No... look I could see you were struggling in Zumba. But the good news is, you managed the footwork... almost. Yes you covered a lot of ground...very fast, but your footwork is quite dainty, it's fairly tight for someone...'

'For someone who's chubby?'

'No... for someone who hasn't danced before.'

'Mmmm well I haven't danced since I was a kid, the dainty footwork might have more to do with the fact I can't open my legs.' He looked bemused, like I'd just imparted a sexual secret. I glanced away thinking to myself, 'why would I say that? I have just told a good-looking stranger that I can't open my legs?

'I mean my leggings have ripped,' I was about to illustrate the problem by opening my legs but fortunately stopped myself. He seemed unfazed and immediately stood up.

'Here just wrap my jacket around your waist, that should keep you covered,' he said, taking it off and handing it to me. 'Look, I came over because I think you might be more suited to my class,' he said, looking at the pony-tails' wiggling bottoms as he spoke. 'It's not Zumba – it's Latin American... Salsa ... the foxtrot - Ballroom with a bit of spice.'

'Oh no, thanks... I think I'll just stick to watching Strictly on a Saturday night.' Despite being interested in his class the whole Zumba thing had knocked what little confidence I'd built up.

'Yes I watch that too... and the US version, 'Dancing with the Stars,' I watch that online. I love it... come to my class and you'll be dancing like the TV professionals in a few weeks,' he teased.

'No. Thanks.'

He looked slightly disappointed and I felt bad, and as he'd just loaned me his jacket I felt I should explain. 'My mum and dad were ballroom champions actually. I never really got into it. I was too young and then it was too late... I just can't.'

'It's never too late... and there's no such thing as can't,' he looked at me. 'Okay – no more clichés, but I'll be honest, I was thinking... if you came along and perhaps convinced your friends to join us you might enjoy it and... well, if I don't get enough pupils my class will close.'

I felt bad for him, but I just wanted to go home.

'I don't know – I've already shown myself up once tonight, I was ten when I last danced. I'm in my forties now.'

'Oh that's right, women over forty can't dance,' he was nodding, his eyes smiling. His skin was quite crinkly, close up he looked older than I'd first thought – still handsome but probably about the same age as me. 'Give it a go, just stay for the first half hour, it's much "calmer" than Zumba and I reckon you'd be good. Thing is, I only have about six students and, I'm not being rude but they are all... mature. I need young blood.'

'You sound like Dracula, and it's a long time since anyone called me "young blood",' I laughed, 'but I just feel weird doing ballroom after all these years... too many memories.'

'Your parents, you mean?'

'Yeah... I just ... I would probably end up blubbing all over the floor.'

'Blubbing is fine... it's emotion. I don't think I'm going to get much emotion from my current class. Have you seen how old my students are?' he laughed. I glanced over at the little group of pensioners and smiled, they looked sweet, but I knew what he meant and I felt a bit sorry for him. I also had his jacket wrapped around my waist and now felt obligated to say yes.

'The first fifteen minutes?' I said.

He nodded and, getting up, patted me on the knee. I thought that was quite an intimate thing for a man to do to a woman he didn't know and as nice as it was I wasn't quite sure how to take it.

Once Zumba finished, the girls wandered over and had a good laugh about the leggings 'incident.' Mandy said Tony was one of her clients and when I told them I'd volunteered us for his class she clapped her hands together, I assumed she must have fancied him – the way she talked she fancied anything male with a pulse. The others said they were exhausted but Mandy and I convinced them it would be fun and we joined the group of elderly couples waiting for the class, with Toyah threatening to 'piss off to the pub', if she got bored. As Tony drew everyone close to begin the class, Mandy complained loudly that her inner thighs were so sore she'd never have sex again.

The whole group, who seemed to be OAPs - looked at her in shock and she looked straight back; 'What?' she said. 'Oh when I said I'd never have sex again... I didn't mean *never*,' she explained, rolling her eyes and looking at the rest of the class like they were mad.

'Glad we cleared that up,' Tony said. 'Hello everyone, I'm Tony and for those new to the class I'm going to teach you all how to dance.'

I doubted it after my earlier 'performance.'

Then the music came on and as someone brought up with music I couldn't help but feel a little sway inside. I knew the tune, and I had an urge to dance like I did at home when no one was around, but I resisted. Tony was blocking out some steps and I could see he knew what he was doing – and he looked good doing it. Perhaps tonight I could learn a few dance steps in his class? It might make me feel less of an abject failure after my Zumba hell? Either way, I was going home to fresh cream sponge cake and Silent Witness... it was only a matter of time.

Tony moved centre stage and asked everyone to get into pairs and we all gathered together like you do at school, grabbing your best friend, in my case Carole. It was a mixed bunch of about ten people including us and though they didn't look as fit as any of the Zumba girls the class seemed keen.

'Now, I want to start with the basics,' Tony started.

Carole nudged me. 'Ahhh he's a bit nervous isn't he?' she whispered, and I could see that his hand was a bit shaky, and my heart went out to him.

'I'm going to show you some salsa steps,' he was saying, 'so wherever you are and whatever song comes on – you can dance!'

He started to sway his hips slowly. I hoped this gentle hip sway-ing wasn't lulling me into a false sense of security... again. If he suddenly started whooping and lunging I was straight out of that door. I was still sporting his jacket around my waist but I wasn't sure how many 'outings' the leggings could take.

'I want you all to feel it, love that soft, gentle music and embrace the rhythm,' he said, turning the music up. 'Just go with the mo-ment. Worrying about what comes next will block your mind, you have to open up, let the salsa in, the stress out – feel it, go with it.'

We were all mesmerised by his swaying torso and his glittering eyes and Mandy was now open-mouthed and winking at Toyah. Both girls' heads were following his tight black trousers, while two older ladies were nudging each other and having a giggle. I sud-denly wanted to giggle too and I thought 'I like this. I like him.' I didn't feel any pressure, it felt like it might be fun and it certainly beat a vigorous session with Martha and her magic vagina.

Tony began by demonstrating a basic salsa step involving a move to the side and back, which we copied several times to his beat. 'One two three,' he was saying as we all did the steps, and I smiled because I remembered the moves so well, I'd watched my parents do them many times. Then the music picked up – a big band Latin sound building up to Ricky Martin singing Livin' La Vida Loca, and I couldn't keep still.

Tony held out his hand to me. I looked around, flattered but confused.

'Lola...I mean Laura, step forward, I want you to demonstrate with me, you seem to be getting the hang of this.'

I walked towards him, our hands meeting mid-air we clasped them together as his other hand went swiftly through my other arm and placed it on the top of my shoulder. I put my arm up on his shoulder, our elbows now touching – he didn't need to tell me anything else, it just felt right. He was tall and strong, very experienced and knew what he was doing which I found infectious. I felt like I could dance too – I was confident with him, like I used to be when I was little and I'd danced with my Dad.

It was a simple salsa step, but as the music picked up we were flying. This wasn't like Zumba, for me it was so much deeper, the rhythm was somewhere in my chest and I was ready for more – so when Tony added another move, I did it too. My stomach was back on a rollercoaster, but it wasn't that scary ride like before, it came from deep inside. I was elated, almost giddy, and so irrationally happy I thought I might burst. Tony's legs were quick, his arms strong as he twirled me around and took my breath away. I tried not to think too much about what I was doing, my body abandoned my brain and I was in another world. I was vaguely aware of the open-mouthed surprise of my friends who were clearly as amazed as me at my fancy footwork.

We whizzed around as Ricky sang, keeping our feet tight, our legs firm and our hips loose and it was like I'd been dancing all my life. I let the music take me as we twirled around and the music swelled and we ended as the song ended, holding on to each other. I was breathless, my heart beating out of my chest with excursion, but also something else, an excitement and exhilaration I hadn't felt for years. In that moment I understood what dancing had been to my parents. I wanted to cry because only now did I realise what they'd lost... because I'd found it.

∗ ∗ ∗

The rest of the class were clapping us and even the last of the Zumba girls were joining in the applause. I must have blushed because Carole shouted, 'Don't be shy Laura – you were bloody brilliant girl!' Still holding me, Tony then asked everyone else to take hold of their partners and 'just dance'.

'What Lola and I did then was our dance – don't be frightened to dance your own dance,' he said over the music, 'no one must ever be afraid to dance... don't worry about how it looks and what other people think of you. Just feel how it feels.'

'I'm not Lola... I'm Laura,' I said as we whirled around some more. He pulled me closer, which felt good but very self-conscious.

'You're Lola on the dance floor,' he said, quite seriously.

I tried not to look into his face – he was so handsome, with brown eyes like my father and the same dancer's posture. I was transfixed and longed to let go and really dance for him. I wanted him to sweep me across the floor the way my father used to and felt just like that little girl wearing my mother's too big dancing shoes. And I heard my dad's voice; 'You be Ginger Rodgers and I'll be Fred Astaire!'

'You're really good...' Tony said quietly into my hair as we waltzed. He pulled me tighter and there was no space between us. I could feel his torso pressed against mine, his hand on my lower back pulling me in – and his hips too close to the gaping hole in my leggings.

'You've suddenly tensed up, are you okay?' He said, looking puzzled.

'Yes... it feels a bit... too close, I can feel your hips up against... me.'

'Let go, Lola. It doesn't matter how close we get, just go with the feeling you have to put your leg between mine.'

Now I felt extremely awkward and completely backed off. I was scared of this sudden intimacy with a man I didn't know, he couldn't possibly be enjoying this with *me*. Why hadn't he picked beautiful but foul-mouthed Mandy instead?

'I'm sorry, I'm just not comfortable with this.' I smiled uneasily and, still dancing, I pulled away slightly to look at him.

'Don't worry I'm not remotely interested in you.' He said this with such conviction I was quite offended. Okay so I wasn't a supermodel like him, but he didn't have to be so bloody honest.

'Oh... I know... I just feel...'

'Look, let me spell it out I don't fancy you.'

'Oh don't worry, you just did. But thanks for making it extremely crystal clear,' I said crossly.

He laughed; 'No... what I mean is – we could both be naked with our hips together and I'd feel nothing,' he smiled.

'Just leave it will you? I get the picture, no need to keep banging on about how repulsive you find me.'

'It's not just you...'

'Okay, you find all middle-aged women repulsive.'

'No. I'm just not into *women*.'

'Oh?'

'I'm dancing on the other side of the ballroom... not literally,' he laughed.

'Oh. You're *gay*! I'm sorry. I just assumed, you're so handsome and – well you don't *seem* gay.'

'Oh sorry, I forgot to bring my rainbow with me,' he sighed, sweeping me masterfully across the room.

I don't know why I didn't realise sooner, but once I knew, I suddenly felt so much more relaxed. And in that chilly Dance Centre on a wet Monday night in October, Tony's dancing was like a splash of sunshine.

We carried on dancing and for the first time in years I really felt like I could let go a little, and I stopped being so self-conscious and just gave myself to the music.

Tony wasn't broad, but he was tall and unusually for me - I felt small and dainty, as I had with my dad, and I know it sounds stupid, but that night was just magical. I didn't know what it was or where it would take me, but at the end of the night when Tony said he felt I had talent and wished I would come back to class, I said; 'Try stopping me.'

I realised that night that it didn't matter who was looking at me or what people thought. And even the fact that I had exposed my thighs to the whole of the Dance Centre didn't bother me. I forgot about Bilton's, my weight, my age – and yes, I even forgot about that sponge cake, which festered in my car boot for days.

Chapter Five

Ping Pong Balls and Crystal Maths

The following Sunday morning, I managed to do 'FaceTime' with Sophie. We texted regularly, but I was keen to confirm visually that she was still alive and in possession of all her limbs. My earlier 'Face Timing' attempts had involved me inadvertently calling the wrong number and demanding that the man who answered 'give the phone to my daughter NOW!' When he said his name was Nattapong and he had never met my daughter, I accused him of abduction and threatened him with 'the might of British Embassy', a phrase I'd heard in a film once. I don't recall the exact conversation, but suffice to say the words 'trafficking' and 'white slave trade' were used by me as I demanded to speak to the leader of 'the drugs gang'. Given that Nattapong was (as it turned out) an operator in a Bangkok telephone exchange this was perhaps a little over the top and when I realised the mistake my face went very hot and I put the phone down quickly.

So here I was chatting away with Sophie who was now in Phuket; 'Are you okay? Do you have enough money?' I asked her as soon as she came on the phone. I was trying not to sound anxious and uptight... which of course I was.

'Yes, Mum.'

'Are you okay for underwear? I can always send some pants out to you... there's nothing worse than being short of pants.'

She giggled. 'Mum, I'm fine for underwear...' Her face was pixelating slightly but I was relieved to see she was all in one piece, hadn't been kidnapped and hadn't had her face pierced or tattooed. I could tick off my checklist and sleep that night.

'I know this next question will annoy you, but I'm going to ask it anyway, Sophie,' I said. Using her name like that might just give me some parental authority: 'You didn't carry anyone's bags through customs did you?'

'No, Mum.'

'Cos last week a British woman was asked to carry a pot monkey through passport control... no one told her it was full of crystal maths. She's now banged up in the Bangkok Hilton and no one can save her. She's being robbed and ravished by Thai lesbians, and made to do all kinds of unnatural things with ping pong balls and prison guards and... '

'Mum, please... it's crystal *meth*. And why do you always feel the need to mention ping pong balls?'

'I don't know, I saw it in a documentary once. I just want to make sure no one's asked you to....'

'No one's asked me to carry a pot monkey,' she monotoned. 'And I haven't been robbed or ravished by Thai lesbians or done anything with ping pong balls. Oh but hang on...there's this porn film called 'Ping-pong Pot Monkey Lesbian killers' and I'm filming that next week with a man I met in a bar'.

'Okay, okay very funny – I know I go on, but I worry about you. Wait until you have children,' I said, provoking a whole new arena of worry in my own head about Sophie having unprotected sex and getting pregnant in Thailand.

I can be a bit of a nag where my daughter's concerned, and I sometimes forget she is an independent woman with her own life. I blame it on being a single mum and the fact there was only ever me to worry about her.

'Oh I miss you, love,' I heard myself say.

'I miss you too, Mum,' came a tinny voice from my phone, and I allowed a second to marvel at technology. I hadn't a clue how it worked, but this little phone enabled me to see and speak to my daughter, the other half of my heart, thousands of miles away. There were a few moments' silence while I gathered myself together and tried not to cry, I missed her so much.

'Do you have a busy week ahead?' she asked, probably guessing I was upset. I felt awful – I didn't want to worry her and make her feel bad, so I put on my brightest voice and smiled.

'Yeah. Really busy. I'm working all week but I'm thinking of clearing up Nan's house later... I've made a start but keep putting it off.'

'I don't blame you, Mum, there's a hundred years' worth of belongings in there – all piled up.'

I suddenly realised going down the 'clearing attic' route might confirm everything she thought about me having a little life, so I changed the subject.

'Oh and I'm going to Zumba with Carole again.'

'Zumba! Wow, Mum, that's hardcore.' I was secretly delighted that I'd managed to impress her – finally.

'Yeah, well it's not actually Zumba... I mean, Carole does the Zumba, I... there's this guy who wants me to join his dance class and...'

'Brilliant. So you've met someone?' She sounded really excited about this prospect.

'Oh, no, it's not like that, he's just the teacher...'

'Oh.' She sounded disappointed and Sophie was the last person I wanted to disappoint.

'We're doing salsa, tango... bit of everything really... like on Strictly Come Dancing,' I said excitedly, trying in my own way to show her that my life was picking up.

'Wow that sounds fab Mum. Isn't ballroom dancing what Nan used to do?'

'Yeah... I haven't mentioned it to her, not sure how she'd take it. She's a bit funny about the past, you know.'

'Yeah. How is she?'

'Oh she's great. Really happy in her posh home – no more phone calls in the middle of the night demanding I go and fluff her pillow,' I was joking, but my mother had been almost that bad when she'd lived alone. 'So Nan's sorted and now you're away, I'm getting my life back on track,' I said, pointedly. I really did need to let it go, but I still felt a little resentment.

'Fantastic. I think it will be really good for you to get out and live a bit, Mum.' She'd obviously missed my dig, it wasn't easy being subtle yet cutting over 7,000 miles and a million dodgy pixels.

I should have been more open like my own mother, who gave it to everyone with both barrels.

'Dancing felt wonderful, just whirling across that floor with a gorgeous, hunky man.' I wanted to tell her all about it, but we were on limited time, our chats always felt so rushed.

'Ooh you said he was just the teacher, sounds like more than that to me – get you cougar!'

'I wish... he's gorgeous... and gay,' I laughed. 'As he pointed out, I could stand there naked saying "take me, take me," and he wouldn't be interested.'

We both laughed at that.

'But Sophie he can dance... oh god his hips are everywhere and I can't wait to dance with him again, I feel young and light and ...'

'Oh Mum, that's wonderful. He sounds lovely too.'

'Yes I'm glad he's not straight – I think I'd feel embarrassed dancing like that with a straight man. It can be very intimate.'

'Yes, very sensual. Hey, and a weeknight too, Mum? You've changed in the last couple of months, you wouldn't normally go anywhere especially when Silent Witness is on.

'Yeah, well there's more to life than sitting in front of the TV,' I lied. It was on series link for me to enjoy at my leisure. I may have been trying to make my life more interesting – but I hadn't gone completely mad.

'So how are you sweetie?'

'I'm good Mum... really good.'

'Show me your birthmark,' I demanded. I always did this to make sure it was Sophie and not an alien imposter (I'd watched too much TV).

'Mum...'

'I want to make sure it's definitely you and not some Thai imposter who's holding the real Sophie hostage in a Phuket sex ring.'

'I can't, Mum... the man who gave me the pot monkey says I must never show my birthmark...'

Sophie loved to tease me about these things, but you could never be too careful. I couldn't see her face properly, it kept breaking up, and I was ready to call the British Embassy but then I heard her giggle.

'Very funny, Sophie.'

'Mum, chill it's all good,' she sighed, holding up her left arm and lifting her T-shirt to show me the small strawberry mark. I put my face closer to the screen and could just see it, which meant my heart could relax a little – my proof she was still alive and aliens hadn't taken over her body. That cute little purply fruit-shaped mark on my daughter's arm was my safety net.

'Sophie... what about eating?'

'Yes, we're eating enough,' she sighed, with a roll of her eyes.

'We? Who's we?'

'Oh ... yeah... me and Carl. He's from the UK, we met a few days ago in Bangkok,' she manoeuvred her phone to show me a young, scruffy-looking lad who seemed to be lying across her lap! He smiled widely into the camera.

'Hi there, Mrs...'

Christ, I thought, he doesn't even know her surname. I hoped to God she wasn't sleeping with him, but the way he was sprawled across her, the body language was speaking for itself.

'It's beautiful here, Mum, there's so much to do and see. There's elephant trekking and later we're going to the Loi Krathong Festival. It's supposed to be amazing... floating lanterns sent out to sea...'

'Sounds lovely.' I couldn't possibly think about elephants and festivals knowing Sophie was holed up with a stranger on the other side of the world.

I was a bit tongue-tied now I knew Carl was with us and feeling rather foolish recalling my earlier diatribe about dancing with a hunk and going red just thinking about it. Had I known this was a three-way conversation with a young man I didn't know I would have tailored it to something more appropriate.

'So... So what are you up to today, Mum?' Sophie tried to fill the silence.

I didn't feel it necessary to inform Carl and whoever else was languishing 'off camera' that I had big plans to remove my moustache and body hair. Nor did I want to share that I was going to spend the day working out some dance steps, then categorizing my CD collection.

'Today? Oh, I will probably meet some friends ...' I said vaguely, trying to sound bohemian.

Sophie sort of smiled but I detected a hint of pixelated pity all the way from Phuket. She knew I was lying. Sundays were days for families and lovers, and apart from my mum (who had gone on a day trip to Southport), I didn't have anyone to spend Sundays with.

'Anyway, I'll get off now, Mum. Keep tango-ing... you never know, you might find love on the dance floor? We'll send you pictures of the festival later... Carl's a photographer.'

'Great... Is he still there?' I hoped he'd gone because I wanted to warn her not to let him take any compromising photos. These days you couldn't do anything without it ending up on the Internet and one night of passion could mean an eternity of online embarrassment. But she misunderstood and assumed I'd asked if he was still there because I wanted to speak to him. Next thing I know, I'm eye to eye with Carl on the face-time-phone-time-thing.

'Hello Mrs... er...'

'Oh... hi Carl. You're there?'

'Did you want me, Mrs...er...'

'Yes. Hi... just wanted to say... bye.' I wished Sophie wouldn't do things like this. Young people today seemed to share everything online – even their mothers.

At this point Sophie managed to squeeze both their faces onto the shot (they were clearly intimate) and they both shouted 'bye'.

I smiled and waved, feeling a little exposed and awkward in front of Carl, but I felt a frisson of pleasure to think my daughter was proud of me. I was proud of her too, she hadn't hung around in the aftermath of her cancelled wedding, she'd moved on and was making a new life, having a new adventure. Seeing the way my daughter had handled her heartbreak inspired me, I wanted to follow in her footsteps, find a bigger life. And watching myself in the full length mirror as I walked through a tango, I dared to believe it was possible.

Chapter Six

Lipstick Lesbians and Lavender Marriage

'Feel these thighs,' Carole was insisting, thrusting her hand under her bum and clutching at the top of her leg.

'No thanks I'm eating,' I said, biting into a bacon sandwich.

'That's what Martha has done for me... the woman's amazing. I wish you could see my pelvic floor.'

'I'm glad I can't,' I said. She'd only been to Zumba twice and was convinced her body's muscle mass was transformed. I didn't say anything, who was I to disillusion my friend?

She sat down with a tray holding a plate of chips and a cream cake.

'I thought you were on The Atkins Diet?' I said, eyeing her cream cake.

'Yes I *am* on Atkins... but the human body needs a few carbs or you'd die,' she said, like she always did when she had abandoned another diet. I took a large mouthful of bacon sandwich, thinking 'I am the kettle calling the pot.'

'Are you staying for Tony's ballroom class after your zumba?' I asked.

'No. But you should. You're really good, amazing... you should keep at it.'

'Oh, I don't know about that, I'm not going to zumba again, but I'm going to give ballroom another go,' I smiled, hoping my success the previous week wasn't just beginner's luck. I didn't want to make a big fuss to Carole in case I gave it up the following week and failed again, but I was excited to get back to the Dance Centre. It felt like the only time I was free from all my worries and could really let myself go.

That evening as I stepped into class, Tony was waiting. 'Oh thank God you came back,' he whispered in my ear, 'I was worried I'd put you off last week, thrusting you into the spotlight.' He gave me a wink then went straight to the mirror and ran his hands through jet black hair. I detected a hint of eyeliner... a little tinted moisturiser too, he wasn't like any man I'd ever met before.

'Come on Lola, it's showtime,' he said, turning from the mirror and doing a little pirouette towards me. Before I had chance to object he'd grabbed my arm and I was standing in front of the class with him.

'I'm beginning to think you're just using me as a visual aid,' I said. Everyone laughed.

'Yes – ladies and gentlemen, this is Lola – my powerpoint presentation,' he joked, gesturing towards me. 'Now, tonight, love is all around us...' he looked left and right. 'Okay perhaps not ALL around us, in fact some of us can never find it – but I'm sure it's hiding here somewhere.' Everyone laughed again. Dancing was a serious business for Tony, you could tell by the way he conducted himself and his thorough teaching methods, but he made it fun too. And given my last, terrible experience of ballroom dancing in Blackpool all those years before, I needed to find the fun in dancing again.

'Anyway, there's no better way of expressing one's love than in a waltz,' he said this in a posh voice and lifted his hand in the air towards me. I immediately remembered the ballroom hold, and lifted my hand up to his and clasped it while he looked out to the class. 'And she says she hasn't danced for years – this one's a hoofer,' he said, slipping his right hand onto my shoulder blade as I placed my left hand on his shoulder as I used to with my dad.

Then the music started and he was stepping towards me as I naturally stepped back. 'Step side close, step side close,' he was saying and I was just dancing. The music and Tony and the ghost of a dancing memory seemed to be taking me effortlessly across the floor. Where had I stored these steps? I'd never been taught to dance, but the memory of my parents dancing had lay dormant in my brain along with the ballroom dresses in Mum's attic and all it had taken was a little memory jog. The steps and the music and the muscle memory seemed to spill from me and through me, the past and the present colliding. I lost all sense of time as I moved around that floor with Tony, it was like we'd been dancing together for years. Something inside had been stirred, a passion awoken, a need that I just knew would never go back to sleep again. And when the lesson came to an end, Tony and the rest of the group clapped me loudly and patted me on the back, telling me how great I was. It felt good. I'd never shone at anything, never been particularly good at school, avoided sports and had just settled into a quiet life. But it seemed I actually had a talent, here was something I could do well, and people were congratulating me.

'I know we joke around, but you really are good, Lola,' Tony said as we packed up after the lesson. I thanked him and tried not to giggle with delight as I walked home on air. It was hard not to dance up Primrose Gardens, not sure what the neighbours would make of it – but I was unable to resist a dramatic curtsy as I landed in the porch.

❄ ❄ ❄

The following week dragged until the next dance class and I thought I'd die waiting. I ached in places I didn't know I had muscles, but it was a good ache, a reminder that I was moving, flexing, coming to life. Opening the doors of the Dance Centre the following week, I felt like I was coming home. A blast of warm air and damp bodies hit my face and Tony waved and beckoned me over urgently.

'Come on Lola,' he said, 'hurry up I need you here.'

I threw off my boots, quickly put my trainers on, and as I reached him, he grabbed me, firmly taking me by the shoulders, positioning me to face him. 'Stand there,' he said.

'What do you want me to do now?' I asked, thinking it was a dance move.

'I want you to stay there and shield me, Lola, do not move from that position. I need you in front of me so I can be spared the horror – the Zumba class are taking off their 80s spandex – I've already seen seven things I can't unsee.'

How did I ever think this man was straight?

I turned to gaze at all the tiny young things stripping off their tight tops and leggings and slipping into even tighter jeans. 'They look fine, better than I do in my big knickers,' I offered.

'Enough... that's all we need, Lola talking about her big knickers,' he rolled his eyes and addressed the little group now forming to take his class.

'Now you know I'm always saying you have to dance your own dance?' he shouted to the rest of the class. 'Well tonight, me and Lola are gonna show you *our* own dance.'

He took my hand and we started a tango which segued into a waltz and being Tony he did a surprise lift, which I didn't feel I was ready for – but apparently I was. It all came so naturally to me which gave me confidence to carry on. So as the music played we just went with it. We swivelled and strutted and spun around the room and when we landed together, me clinging to him, one leg wrapped around him, my whole body alive with movement.

'Now you can all do that,' he started, but they were shaking their heads and saying how they'd never be able to dance like that; 'I'm a great grandmother,' said one of the ladies, I can't make my legs do that!' At this the others laughed.

'Yes you can – everyone's at a different... level, but what I want to do is give you the basics and you can then dance your own dances.'

There were now five couples in the class including me and Tony. One of the couples was two older ladies who Tony called the Golden Girls. 'Come on Blanche,' he shouted, 'get those legs up... you didn't have any problem getting them up for that silver fox you were with last night did you, love?'

Blanche and her friend (Tony christened Bea after the tallest Golden Girl) would scream with laughter at his cheeky comments.

'You should be on telly, Tony,' Bea shouted back between giggles.

'I am love – I'm on top of that telly when Poldark gets his shirt off!'

The other students were two married couples in their sixties and a slightly younger couple who wanted to learn to dance for their wedding. And like Tony said, they were all at different levels, but the best thing about the class was that we all loved dancing and it didn't matter how good we were.

Tony went back to basics with the steps again, but adding more moves as we went along and turning a few simple twists and turns into a dance. He was such a brilliant dancer he made me a good dancer – and whizzing along that floor I felt light and beautiful and young again. He was funny too, and when he wasn't addressing the rest of the class directly and making hilarious comments, he was whispering in my ear as we went. 'Lola – I reckon the Golden Girls are lipstick lesbians, what do you think?' he hissed.

Tony had a theory about everyone – insisting the two married couples were swingers with each other and the younger couple weren't even in love.

'A lavender marriage, Lola, mark my words,' he hissed while sweeping me across the floor.

'Really?'

'Yes. He's so gay he can't drive straight!' he sighed, twirling me around. 'He's only here because he wants me.'

'Wishful thinking,' I laughed.

✿ ✿ ✿

Over the next few weeks dancing began to seep back into my life like chocolate fudge sauce on ice cream. It melted into each day, bringing excitement and happiness I'd never known before – and I couldn't take the smile off my face.

Dancing helped me to lift the dullness of my life, like wiping it clean and sprinkling on some glitter. I could also see how dancing helped my parents forget their problems – it was pure escapism. Dressed in their dancing finery under a glitterball, they could forget about the unpaid bills and the bailiffs at the door. If Mum ever showed concern about money, Dad just told her she was beautiful and bought her another dress. We often had no electricity – but I had beautiful toys and we dined in the finest restaurants. I learned how to say chateaubriand before I'd learned to say 'cat' and an 'amuse bouche' was something I came to expect before the beans on toast when having tea at friends' homes after school. I remember one particular occasion that sums my Dad up - we had no food in the house and Dad had just £5 in his pocket until pay day; 'I'll pop out and get a loaf or something,' he'd said. In those days £5 could have bought a couple of basic but nutritious meals for a family of three, but Dad came home with three of the finest French patisserie I've ever tasted and six ounces of loose Earl Grey Tea. We enjoyed this on fine china with linen napkins. 'This is what it's all about,' he'd said, handing me a pastry fork as we dined by candlelight.

It was only eight weeks since that October evening when Carole and I first arrived at the zumba class, yet so much had changed for me. I suddenly felt like there were possibilities for me and after all this time I might actually have a chance of a different, bigger life. And as the frosty mornings of winter arrived stripping the trees of their leaves and plunging late afternoons into darkness I was coming alive. To me it felt like summer standing at my checkout, music in my head and steps tingling my toes. I had something more than my job now and I didn't care about loyalty cards, or someone sneaking in the 'ten items only' aisle with fourteen bottles of Coke. And in the middle of winter life was sunnier, more intense. There was always something to look forward to, a new dance, a particular step, a lovely piece of music. Tony had asked if I'd be his dance partner permanently and I was delighted, and we now practiced together several times a week. I loved his dancing and enjoyed his company too – we were becoming good friends.

He gave me a playlist with music for all the different dances we were doing and each night I'd put them on at home and practice. There must have been about thirty tunes on the playlist – I samba'd to Barry Manilow's 'Could it be Magic?' Tangoed to Eminem and Rihanna singing 'Love the way You Lie' and giggled to myself dancing the Cha Cha to Tony's favourite song, 'It's Raining Men'.

I even practised at work, behind the till, with the music going through my head, my toes tapping under the checkout. I was beginning to feel my hip bones and delighted in a secret hip swivel as I passed the items through the scanner. When I was offered an extra late shift stacking shelves, I leapt at it... literally. All that shiny floor space! As soon as it was quiet, I flew down the Pet Food aisle doing the Cha Cha, with Carole being lookout and singing 'It's Raining Men' at the top of her voice. The following week I called Tony and told him to come to Bilton's so we could work on a particularly difficult lift. We still used the room at the Dance Centre, but we had to pay for that, so in between sessions this was free space – a gift for hard-training dancers. I volunteered regularly for late night stacking duties, and Tony would turn up and we'd rehearse for a couple of hours uninterrupted. The cereal aisle was perfect, it was long and wide and as Tony pointed out, 'we can really get a run up into our lifts'. He was an amazing dancer, a wonderful teacher and had the body of an athlete and the strength to lift me up over gondolas of half price biscuits and special 2 for 1 offers on Dog Food. I even began to see Bilton's supermarket in a better light – everything was so much livelier and lovelier when dancing was involved.

Chapter Seven

Her Name was Lola, She Was a Showgirl...

In those first few months I cleared Mum's house, put it up for sale and while Sophie travelled the world, Mum enjoyed life at Wisteria lodge and I had started my own journey. Tony and I worked on all our dances and I mastered most of the basic steps relatively easily. It sounds dramatic, but it felt like I was born to do this. Much of my spare time was now devoted to training and I attended classes for practice, helping Tony demonstrate steps and helping the other students if they were struggling.

However, there was one dance I just couldn't seem to master. Tony was teaching the Argentine Tango and we'd blocked through the basics and demonstrated it to the class, but for some reason I didn't enjoy it. I loved watching it on 'Strictly Come Dancing,' my favourite Argentine Tango performance had to be the wonderful Vincent Simone and Flavia Cacae. They were magical, the chemistry, the passion in the movement and the way they flowed together was just magical, mesmerising. I would watch it again and again online to try and understand the steps, the emotions, but so far the magic had eluded me. The Argentine Tango is a sensual dance, telling the passionate story of a prostitute and her lover (or customer, depending on your interpretation) and involves intimate, hip to hip contact and for the woman to open herself up to her partner physically and emotionally. I found this difficult. I didn't know why, but I felt stiff and awkward and just couldn't relax into it like I could the other dances.

'Jesus Lola, you're dancing like a bloody truck driver tonight,' Tony said after everyone had gone home.

'I know, I just find it really hard to let go,' I said. So he took my arm and pushed his hips against me and I squirmed. 'I'm really uncomfortable,' I said, pulling away.

'Come on Lola, you're about to have mind-blowing sex with your punter... he's probably paying you a fortune, if the sex isn't working, think of the money.'

'I'm sorry, I feel self-conscious. I find this dance so... intimate, so personal. Dancing in front of people is hard enough as it is and I can only do it in front of our class because I know them all now.

'You won't know your audience when you're dancing in that ballroom girl... under that glitterball.'

'Mmmm I don't know about that. Doing the Argentine Tango is like foreplay – which is something I *won't* be doing in a big ballroom with an audience - or glitterballs!'

He laughed; 'Oh Miss Prissy, just let go of Laura and bring on Lola the showgirl.'

'I don't really see myself as a Lola... a sexy woman. It's not in my nature to flaunt my sexuality in front of others...' I explained, wondering if I still had such a thing as a 'sexuality.'

I'd had a difficult and painful love life which started at sixteen when I met the love of my life Cameron Jackson. He was tall, blonde, and just a little wild without being dangerous. I'd loved the way he wore his school tie around his head like a bandanna (it *was* the eighties). Life was difficult for me at home and Cameron saw me through sixth form, hugging me when I felt low and providing me with a wonderful sex education. He was insatiable, but I suppose at sixteen everyone is – and there was nowhere we didn't have sex. The back row of the cinema, his parents' bedroom, up by the wall at the back of our house, and everywhere and anywhere in between. It was more than just lust though and even when he left to go away to university and dumped me after the first term I still thought about him. He'd been my first love and I'd been devastated at the time, which had led directly to my next traumatic encounter with love, which is why I was still single.

It was hard to explain, and I didn't want to share it just yet with Tony, but I hadn't had sexual contact with anyone for years. In fact, I hadn't had much human contact, the only time I'd hugged anyone was Sophie or my mum and sometimes I even found the waltz a little overwhelming. That's why I was able to dance easily with Tony, it wasn't about sex, or intimacy, it was about friendship, and our mutual love of dance.

We tried the Argentine Tango many times over the next few nights, but I just found it impossible. Perhaps it was just all too much too soon, and given my history with men I wasn't ready to flaunt myself, to see myself as a sexual being again. Perhaps I never would?

'Okay, we don't have to start so close, let's try and do the leg hooks again, if we can do that the rest will fall into place,' he said. 'I'm going to hook my leg around yours like this,' he slowly moved one leg under my leg and lifted it, 'now go with it,' he said, moving his legs around mine. And I tried, so hard – I concentrated while attempting to let myself go which was just impossible and resulted in a tangled mess of my legs ...and my emotions.

'Lola, I don't get it. We do lifts and pivots all the time and you waltz like a dream! You can swivel your hips and your knees and your ankles for the Charleston... what is it about this tango you just can't get?'

'I don't know,' I sighed, exasperated. 'It seems the harder I try the more impossible it becomes for me.'

'It's like there's a blockage, it's not about here,' he said, pointing to my legs, 'it's what's going on in your head. Or perhaps you just need a hot night with a passionate man... mind you don't we all?'

I rolled my eyes and tried not to blush.

'I know you've got that passion in you, it just needs to come out,' he smiled. But I could see he was frustrated, and so was I.

After class, Tony asked if I fancied going for a drink and as I had no one to go home to and I wanted to talk dancing, I said yes.

In the pub we ordered two white wines and found a comfy seat. I was exhausted after all the dancing – it was a good feeling, but I'd ache in the morning. After Tony's class I always felt tired, but exhilarated and energised. I wanted to talk about what we were going to do next week and I had one or two ideas to add a few turns and steps.

'We really need to crack the Argentine Tango, Lola – and we will, you just need to open up and become the firecracker I know you are.'

'Not tonight,' I smiled.

'Okay you can have a few hours off. But I want you practising tomorrow. Wrap your legs round the customers at Bilton's, they'll think it's their birthdays,' he laughed.

I giggled; 'I find it hard enough to wrap my legs round you, God help me trying to do it with a stranger. But sometimes I wish a straight guy could make me feel like you do on the dance floor,' I said.

'I wish a gay guy could make me feel like you do on the dance floor,' he sighed.

'I'm now waiting for you to say something funny and bitchy and outrageous,' I said, smiling.

'Hey, Lola I can be genuine you know, and I meant that. I take the piss out of everyone, but that's me. Some people can't take what I have to give out, I'm honest and if I don't like something I say it, but I'll also say if I like something too. And I think you have a real talent – I saw it among the sweat and spandex in that twisted Zumba class. Jeesus – there's you staggering around like an old drunk and Martha screaming about pelvic floors and women's parts with her headband and her barrel chest. She looked the spit of Cher's grandmother!'

I was a bit surprised again at his brutal honesty, but laughed at the thought of Martha, who took herself, her vagina and her Zumba so seriously.

'I can see you and me dancing at Blackpool one day,' he smiled.

'What?' I had no intention of doing any competitions and certainly not at Blackpool. The bad memories of that place would surely be too much for me. 'No. I enjoy dancing but I have no ambition to compete.'

'Mmmm. No ambition. You just said it. Love...' he leaned forward and held my arm, 'there's no point dancing if you don't want the glitterball.' He kissed me gently on the cheek.

'What about just dancing for the joy of it?' I asked.

'Well you could... I suppose, but what's the point in that? The fun is in competing, in taking down all the other bitches,' he laughed.

'I don't want to turn a lovely hobby into a pressure, something I worry about and...'

'Too late.'

'What d'you mean?'

'You've already gone over the line – I could see it tonight. It's more than a hobby... isn't it?'

I was amazed that Tony knew me so well and I nodded. 'Yes, and I want to dance. I want to dance for my dad and achieve stuff he couldn't. But I know my limitations... and I don't want to fail.'

'Oh limitations and failure she's talking now... wow calm down, love, you're on fire.' He made a loud sizzling noise and everyone turned round.

I couldn't help but laugh through my embarrassment. 'Just because I'm not flaunting it around and going on about winning and sex all the time doesn't mean I don't have fire and...'

'There you go, a bit of anger gets you going doesn't it... you came alive for a minute then. Stop being so scared. So... you might fail, but you might fly too.'

He patted my knee; 'You work it girl... and bring it to Blackpool Winter Gardens.'

'Tony, I know how big the Blackpool competitions are, I've been there."

'Yeah, they are huge. But we can start next year with a dance display, then work up to a competition the year after.'

'Mmmm.' I wasn't sure. 'They are international competitions and brutal, involving virtually full-time training. It's okay for you, but I've got others to consider – my daughter's travelling round the world and I've got a mother to visit and... oh yes and I have to keep my job because my trust fund alone won't keep me in designer dance dresses.'

'Yeah my trust fund's a bit meagre too – which is why I'm Tony Griffiths working in a dress shop by day – but by night I'm "Tony Hernandez, Dance Diva".'

'That's funny – my dad worked in a gentleman's outfitters, always said he'd give it up one day and start a dancing school.'

'Me too! Teaching this class is just the beginning for me, one day I'm going to kill Tony Griffiths, bury him under the patio and be Tony Hernandez full time. I'll be teaching at the "The Tony Hernandez School of Dance",' he wrote it in the air with his fingers. 'Like your Dad, I just do the day job to supplement the dancing, but one day that'll change.'

'Well, Dad never made it I'm afraid... fate had other plans.'

'Oh, that's a shame... what happened?'

I shook my head.

'It's okay,' he said, finishing his drink, 'just don't let your parents' lives decide yours. My dad was a big butch lorry driver and look at me? God only knows where I come from, but my parents always let me be me – may they rest in peace. My mum used to say, "Life is to be lived, not regretted. And I'm determined to live mine dancing".'

'I envy you your ambition...'

'It's not exclusive to me, Lola, you're allowed some too, you know.'

'Yes, but I don't have the money or the training to open a dance school. As for the competitions, once you start, you just end up on the road all the time... it's a half-life.'

'And working in a supermarket all day and going home and worrying about your daughter who's on the other side of the world isn't a half life?'

I was offended, I'd known him six weeks and though I felt close to Tony I was hurt to think he thought of me this way and felt he could openly criticise me; 'Tony, you don't know me. You don't know anything about my life, and yes you might get off on "telling it like it is" and letting people know what you think, but sometimes people don't want your opinion. I'm fed up of people telling me I'm not living the "right" life, that I'm not going anywhere. It's enough with my mother and my daughter telling me I'm a failure and now you're telling me I need ambition and... and a... shag!' I'd said this quite loudly, with some passion and caused a slight ripple around the snug in the King's Head, but all the hurt I'd felt after Sophie's comments had been bottled up until that moment. Then I started to cry.

'I'm sorry, it's just that everyone's criticising me and I thought you were my friend. I thought you understood that I feel battered and bruised and... I can't take much more,' I said between sobs.

'I'm so sorry,' he said gently, 'but just because I'm gay it doesn't mean I get it. I sometimes find women as weird as straight men do. Tell me what I don't understand.'

'Look, I love dancing, I live for it. Since I started your classes my life has really changed, I can't wait to train and I spend my days at work just thinking about dancing, it's all about the dancing... and everything else is about the waiting.'

He nodded, encouraging me to continue.

'I do have ambition and I do want a better, bigger life but so did my parents once but it never happened for them. You're right – I am scared of pushing too hard because I'm scared of falling flat on my face and sometimes life's bigger than we expect and things happen and people let you down or leave you and...'

'So tell me,' he said gently, 'tell me about your parents.'

'I don't know why my parents' dream failed, but I'm scared if I chase the same dream I'll fail too,' I said, going on to tell him how despite wanting it so badly, Dad had never got to Spain. I explained about finding the letter and how it seemed there was a problem in their marriage but I didn't know what it was.

I'd obviously been too young to understand what was happening and after Dad left us, we just got on with it. The world was a different place then, and Mum was heartbroken but never talked about it, so we just fought on, struggling for money, in a permanent state of shock in our insular little world with no outside help.

I'd been so lonely during those years. As a teenager I had friends at school but couldn't commit to nights out or really let myself go because I was always worried about Mum. I hated leaving her and at the same time didn't feel I could invite my friends round because our house was Mum's sanctuary, where she'd cut herself off from the world. As for boyfriends I had only Cameron during those teen years and when he smashed my schoolgirl heart I almost gave up on loving anyone again. But I was young, and still had a little hope so when I met a handsome, twenty-four-year-old musician at a bus stop I was ripe for the picking. John was bohemian, he didn't live by rules and he seemed to know all about the world. He smoked roll-ups, wore his hair long, his leather jacket loose and for a few months with him I felt like a rock chick.

So when John said he had an uncle in Melbourne and a dream to live in Australia, I offered to go with him. I had nothing to keep me here except my mum, who was too wrapped up in herself to care, and John and I talked long into the night about leaving the cold and the memories behind. We'd been together about eight months when I fell pregnant, I was surprised but not too worried. We'd already committed to a future together and this would just cement our lives further, but when I told him, the look on his face told me everything I needed to know... he rolled another ciggie and asked me how much I'd need to 'get rid of it'. From that moment I started a different journey – one I'd be taking alone. He went off to Australia and I stayed behind, I never heard from him again. I have never once regretted my decision to have my daughter, but John left me with a mistrust of men.

Over the years I'd had the odd fling, but I'd been wary after John and scared stiff of being let down again. It's not unusual for a young person to have their heart broken a few times before finding 'the right one', but I'd always imagined I'd find a partner and live happily ever after. Until my thirties I held out for it – but now I was tired of waiting.

Sharing my life story with Tony in a wine bar full of people wasn't easy, and I was trying hard not to burst into tears again.

'And in the past few weeks as I've started to dance I've realised that there's a little bit of me that sparkles, and isn't quite so world-weary and battered as the rest of me. When I get on that dance floor, that little part of me grows and I'm stronger, more confident, in charge of my body... my life too, I suppose. It's so empowering and I know now I don't need a man to change my life – I just need courage, like the Lion in Wizard of Oz.'

'Yes... that's exactly it. I know just what you mean, I feel like the real "me" is the one on that dance floor.' He smiled, 'But if you're the lion, can I be Dorothy? We did that play at school and I was born to play Dorothy, but those tyrants made me play the tin man... the tin man!?'

'I guess we all have our disappointments in life,' I tried to laugh, but my nose was running and my eyes were streaming. 'I'm sorry, but telling you all that stuff was like a detox,' I sighed.

Tony gave me a handkerchief.

I took it gratefully and wiped my nose. 'Is it scented?' I asked through my tears.

'Yes... spring lavender, sweetie.'

'Who in the twenty-first century even has a handkerchief... let alone a lavender one?'

'I do. Now can you just move away a little, your saltwater tears are dripping on my Armani jacket.' I looked up through mucus and tears and he was smiling. 'I'm only joking... not about you leaning on me – about it being Armani. It's Primani and the last thing it needs is you blubbing all over it, you crazy bitch.'

I laughed, and touched his arm; 'Thanks for listening, Tony.'

'Thanks for letting me. I know I can be a bit of a prickly old queen, but I can see you've been through it and it explains a lot. But don't forget, Lola, you're a big, strong woman.'

'Less of the big...' I laughed.

'A *big* strong woman who's discovering what she wants,' he widened his arms out to stress the hugeness and I wafted him with his hankie.

'Some people watch the dancing on TV and think "Ooh I want to dance like that – I'm going to find a class – I can see myself in that glittery frock." Ballroom magpies, love – they just see the glint and head straight for it, but there's no substance, no willingness to put the hours in. You know because of your mum and dad that dancing isn't all about the sequins, it's about blood, sweat and tears... and a few sequins if you're lucky. But you know all that and you're determined, and whatever you might say about not being ambitious, there's fire in your eyes, babe.'

I was touched by his observation.

'Now, I know it won't be easy, but let's seriously think about dancing at Blackpool, focussing on that goal will give us both something to aim for and train for... it will be our Copacabana.'

'Her name was Lola, she was a showgirl,' I smiled.

'Yes... and he was called Tony... oh we were meant to be you and me. Oh...'

'What?'

'I just remembered what happened at the end... it was tragic, she was very, very old and kept hanging around the dance floor.'

'Yes – and he was dead, because he kept saying how old she was,' I warned and we both laughed loudly then quietly hummed the song together.

Tony was right, I had found what I was looking for, but it would be good for me to focus on a goal now. I had, for so long lived in fear of heading into the light and here he was a knight in shining armour offering me his hand. He was holding it out to me, a goal, something to aim for, something to achieve – no excuses, no 'tomorrows', we start now. I was me and though I could learn from the past and be inspired by my parents – it wasn't *my* future.

I felt a surge of excitement and fear pulse through me. 'I think I might just consider competing,' I said, biting my lip, 'after all, I've got a great partner. I can almost taste those sequins.'

'Babe, you have the very best partner, and you were born with sequins running through your veins, I don't know how you kept off that dance floor all these years.'

'Yeah, life just got in the way. But now might just be my time. And the more I think about it the more I want to do everything my parents didn't... for them.'

'That's good Lola, but you have to do it for yourself as well. You have to free yourself, love, I've had some traumatic love affairs where I thought I'd die when they dumped me – but I always had the dance. It's a refuge in a cruel world and it sounds like there's some painful memories tied up in there, so use them – channel your feelings, take hold of them. I sometimes think you're pushing them away – embrace them and dance through.'

What he was saying made sense and I felt a light go on somewhere inside me.

'Oh listen to me going on, I suppose I'm just worried you'll do what my other partners have done, train and go through hell only to give up halfway through.'

'I won't. I can't give this up, I'm doing it for my dad but also for me.'

'Yeah. I think we should celebrate that. Do you want another white wine or shall we go all out and have a couple of pink ladies?'

I nodded and off he went to the bar for the next round, and after much laughter and several more pink ladies, he bundled me into a taxi home. I look back on that night as being pivotal in my commitment to making dance my future, and filling my life with sequins again. It was meant to be and my life had been leading up to being back on that dance floor. I was elated, tipsy, giggly... and just a little bit scared.

Chapter Eight

Christmas Wishes and Online Kisses

It was almost Christmas and as Sophie would be in Bangkok I was contemplating my options. 1) A Christmas with my mother and her friends at Wisteria Lodge where a pantomime involving all residents and their families would be taking place? 2) A day with Tony at his sister Rita's house, followed by an evening on Grindr selecting Tony's next shag? Or 3) A day home alone with some good DVDs, whatever I wanted on the telly, a nice dinner and the 'Strictly Come Dancing Christmas Special.' It was a tough one and I came to the conclusion that home alone was the winner.

And it was surrounded by fairly lights, my tree twinkling in the corner and a small turkey crown roasting in the oven that Cameron Jackson, my first love suddenly came back into my life. I don't mean he was actually in my living room, but he requested my friendship on Facebook. I had no idea he was even on Facebook, I wasn't a regular user and had only joined because it was another portal to Sophie, so receiving a request from him on Christmas day was wonderful. It felt like... well, Christmas!

I immediately found his page but couldn't see anything until I'd accepted his friend request. When the photos and comments suddenly flooded the screen, I was overcome with emotion. It was so weird seeing someone I'd known almost thirty years ago, and through the slightly greying hair and the leaner, more lined face, I recognised the schoolboy I'd once loved. It was also weird to think how people's lives go on once they've left ours. It seemed like his life had been full-on – even his most recent posts gave a sense of a life very much being lived. There were pictures of him doing charity runs and at parties, shots of him smiling in sunglasses from foreign beaches and just seeing him again made my heart flutter a little. I looked closely at some of the blurry photos to see if there was a wife, but it was hard to tell, no one was tagged. Then I remembered the relationship status at the top left side of the page, and to my relief there was nothing that said 'married' or 'in a relationship'. I imagined he would probably be in a relationship of some sort, but today wasn't the day to see him in a clinch with a pretty wife. To see 'married' as his status when I was all alone on Christmas Day might have put me off my chocolate covered brazils. I scrolled through his page, hungry for information, for any indication of where he worked, what he was like... who he was sleeping with? I gazed closely at smiling summer photos of him with a football and a younger man (his son?) on a beach. There were palm trees, so it was obviously somewhere far away and exotic... definitely nowhere I'd ever been. I scrolled down anxiously taking it all in. Cameron in sunglasses leaning out of a car, in a sunny pub garden with his brother, standing proudly behind a smoky barbecue with a pint in his hand... several smiley kids in the forefront of the photo.

Then my heart plummeted even further when I spotted a recent photo of him with an attractive young blonde. They were stood by a Christmas tree, he had his arm around her and she was positively twinkling, who could blame her? He still looked good. I put my glasses on I could see he'd tagged her, so I did what any self-respecting Facebook stalker would do and clicked straight to her page. Sadly as I was met with a disappointing blank because I wasn't a FB friend and couldn't see her details. I had the only detail I needed though, her name. Holly Jackson... his wife. Great. Like everyone else I'd known, Cameron had moved on with his life and was settled with a perfect partner, a handful of kids, family holidays, friends, barbecues and bottles of wine all summer. I suppose I'd just assumed as he'd requested my friendship on Christmas Day he must be messing about on Facebook and therefore alone. But he just wanted to add me to his list of friends and show off about his holidays and his family and his lovely big life. It was only a 'friend' request, I told myself, checking my tiny turkey crown, opening a bottle of wine and taking a big slurp. I didn't want to chase after someone out of my league and get embroiled in some online thing that might lead to more heartache – he wouldn't fancy me now. He'd loved the younger me, someone who was a bit more lively, fresh-faced with no wrinkles or strands of grey – someone quite different – a girl from another planet.

Seeing Cameron's happy ever after was quite a dampener and gave me doubts about myself that even the 'Strictly Christmas Special' couldn't quite eradicate. And before going to bed I couldn't resist checking Facebook again – and as the screen flickered to life I could see a red sign over the private message logo. I gasped slightly and my heart fluttered a little as I opened up the message and saw it was from him. It was like reaching back through the past, touching something that had once meant so much to me, and I felt quite overwhelmed as I read his words.

Hi, it's you Laura isn't it? I saw your photo you haven't changed, you're still as good-looking as you were at school! ☺

I flushed slightly – and it wasn't the wine or the menopause. He was still as cheeky and flirty as ever then – even if he was married. I sat down with the laptop on my knee and replied.

Hi, yes it's me! I saw your photo too and I remembered how you always wore your school tie around your head. How are you?

He responded immediately, saying he was fine, and he now wore ties round his neck. I asked if he was enjoying Christmas with the family (my not so subtle way of checking on the health of his marriage). He responded by saying 'I'm spending Christmas at my mother's, which I found interesting – particularly the 'I' instead of 'we.' He asked if I was married and so I felt it was okay to ask him, but when he said he was divorced, I thought 'I'm not being made a fool of here,' so I challenged him in a light-hearted way about the beautiful blonde on his timeline.

'She's my daughter, Holly, she's seventeen,' he said, with a smiley face logo. I smiled to myself, relieved he wasn't married to a gorgeous blonde.

He explained that he was now divorced from Holly's mother – which I have to admit pleased me and I told him all about Sophie.

I intimated that I'd had endless lovers, countless offers of marriage but none of them were right for me (well, a girl needs good PR). We messaged each other for hours, sharing memories of school and of our relationship too and the years just slipped away. We'd grown up together and been through the whole teenage thing and I found him just as easy to talk to as I had then. Cameron and I had a bond I suppose - both virgins when we met we discovered sex together, which was quite a special journey to share with someone. He'd always be special to me and I enjoyed our trip down memory lane. He reminded me of a time when the chemistry teacher found us snogging in the lab, and how his parents came back early one night almost catching us in their bed. We had been through a lot together in those two years, and had gone from schoolkids to young adults. It was funny to think that this man I was writing to knew everything about my early life, my young body and was back here chatting to me. I'd never expected to hear or see Cameron Jackson ever again, he was so deeply embedded in my past it was as though he didn't exist outside that time of flavoured lip gloss, first kisses and fumbled sex.

Eventually we said goodnight, both promising to keep in touch, and as I closed my laptop I thought about what Sophie would say when I told her I'd been flirting online. I was so pleased with myself, I was a thoroughly modern woman with a job, a life and now my own online 'friend'.

Over the next few weeks I kept in touch with Cameron. He was a breath of fresh air, always talking about the past, reminding me of a time when anything could happen. We'd had the world at our feet, yet like most kids that age we didn't realise or appreciate everything we had. Though he hadn't changed, he was still funny but he obviously had an important job at the local council and he loved his two kids Holly and Jack. It was good to talk to someone without the distractions of work and family – in our little online bubble we could communicate privately without the rest of the world even knowing about it. I got the feeling he yearned for the past and all the freedom we had when we were younger. 'When you're young life seems to go on forever, you wait for birthdays and Christmas and think they'll never come, but you spend the second half of your life holding them back,' he wrote in one of our chats.

I felt the same, and meeting someone who had been such a big part of my life during that heady time reminded me what it felt like to have future and all the infinite possibilities it held.

I found the combination of dancing and Cameron to be quite a delicious cocktail and when I told Sophie she was actually impressed.

'Oooh, Mum, you dark horse,' she said. 'I think I'll have to come home immediately before you do something you regret... I hope you're taking precautions?' she said, impersonating my voice.

I laughed. 'If only that were necessary,' I sighed. 'Firstly I doubt I could get pregnant at my age and secondly he is merely an online flirtation... though we have exchanged phone numbers, which in today's world is probably the equivalent of getting engaged.'

We laughed about it, but if I'm honest I think even on that first night I'd begun to warm up that little piece of Cameron that had been left in my heart.

Meanwhile, Tony was constantly telling me to stand straight, his hand always in the small of my back metaphorically and physically moving me forward. He would sometimes cook for me in his cramped little flat and over delicious salads and fish dishes we'd talk about dancing. Even sitting at the table, our fingers would dance across the surface to explain a move, our arms showing the other one a particular hold, a finger click.

Tony was keen for me to make the very most of dancing and helped me to change my own rather fatty diet for something more healthy. He was like a personal trainer, always telling me I could do one more step, eat one less cake and that I was capable of anything.

'You can do it, Laura – so stop saying you can't,' he'd say crossly if I ever even hinted that I might just throw the towel in. We worked hard, trained until the sweat dripped from our faces and my limbs screamed for me to stop, but we pushed through and I felt better for it. My body was beginning to feel firm, my legs strong and Tony said I was building stamina because I could dance for hours and never complained.

'One more run through,' he'd say, holding out his arms or just standing in his opening pose and I would willingly follow his lead. And as much as I needed him, I realised Tony needed me too. Until we met, we'd both spent Sundays alone and when Tony felt like hell at midnight wondering where his life was going he now had me to call. I can't tell you how many of those midnight calls I received where Tony had to be talked through a man problem or even a dance we were trying to crack together. I'm convinced we were the only people in the world who could call each other without even saying hello and start with 'that back step into your tango was stiff tonight...'

I even kept a calm communication with Sophie and stopped leaving frantic messages on her phone. I held back from declaring an international emergency and demanding to speak to the British Ambassador of wherever she was if she didn't respond immediately to my texts. She was, is my heart and I would always worry about her wherever in the world she was — but I could channel it now and give my inner parent paranoia a day off every now and then. My energy and time was now being taken up with the dance and I was filled with an inner calm like I'd never felt before.

I began to like the way my body was changing too —I'd lost weight, and at forty-four I felt more confident than ever about my physical self. I'd never enjoyed walking into a room or being noticed, so I'd kept myself to myself, happy to stay in the background. But now I didn't try to hide, staying under the radar in case I was noticed, I wanted to be noticed and the physical confidence was making me a stronger person. At work, when Julie reminded Carole and I 'no chit-chatting on the floor, ladies,' when we were actually on a break, I didn't nod and scuttle off like before, I squared up to her. 'We are having a conversation Julie — not a "chit-chat", as you put it. We are two trusted, mature employees having a short break in a very long day and I speak for both of us when I say please will you not address us like we are three years old.' She was taken aback and so was I — but she never said the c word again in my presence.

Carole was amazed; 'What's got into you?' she'd gasped.

I shrugged, but I knew it was down to the dancing. For me there was no more hiding behind a smile and being afraid to speak up because I was scared to rock anybody's boat. In the past I felt like I had to apologise for being me, for not being good enough, or slim enough or strong enough. I'd felt like a disappointment to everyone, but I wasn't a disappointment to Tony, he said I was 'a bloody revelation'.

'You are looking good, girlfriend,' he commented with a whistle one night as I arrived in new jeans and trainers for a training session. I'd let my hair grow a little, had it shaped and spent more than I normally would on a sea blue cotton jumper. I wasn't wearing my glasses and Tony said I looked ten years younger. I was taking more care over my appearance these days because I didn't feel invisible any more and wanted to look my best.

'You are doing so well I want to try the Argentine Tango again,' Tony said.

'Really? So soon?' I sighed. I'd just begun to feel really sure of myself, and I didn't want a night of leg-locking if it led to my confidence being knocked because I couldn't do it and losing what little self-esteem I was building. 'I don't feel ready, Tony, I just need to practise at home on my own a bit more... let's give it a week or so...'

'No, you're putting things off again, Lola – I thought we weren't going down that road of saying 'I'll do it next week, tomorrow.' I don't want to hear your theories on why it won't work, I just want you on that floor gagging for it,' he snapped, 'just listen to the music first, let it flow through you, imagine you're having sex with a gorgeous straight guy,' he winked.

So we tried again, but still I couldn't 'feel' it the way I felt the other dances.

'I know you thought I was joking when I said you needed a good shag, but girlfriend you so do,' he said afterwards. 'Why don't you get Facebook guy over and offer him your body on a plate?'

'I'm not sure it's as simple as that,' I laughed. Tony knew all about Cameron and though it was still just an online friendship with flirting Tony couldn't wait for each instalment.

'I'm not spoiling what Cameron and I have got...'
I started.

'Love, you haven't got anything – yet, but just think what you could have if you got him naked on that velour sofa and practiced the tango on him.'

'Yes and I'd probably fall off the sofa mid-'tango' knowing my luck,' I laughed. 'But seriously, I've been hurt in the past and... I don't want a man coming into my life and...'

'Whoa girl. Who said anything about a relationship? I'm talking about a night... or just a couple of hours of red hot passion. Trust me it will be like a dam bursting...'

'Oh what a lovely image...' I sighed.

'Don't worry, we'll nail that tango – but you have to get nailed first, girl... you just need to have sex... with anyone. Okay?'

'Yes. I'll pick someone up on the way home,' I said, thinking how it must have been so easy for Tony. He was a gorgeous gay man and he didn't get it that an average middle-aged woman couldn't just pick up any man she fancied like he did.

'When are you going to believe that you're attractive ... gorgeous even? Lola, you just need to believe it.'

His smile made me smile – I liked Tony's approval, it made me feel good about myself. Our friendship was special – it wasn't complicated by sex or rivalry or jealousy we just spent our time laughing and dancing – and what's not to love about that?

Chapter Nine

Shattered Dreams and Flesh Tinted Pixels

In between long shifts at Bilton's, Tony and I worked on our 'repertoire' as he called it.

'We need to be eclectic, not predictable or complacent – always offering a little surprise here, a quirk there,' Tony said.

'My dad always used to say stuff like that... about dancing. You remind me of him.'

'Really?'

'Yeah, there's a song that's been going through my head for years, I think Luther Van Dross sang it, it's called "To Dance with my Father Again".'

'Yes I know the one you mean, it's really slow, makes me want to cry.'

'Me too – I suppose it's about being able to say goodbye. I never said goodbye to my dad and if I could have anything – I'd have one last dance with him.'

Tony smiled. 'I think we could dance to that song you know, a waltz?'

'I would be a blubbering mess.'

'Me too,' he laughed.

'It's not just the dancing though. I know it's not the image you want, but like him you make me feel safe, like my dad did.'

'Safe? Try telling that to the hunky builder who's doing my brickwork. He looks scared to death every time I go near him.' Typical Tony, he found it hard sometimes to take compliments and would turn them into a joke.

'Don't go near him then,' I said.

'I can't help myself. I stand behind him when he's on the ladder and pretend to be ever so interested in his work, but really I want to look at his cute bum. I found him on this website that said his work was "robust, pleasing to the eye and largely maintenance free". I thought he was describing himself, I didn't realise it was actually a builders' website. So when he turns up on my doorstep in a big hard hat with a bag of tools I thought I'd died and gone to heaven.'

Tony's whole approach to life was just what I needed after a lifetime living with Mum's melancholy. He never took anything too seriously – though everything was high drama, the most horrendous thing could happen and Tony would turn it into something hilarious. Even when he discovered his latest boyfriend was involved in internet porn he'd called me to tell me through his tears and we ended up laughing.

'He shattered all my dreams, Lola,' he sighed. 'I opened up that computer and was faced with the motherload of flesh-tinted pixels.'

I wasn't quite sure what this meant. 'Oh... is that so bad?'

'Bad? Lola he's been looking at men having sex online.'

'I repeat... is that so bad?'

'It is when I zoom in and see he's one of them!'

'Oh that's bad,' I said, 'what a betrayal.'

'Darling you are so right – a betrayal. I wish I'd thought of that word when I lambasted him with a million Fs... it's very Joan Crawford isn't it? Betrayal?' he said, in his quivering Joan Crawford voice.

'So it's over with Adrian and time for a fresh start,' I said.

'Yes, truth be told we'd fallen out of love and there's nothing sadder than watching someone you once loved become a stranger. Except maybe over-tweezered eyebrows?' he suggested as a quick aside. 'Anyway, I'm going to wash that man right out of my hair, and do you know the first thing I did when he dumped me – before calling you, Lola – I went online and booked a trip to Spain later this year.'

'Lovely. For a holiday?'

'Not just a holiday. I've always wanted to dance flamenco – and I promised myself I would learn properly, which means going to Spain. I feel if I can get the basic steps and rhythm down then I can play around with it and do flamenco a la Tony. Oh I wish we could go together, but I got the last place on the course.'

'Ooh I've got goose bumps, that's really spooky because my dad's biggest dream was to learn flamenco in Spain. How weird is that?'

'Yeah weird – but I doubt he wanted to wear the frills like I do,' he laughed. 'You should come with me next time?'

I smiled at the thought of Tony camping it up in the huge frilled sleeves worn by the male flamenco dancers.

'Yes, I'd love to go to Spain, maybe one day,' I heard myself say, in my father's voice. Like my Dad I was putting things off, standing on the edge unable to jump and I wasn't sure I'd ever summon the courage to do it alone. 'How long will you be away?' I suddenly panicked, I couldn't dance without my partner.

'Only a couple of weeks, I'm going to a place called Escuela Carmen de las Cuevas. It's a fabulous flamenco school set in the Sacramento caves... sounds totally gorgeous doesn't it? Atmospheric, authentic, and you know me, honey, I like to keep it real.'

I could only imagine how it would feel, to really get inside the dance and live it in the place it was born. I felt my stomach fizz just thinking about it and wished I could go with him. But there were no more places on the course and I wasn't ready yet, but I promised myself I would go to Spain and learn Flamenco – one day.

'I've booked it for August 16th which is of course the birthday of our lady Madonna Louise Veronica Ciccone. And just like Madonna I will return with a taste of flamenco and a string of Spanish lovers... I can't wait.'

'It sounds wonderful,' I sighed. 'I'm really happy for you... I'll definitely come with you next time.' I was envious of his confidence and his freedom to just take off, I had commitments, I couldn't leave Mum and what if Sophie suddenly needed me?

'Yeah Lola you're coming with me next time. And I won't let you put it off like you said your dad did... but it's tough, so you have to be prepared to fail... and try again. That's good advice isn't it? I got it from a book.'

'Which one?'

'Oh I don't remember what it's called, I buy a self-help book every time I'm dumped and it's happened so many times the hundreds of titles merge into one. It was called something like,' he breathed in, gave a dramatic pause 'Feel the Fear and Shag Him Anyway!' We both laughed.

It amazed me the way Tony had just stepped into my life, and though we'd only known each other a few months it was like we'd always been friends. Tony had even received my mother's approval on a recent visit. We were like an old married couple except for the sex, but as Tony said, old married couples don't do it anyway – so in essence we were the very picture of a couple who'd been married for years. I just had one little shadow on the horizon... I still had to talk to Mum about Dad's letter. I'd been to visit her a few times but had put off 'the conversation' I didn't want to bring up painful memories from the past, and even if I asked her directly she'd have every right to refuse to tell me about what happened between her and Dad. Part of me was scared to know the truth, I'd always seen my parents as the perfect couple with the perfect love. Would I feel differently about them, about Dad, if I was told this wasn't the truth? I was torn between being frightened to ask and have my illusions shattered – and desperately wanting to know what had happened. I had to talk to Mum and let her know I was dancing ballroom too, another conversation I'd been putting off, but wanted to keep that to myself a little longer. Dancing felt to me like a beautiful, but fragile bird in my hands and I wanted to protect it, protect me from destroying it. There was every chance that Mum might criticise me, and make a comment about me dancing that would spoil it for me. So for now I would keep that little bird in both hands and close to my heart.

Chapter Ten

The Fine Tart of Sexting

'Do you still go dancing?' Carole asked over lunch. She was drinking a strawberry meal replacement drink and I was having a chicken salad.

I nodded. 'I go nearly every night now, I can't get enough.'

'Is that gorgeous Tony still gay?'

'Yep... it's not a moveable feast, Carole. It's like me asking you if you're still hetero.'

'I know, but it seems such a waste. You'd make a gorgeous-looking couple, both dark haired, dark eyed, and you've gone all... "glossy". Makes me wish I'd stuck with the Zumba if I could get a figure like yours, but the human body can't do that every week and live.'

'No,' I said, doubtfully. She'd only managed a couple of weeks at zumba class, she said it wasn't possible for the human body to survive the sheer physical punishment of Martha's sessions.

'Have you heard from Cameron?' she asked.

I'd told Carole about mine and Cameron's online liaisons and she said she remembered him vaguely from school and his sister was a member at her slimming club. Carole left school before the sixth form so wasn't around to witness our passion at the time but was fascinated to know every detail now. I enjoyed chatting to Cameron, it was just flirting, but it made me feel good about myself. We talked more about the past than the present and he seemed reluctant to talk about his ex wife or the divorce, he was more interested in flirting and making suggestive comments. I understood that he might not want to share the pain of a broken marriage with me and I was just glad I finally had someone I could talk to and tell my troubles at the end of the day. I also enjoyed the frisson of our flirty chats, recently his messages had become a little raunchier. Sometimes in the middle of the night I'd get a text asking if I was lonely and needed company in my big bed. But it was all very light-hearted and I didn't mind, I quite enjoyed feeling wanted, desired again after such a long time – even if it was just online and just for fun.

Carole loved to hear about my online flirting. 'As Jason and I gave up sex for Lent about fourteen years ago and never bothered to reinstate it I shall live vicariously through you,' she'd said. So, having known about it for a few weeks, Carole wanted her usual update over strawberry slimming milk.

'Do you think you'll meet up?' she asked, opening up a large block of Cadburys chocolate.

'I don't know, I'm not sure I want to, it might spoil things. We don't really talk about anything serious. It's just memories about school, about the teachers and it just takes me back, makes me feel good. I didn't have a very happy time when I was younger, but

Cameron was a little bit of light in the darkness,' I sighed. Neither of us had ever mentioned meeting up and that was fine with me, I enjoyed what we had for now, and like my dancing I wanted to take each step one at a time.

'Well, I suppose if it stays online it can't do any harm,' she smiled.

'It can't do any harm even if we meet up... can it?' I had considered the possibility that one day he might suggest we get together. I'd even wondered if I should suggest it myself – it seemed the next logical step, but I was too nervous. And I didn't want to spoil what we had.

✳ ✳ ✳

That night when Tony and I stopped for a ten minute break, I had a sext from Cameron that was particularly explicit. He asked me if I'd give him a private dance... naked. I was flattered, but a little taken aback - I could feel the blood rushing to my face as I read it, but when I showed Tony he said it was 'positively tame, dear'. So I decided to be a little daring and sext Cameron back. I wasn't comfortable with sexting and quite frankly at my age I felt a bit silly texting sexual stuff. Tony was the expert – but I didn't want to ask him what to say because he would snatch the phone off me and send something so X-rated Cameron would be horrified and probably take out an injunction against me. So I wrote it without help and went for something playful, but suggestive.

'Hey, I'm doing the Argentine Tango. It's like making love on the dance floor and it made me think about you and how I would love to be your private dancer. I'm not wearing any underwear – and I'm very, very hot!' I typed, feeling that was just the right balance between playful and raunchy, and I pressed send feeling outrageous, but pleased with myself.

When Tony wandered over with two bottles of water, I showed it to him. 'You see, I can let go... I may not be from the underbelly of Brazil, but I'm a total tart when it comes to the art of sexting,' I smiled, proudly.

'Yeah... ooh that's good, babe.'

'Is it raunchy enough?'

'Yeah... but who's Carl?'

'Carl? He's Sophie's boyfriend why?'

'Oh, love. That's... that's not okay,' he was deadly serious.

'What do you ...mean?' I looked down at the message which, in my urgency, I'd mistakenly sent to Carl instead of Cameron. I'd asked Sophie to give me his mobile number so I could call if I couldn't get hold of her. Both Cameron and Carl were in my phonebook under C – an easy mistake to make. So, I'd just sexted my daughter's boyfriend, informing him that I was hot, would love to be his private dancer... and I had no pants on!

'Shit. Oh shit. Oh my God, Tony... Tony what can I do?' I said, throwing the phone at him like it might scald me. 'Make it stop. I don't want to be Carl's private dancer... what can I do? It's a long way to Phuket, can I stop it getting there?'

'No, love. It's gone,' Tony was shaking his head and looking at the screen, then he started smiling, 'but if he sexts you back you're a cougar – if he doesn't you're a gonner,' he roared with laughter.

'It's not funny, Tony.'

'Not funny? It's bloody *hilarious*,' he laughed.

'Oh God, imagine if Carl leaves Sophie because of her inappropriate mother? Oh Christ, Christ, shit... she's sent me a message.'

I opened it and we both peered at my phone.

'Mum. Really?'

There were no words I suppose.

'Oh how entertaining,' Tony laughed when he read it, 'she'll be upping her game with old Carl now, thinking mummy wants in on the action.'

'Stop that...' I said, desperately texting Sophie to say it was a mistake. 'I'll have to FaceTime her later and explain everything. Oh God and Carl will be there... looking at me on screen...wondering how I could do such a thing.' I felt sick.

'What will you say?'

'I'll tell her it was you.'

'Oh that's a great idea - her mother's gay friend, who doesn't know Carl or Sophie, just took it upon himself to text and offer pantless private dancing. They'll believe that... much.'

'Oh I've told Sophie what you're like – nothing would surprise her. Let's get on with the session, it will take my mind off what I've just done.'

'Okay, but only if you put your knickers back on.'

So Tony had another good laugh and we got back on the floor, forgetting about men and my major faux pas doing the thing we loved most – dancing. Despite my lack of bedroom action, we gave the Argentine Tango another go. Our dance began with a flirtatious leg hook followed by a dramatic battle of wills, a pull towards and a push away. A lift high in the air, my legs wide, toes pointed, then a landing, and Tony throwing me across the room, me coming back for more and miming a slap across his face. But when we got together it was electric, and I felt such a depth of intimacy, a closeness I'd never felt with anyone. The dance climaxed with us both in absolute sync, our legs a perfect mirror, our brains and bodies working as one. And so we danced and danced until we couldn't dance any more. Tony hurling me around the dance floor, making like a big butch cowboy, while I strutted the steamy streets of Brazil – in a dance centre in the West Midlands.

'That was so much better – Lola you're nearly there,' he said, as the dance ended. He was breathless and sweating, wiping his forehead with a towel.

'Yes, I really felt it then, I just let it carry me away – almost. Ooh it's so exciting Tony!'

'I told you Lola you just needed a little bedroom action... and all that sexting is opening those floodgates... now you just need a hot night of passion and you will be living it girl!'

I walked home that evening, the January night was freezing cold but I was warm inside was and feeling every muscle, every sinew in my body, thanks to dancing – something I was good at, something that made me truly happy after all these years. What a brilliant day, I thought, despite a sexting scandal involving my daughter's boyfriend that I needed to unravel as soon as I got in.

Tony was right, all I needed now was a night with a man to finally make me come, throw off the shackles and become the dancer

I knew I could be. alive. But like the Argentine Tango, the thought of getting physically close to someone and letting go was scary.

❊ ❊ ❊

Dance had become my respite from a humdrum life watching Weetabix on a checkout belt, my escape. Before now I'd spent my days imagining other lives from the contents of someone else's basket – and wondering when my daughter would call. But now I thought about the dancing and couldn't wait to get on the floor, become Lola and leave Laura the checkout girl behind. Dancing The Argentine Tango with Tony, I was hot and vibrant, a wild young thing on the streets of Buenos Aires, flirtatious and effervescent in Cuba dancing the Cha Cha, I was breathless with enthusiasm, passion and a lust for life. I could also be serene and ladylike, a rich, titled woman, royalty even, gliding through a European Palace at the turn of the century during a Viennese Waltz. I could be anything and anyone when I was dancing.

Sometimes, when we were quiet I would abandon my checkout and grab Carole or Rocky from security and make them dance with me. Rocky was great, because he was sturdy he could take my weight and I could try out all sorts of moves on him, like a kid on a climbing frame. We almost caused a furore in toiletries when I was trying out some leg hooks which involved wrapping a leg around your partner's knee and vice versa. It was complicated and you had to go with it but the minute you thought about the process everything collapsed – including the dancers! Tony and I had a few close shaves where we got caught up in each other's legs, but we recovered and I turned round to see a small audience forming around the shampoo and conditioners. Rocky loved it and played to the audience, and when we finished they clapped and cheered and I felt utterly embarrassed because I'd been so engrossed in the dance I hadn't even noticed. After that I would get requests at my till – 'Go on love, show us your tango,' the old ladies would say and others would ask if I would teach them. Of course I had to decline, but it wasn't unheard of for me to hold an impromptu tango masterclass at the back of the freezer aisle on late nights when the bosses had gone home. I was also happy to dance alone wherever I might be – in private of course, and during those times, I was sure Dad was there, guiding me through those tricky steps.

❄ ❄ ❄

'You're late,' my mum said as I opened the door to her apartment.

She was sitting by the window looking through Heat. 'Kate Middleton's looking thin...' she sighed. 'I hope it's not going to be Diana all over again... at least you've never had that problem. The opposite in fact...'

'Do you like my dress?' I asked, refusing to let her negativity affect me and stopping her elaborating further on my 'curviness'.

'Yes it's very nice, you look lovely,' she said, looking up from Kate Middleton and suddenly smiling.

I was taken aback, even when pushed, it wasn't like Mum to compliment me – I must have looked quite good.

As I'd lost a little weight, I'd bought a new dress. I hadn't even admitted it to myself, but I'd bought it with Cameron in mind. I'd seen new photos of him on Facebook at yet another party and he looked good. So I bought the pink and blue floral dress which showed off my emerging waistline but wasn't too low cut or too short. I liked it so much and I planned to ask Tony to take a picture of me wearing it so I could casually post it on Facebook in the hope Cameron might see it.

So given that Mum was smiling when she saw me in my dress, I reckoned she was in a good mood and I decided it might be a good time to mention Dad's letter. There would never be a good time to confront my mum about secrets in her marriage, so I had decided just to go for it. After a cup of tea and some polite small talk, I broached it, easing in gently: 'Mum... when I emptied your attic I found some lovely dresses.'

'Oh good – I'm glad you found them. They were beautiful, very expensive at the time.'

I was relieved, this was a good start, in the past Mum would have shut me down at the mere mention of dancing dresses.

'Yes – I found other stuff too Mum... memories, one or two things of Dad's... a letter.'

'What did you say love? You're feeling better?'

'No Mum – a letter, I found a letter in the attic, from Dad.' I shouted, knowing she sometimes used her deafness to avoid having difficult conversations. And this seemed to be one of those occasions.

'Do you remember Dad sending you a letter?' I asked loudly.

She looked up at me and for a second I thought she might give me an answer; 'Oh... oh you're wearing your glasses,' she put her hand to her mouth like I was wearing a Halloween mask.

'Yes – I always wear glasses, I have done for years.'

'Oh but not with that lovely dress... you're spoiling it. You should get some of those nice blue eyes like Janice.'

I gave up on the letter. There was no point, whenever I tried to talk to her about the past she just shut me down with a veiled insult or pretended she was deaf. Janice was my slim and pretty cousin who also happened to be a bank manager, married to a surgeon. Just hearing the name 'Janice' made me feel fat, ugly, poor and unsuccessfully single.

'Okay, I'll get nice blue eyes, a good job and a husband just like Janice's if you wear a hearing aid.'

'Lemonade?'

'Yes, Mother – lemonade,' I sighed, defeatedly adjusting my glasses.

I only ever took them off for dancing and Tony said I looked so much better without them, he said I was Lola without my glasses. Perhaps Mum had a point and I should think about wearing contact lenses - 'nice blue eyes' like Janice?

We were so very different, Mum and I. She'd always been a free spirit in her own way, living a life on the road with Dad, never imposing rules on herself or others. And now I wondered what else she'd been doing, what other rules might she have broken in her marriage? And would she ever reveal the truth? I remember when she was younger catching the admiring glances from men other than my father. Thinking about Dad's letter made me re-alise it would have been easy for a woman like Mum to have an affair. Perhaps she craved the attention? Perhaps Dad was busy at work and didn't have the time or energy for her? She'd always been pretty high maintenance.

I on the other hand wasn't high maintenance because I was the overweight, uptight daughter. It occurred to me that despite my caring and being there for her, ultimately I had just been another disappointment in Mum's life.

'Cheryl Cole takes her mother to all her awards ceremonies,' she was saying. 'Took her on holiday to a five star hotel in the Maldives, she did.'

'Well, when I next win an international award for singing and stay in a five star hotel in the Maldives I'll be sure to take you with me,' I said. Christ it was hard enough competing with cousin Jan-ice, now I had bloody Cheryl Cole or Hernandez Versini to live up to. Perhaps I should just get a massive rose tattooed on my arse and be done with it.

Chapter Eleven

Dancing Like Nobody's Watching

One evening when we were in the dance centre, training, another class came in and started watching us. Tony seemed to feed off the audience and the more they clapped, the more experimental he became. He was a showman, but I hated an audience and I could feel myself stiffen as more people gathered around. When (at my insistence) we stopped for a bottle of water, I could see my usually patient mentor was irritated. 'What's wrong with you Laura, you're all over the place.' Addressing me as Laura was a sign of how annoyed he was.

'Tony I can't... not with everyone looking at me.'

'You CAN. You've stood at the side of the dance floor all your life like a bloody wallflower, just watching everyone else dance past you – now it's your turn girl, so get off your arse and out there. Pretend we're alone, just you and me and the stars... dance like nobody's watching.'

I'd heard the phrase before, and hadn't really thought about it – but now it spoke to me.

We went back and danced some more, and with everyone gathered round, Tony 'threw' me to the floor. Then he 'dragged' me along, which was as much of a surprise to me as the 'audience', but within seconds I was with him, we were organic, and I just knew what he was trying to achieve and went with it. Then as he lifted me, I held out my arms like a bird, sure of myself, confident my body and my mind could take me anywhere I wanted to go. And in my head we were alone in a huge, empty ballroom, just me, Tony and the glitterball. A sea of shiny floor, an ocean of music – and nobody watching.

'That was more like it,' he said later as we got changed. 'You've cracked the technical aspect, that's the easy bit – now you have to perform, Lola!'

I wasn't quite sure what he meant – I thought I'd been 'performing' on the dance floor for months. But pretending no one was watching had helped me through the fear of facing an audience, worrying what they thought of me.

I'd finally realised it didn't matter what people thought about my dancing, it didn't matter if I won a competition or lost it – what mattered was it made me happy. And what made me happy was my daughter, my dancing and my dreams.

That evening, Sophie called me to tell me she and Carl were extending their visas.

'I'm happy that you're so happy you want to stay,' I said, surprised at my own reaction. This news would have sent me into paroxysms of grief and worry six months before. But now I had my own, much bigger life, and I was able to let Sophie go, encourage her to chase her dreams and not see death and danger round every corner.

'Oh Mum I was worried about telling you. Thanks for being so understanding.'

'It's great that you're having such a good time... you needed this opportunity to move on, love,' I said.

I could see her nodding on the screen.

'And what about you, Mum? Anything happened with that old boyfriend?'

'No,' I said, feeling a little foolish... I'm sure she thought I should be sleeping with him by now.

'Oh Mum, why don't you just go for it? What are you doing messing about on Facebook when you could be with him for real? Why not arrange a meeting, nothing too heavy, just a few drinks or... whatever?'

'It's okay as it is,' I said, though I wasn't convinced.

'Well... what exactly is it?'

'Old friends... just chatting.'

'Well that sext you sent to Carl was more than just friends chatting... you can't fool me, I know it was meant for your old boyfriend. I can't believe you haven't gone any further and tried to get together. Mum, you need to be a bit more... random.'

I went slightly pink at the mention of my sext mistakenly sent to Carl, but she had a point. I was all about courage and confidence these days, so why wasn't I applying it to my non-existent love life? Yes I had the dancing, but wouldn't it be even more exciting now to add a bit of romance, sex even? After all Tony had been telling me for ages that all I needed was a hot night with a passionate man...or a passionate night with a hot man. I'd take either.

I came off the phone with mixed feelings, but after a couple of glasses of wine and a need to impress my daughter with my 'randomness' (whatever that was), I called Cameron on his mobile. We'd never gone beyond texting, so this felt like a big move, escalating our online intimacy into something real. My mouth was dry as I held the phone to my face – which was hot.

I heard the phone click and jumped in straightaway before I chickened out: 'Hi... it's me...' I started, then his answer phone kicked in. I was so nervous but the wine had given me more courage than perhaps was wise.

'What about we stop this texting thing and actually get together?' I said. 'We could meet up and have a few drinks and a laugh? I understand if you'd rather not, but it might be nice to meet up after all this time?'

I waited and waited but he didn't call back, so I went to bed with the phone under my pillow just in case.

❊ ❊ ❊

The next day I told Carole what I'd done and she raised her eyebrows over the large, cold pork chop she was eating.

'Really?'

'Yes, I just think it's time to say "yes", to stop making excuses... and like Sophie said, it can't go on forever just texting and talking on Facebook.'

'I suppose you're right...'

'Along with the Paso Doble, I think about him all the time.'

'I think about food all the time,' she said, tossing the pork chop bone back onto her empty plate like Henry VIII.

'Atkins?' I asked.

'Yeah... I had high hopes for this, Mary in Home Electricals lost 3 stone, but there's only so much red meat a woman can take. I found myself in the kitchen at three o'clock this morning with my mouth around a huge piece of rare steak, blood dripping everywhere – it's all getting a bit "Rosemary's Baby". Imagine if one of the kids had walked in on me alone in the dark ripping at flesh like a deranged caveman? It doesn't bear thinking about. Nothing else for it, I'll have to come off the Atkins – I mean, the human body can't live without carbs... it's... it's *inhuman.*'

'Cake?' I said, knowing where this was going and getting up to go to the counter.

'Yeah... okay, I'll keep you company with a slice of cake. Chocolate fudge,' she said calling after me, 'with thick cream... God knows I need the calcium.'

❄ ❄ ❄

Later that day I received a text from Cameron. 'Meeting up sounds good, but I work in the evening (he was an accountant, he probably took work home) so it's difficult to go out at night.'

I was disappointed, but I understood. 'It's ok,' I texted. 'I work nights too – perhaps you could come to my house after work one evening? It doesn't matter if it's late. It's not like I don't know you – unless you're a serial killer accountant now?'

'Ha ha, yes, that sounds good.'

'Tomorrow night?' I texted, feeling very daring and... random. Wait until I tell Sophie about this.

'Yes. Tomorrow is good.'

I was delighted, his immediate response was a good sign so I texted my address and he said he would be over about ten after he'd finished work. Then I sat back and thought about the possibility of actually meeting him, what we'd say, what he'd think of me now – and I wanted to text back and say 'forget it.' I was so nervous, but at the same time glad Lola had kicked in somewhere and I'd found the courage to ask him to meet – and that he'd said yes. He'd obviously just been waiting for me to make the first move. Now I had to start planning tomorrow evening, my outfit, the setting and, *oh God*, the lighting – after almost thirty years I would need very dim lighting.

Chapter Twelve

Cameron, Cava and Candlelight

The following evening I planned to leave dance training slightly earlier than usual so I could get ready for Cameron. He'd only seen photos of me, and they were only the ones where I looked good and not like me at all – so I had to make an effort so he wasn't disappointed when he saw me in the flesh.

As always I'd been lost in the dance, stayed longer than I meant to and came straight out of a vigorous Paso Doble and screamed when I realised the time. Not one to be outdone by drama, Tony screamed too and ushered me out of the door saying, 'Go… go like the wind to your rampant lover,' in a very loud voice which caused a few ripples in the waiting 'Advanced Zumba Class'.

Arriving home at 9.30 I'd left myself only half an hour to get ready and to set the scene. I wanted Cameron to find me attractive, but I also wanted to impress him, to show him I'd grown up and had a successful life since he last saw me. He knew I danced but he also knew I worked at Bilton's so I wanted to present him with an artsy interior. I didn't want him to see the home of a supermarket checkout girl, I wanted him to see a woman at one with art, nature and herself. So I tidied the house and put a large piece of driftwood in front of the fire to hide the fact it was ugly and electric - and at the same time to impress on him my oneness with nature. I'd also prepared a small tray of smoked salmon canapés and dipped strawberries in chocolate, which I hoped wouldn't be too over the top. I would make out like this was my usual snack of choice and nothing special. I'd even bought some scented candles from Homeware and dotted them around the living room. I closed the curtains, lit the candles and took the food and drink out of the fridge, placing it carefully on the coffee table.

I then ran upstairs, two at a time, to slap on make-up and slip into something gorgeous. I wanted his first sight of me after all these years to be one he wouldn't forget – in a good way. So that day, between finishing work and going to dance training, I'd popped into town and I'd spotted what my mother would call 'loungewear', in chocolate silk. They were like posh pyjamas really and I could see myself greeting Cameron in these, thinking they would give just the right message, available, but not in your face.

So there I was in chocolate silk by candlelight, the dipped strawberries and my body, ripe and ready to hand to him on a plate. I put some music on, forgetting that Tony had been round the night before and downloaded Wham, 'I'm your Man', which sent me into a panic because that wouldn't play well with the cava and candlelight. I was going for mature and sophisticated and the lyrics 'If you're gonna do it do it right - right? Do it with me' were not going to be my opening number. So I frantically searched through Tony's gay anthems, 'YMCA,' no, It's Raining Men,' no, 'Relax,' absolutely not - then I found some Dido and was calm again.

I stood for a while, not wanting to crease the silk. It was almost ten and he'd be here any minute so there was no point sitting down. After a few minutes I leaned on the sofa like a mannequin, keeping all my limbs straight, but despite a newly strengthened core I couldn't last for long in that position. At 10.13 I shifted the ice bucket a little to the left and stood back... at 10.21 I moved the glasses slightly to the right and spread the napkins out like a fan. I took a strawberry and stood back eating it, the bitter sweet fruit meeting the gooey chocolate was a deeply moving experience and I had to stop a moment and take it in. Then I saw it was 10.39 and my heart started to feel heavy and anxious. At 10.53 I arranged everything as it had been before I had moved things. I just wanted everything to be perfect, but it was now 11.01, and he was over an hour late and the cava would be warm and the strawberries would be gone because I was peckish and slightly anxious, not a good combo.

At 11.07 I checked my phone again. Perhaps he'd texted me to say he was running late? But there was nothing. I checked Facebook quickly, hoping he didn't turn up now to see me through the window, my bespectacled face lit by harsh phone light, screwed up and scrolling his timeline like a crazed stalker. But there were no clues on Facebook so I took another strawberry and rearranged the smoked salmon. It was only nineteen minutes past, he would be here in a minute... or two. At 11.32 as I finished off the last strawberry, I couldn't shake off the thought that he might not turn up. No, I'd give him a bit longer, he might have been held up at work – and I had all night.

By two a.m. I was tired, fed up and I'd run out of excuses for him. I didn't text him, what was the point? Perhaps he never intended to come over? Perhaps he just got a cheap thrill out of contacting old girlfriends and making lewd suggestions?

And as I emptied the last of the cava and scoffed the final smoked salmon canapé I faced the fact that he wasn't coming and that all men ever do is let you down.

Chapter Thirteen

Whatever Happened to Baby Joel?

'On the bitch mode scale, I'm calm – only like a two right now, but ask me again in an hour when he hasn't texted me back.' Tony was blowing my hair in between huge gasps of furiousness. 'I texted him at ten past four,' he continued, tugging a little too hard on my roots as he pulled the brush vigorously through my hair. I wanted to say 'ow' but he wouldn't have listened, he was completely off on one about his latest dating disaster; 'I said don't worry about me, sugar tits, not that he was. I said I watched "Whatever Happened to Baby Jane" on Netflix in case you were wondering what a fucking white-knuckle thrill ride my evening was when you were a no-show. I think he got the message.'

'Good for you,' I nodded. Tony's complicated and free-flowing sex life often involved his ex-partner Joel who'd once broken his heart but turned up every now and then for sex. Tony was handsome, he could have his pick of men and enjoyed various 'gentlemen callers' with different talents and varied abilities in the bedroom – but he would drop them all for Joel. Deep down, Tony knew Joel was using him but was in complete denial. Whilst I'd been waiting for Cameron, Tony had been waiting for Joel, who didn't turn up either. Tony knew exactly what I was going through and it made me feel better to know I wasn't alone in all this relationship madness.

'I hope you gave that Cameron short shrift too,' he hissed. 'There's me on my pink velour sofa looking chic as hell, and there's you, dressed in cheap loungewear, house done up all candlelight and driftwood like something from "Blair Witch," And he doesn't even bother to text. They are all the same, bloody men, letting us down.'

I wasn't sure what I resented most, the Blair Witch comment (I was going for Kelly Hoppen), or the reference to cheap loungewear.

'Short shrift? I can't even find him. I refuse to text him and come over all desperate. But I went on Facebook this morning and he's gone, completely disappeared into thin air, it's like he never existed. His account's not even on there' I said.

'Facebook's like the wardrobe in bloody Narnia sometimes. You're convinced you've had the most amazing adventure then someone deletes everything taking the fucking wardrobe with them so there's nowhere to get in. What a tosser,' he spat, taking his frustration out on my poor hair – wasn't I suffering enough.

'Oh... ow!' I was gritting my teeth as he untangled a tricky knot – with vigour. 'I'm used to it Tony. I don't know why I bothered. How stupid I was to be taken in by him. I told you, I don't want or need a man in my life, I'm fine as I am. I'd just like someone to hold me every now and then, tell me I look nice... someone who's there for me.'

'I'll be there, Lola,' he smiled, kissing the top of my head. He meant it too and it made me realise that the Cameron's of this world will just disappoint you and let you down. While waiting all night for him I'd recalled a few times when we were younger when he hadn't turned up as promised and I sometimes wondered if he'd cheated. Perhaps those lovely salad days of loving Cameron weren't quite as lovely as I'd remembered? As a young woman I'd probably put up with far more than I would now and for me Cameron hadn't only left Facebook, he'd left my life and my head too.

I thought about this as Tony continued to rant and pull at my hair. We were in my kitchen and he'd turned up to walk with me to the dance centre for our usual session, but wanted to talk me through flamenco while he made me look ten years younger with a bit of hair mousse and a lot of pain and heat, because he said I looked 'rough as old boots', which was nice. I think he just wanted to try out his new hair mousse on my hair rather than his – I was the guinea pig.

'It's only a couple of weeks before I go on my flamenco odyssey and I've been reading up about it online. It looks like a fortnight in heaven and hell, my love – long arduous days of training, difficult steps and the *compás*... oh my God don't talk to me about the *compás*. I will be exhausted... but fabulous.'

'You will. What's *compás*?'

'It's the rhythm of flamenco, it's not like anything we do. The dance is originally Moorish and so the music's alien to our ears – and our toes.'

'Oh it sounds so exciting, and intriguing too. Why don't we practise together before you go?' I said, excitedly. How I longed to go with him and bask in the sunshine and the dancing.

'You read my mind. Already thought of that – you and I are going to do a little flamenco this evening, my love... I've been on-line and checked out the steps. I've downloaded some music and I think between us, you and I will be able to make it sizzle.'

He finished my hair, which looked good, and before leaving for the dance centre I ran upstairs and, grabbing my handbag and putting Dad's letter in., I wanted Dad with me tonight, the Flamenco was a dance he'd longed to do and I just wished I could dance for him, with him. I adored the difficult Argentine Tango and the smooth and wonderful waltz – we were planning to enter both dances for Blackpool the following year – but this was the flamenco and it was different. It was also something close to my heart.

Waiting for the studio to clear, I thought about how far I'd come since that first class a few months before. I could barely walk the next morning, I'd ached everywhere. I still ached after every dance session, but it was a good ache, a reminder of something I could do rather than something I couldn't.

Eventually everyone had left, but some of the Zumba girls asked if they could hang around and watch, which meant we suddenly had an audience of about thirty people watching us attempt a dance we'd never done before. Tony could tell I was nervous and kissed my cheek, then with the most gentle and loving look on his face, he said, very quietly, 'Remember what I told you – dance like nobody's watching.' I looked up at him, smiling, then he burst the bubble, 'Now no whingeing and move your tight little arse onto that dance floor – or I will kick it!'

I smiled sweetly at him through gritted teeth. I would 'perform' with confidence, and no one would know I hadn't a clue what I was doing. Tony took my hand and led me forward into our arena.

'Now, I've been reading up on it – flamenco isn't like anything we've ever done before,' he explained. 'It's not just a dance, darling, it's a culture, an art form, a lifestyle – people take a lifetime to learn flamenco so don't expect to get it on the first try.'

I nodded, even with the spectators it was all so exciting, and though I knew it would be a huge challenge, I was keen to learn some of the basics.

'In true flamenco there's a dancer, singer and a guitarist, but we're going to make do with my iPod, my hips and my passion. Okay, Lola?' he turned on the music and started to clap out the rhythm, then after a little while we did a little stomping and I imagined I was wearing a long, frilly dress like my doll, Senorita. I attempted to flurry my wrapover skirt into a frenzy, which didn't have the desired effect, but it made Tony laugh. As the music continued, we just kept going, our own improvised flamenco, twirling and stomping and clicking our fingers in the air and laughing like two little kids. Eventually, we slumped against the wall, sweating but still smiling. I grabbed my water bottle. 'It's thirsty work, flamenco,' I said.

Tony laughed. 'I'm not sure what you just did there was flamenco, love. Let's give it another go shall we?'

So we got up and started again, this time a little calmer. The strains of the guitar soothed and inspired me and I felt like I knew the dance. Of course I didn't, but as we both stamped on the floor and raised our arms, straightened our posture it began to feel like something Spanish. Then Tony started with the 'Olés' and the Zumba girls started clapping and shouting 'Olé' too.

Tony didn't need much encouragement to put on a show, swirling around, stomping, and shouting random Spanish sounding words I wasn't convinced were actually Spanish. But the 'audience' seemed genuinely enthusiastic about what we were doing. This time I wasn't intimidated but inspired by the clapping and the sounds of approval – and I carried on, stamping and clapping to the rhythm. I really loved it, and despite feeling self-conscious, I curtseyed when Tony bowed, and I felt a rush of blood and emotion in my chest and the sting of tears in my eyes. The applause was for us, for me – I'd never realised how bloody wonderful that could feel. I felt I'd finally broken through the barrier to becoming a better dancer... and maybe a braver person.

Chapter Fourteen

Dancing at the Deep End

Tony was excited about a new venue he had found for us to practise in and was driving along the M6 to a leisure centre near Walsall. I still hadn't heard from Cameron since his no-show and the fact he hadn't texted me at all since it was clear he had no plans to take anything further. I had resisted texting him and if I'm honest was still hoping that he'd text with an explanation. But the day before I'd found out the truth and I needed to share it with Tony, who I knew would understand and be totally on my side. There was no way to sugar coat it, so I jumped straight in. 'Cameron's married.'

He was overtaking a lorry and I wasn't sure if he was concentrating or just taking this news in, but after a few seconds he exploded.

'You are kidding me? Tell me it's a joke?'

'Well if it is I don't think it's a very funny one,' I snapped.

'How did you find out?'

'Carole told me. She wasn't sure – but she had her suspicions because she was at school with his sister. So she made a point of standing with her in the queue to be weighed at Slimming World and somehow got the conversation onto Cameron and his family. She should have worked for MI5, anyway within minutes his sister had sung like a canary about his wife and three kids. Carole even found out they are about to celebrate twenty-five fucking years of marriage next week.'

'Bastard!' with that Tony slammed his fist hard on the steering wheel.

'It's okay, Tony... I just feel stupid. I can't believe I was taken in.'

'He took advantage...'

'No he didn't. I wish he had. I just got carried away... it's easy to start seeing more in an online friendship... a "goodnight, gorgeous" becomes a relationship.' I didn't add fuel to the fire and remind him that Cameron had lied and told me he was divorced.

'Babe, that's an engagement where I come from,' he sighed. 'But don't beat yourself up, Lola, it was the first sniff you've had in decades...'

'Years... not decades, I'm not that old... I don't sniff at men like a dog either.'

'Oh come on love it's been a while. Decades... he was desperate and you were needy... and sniffing around him like a dog,' He started laughing at his own imagery.

I reached out and slapped him. 'I'm not needy or desperate... and I don't need a man.'

'No you don't – you've been responsible for your own orgasms since 1992...' he added.

'Thank you for that.'

'But you're okay aren't you, Lola?' he said, more seriously now. Joking aside, he knew this had knocked my confidence and was worried I might retreat back into my safe little world.

'I am fine. I enjoyed talking to Cameron, it was good sharing our memories. I'd always looked back on my teen years as being overshadowed by my mum's sadness when Dad went. Cameron reminded me that I was young once and had dreams and... I feel like I'm now picking up the threads all these years later... and I don't need a man to help me do that, in fact they just muddy the waters.'

By the time we arrived at the leisure centre, it was dark and empty, almost spookily quiet. Tony opened a door and led me into a changing room where the stench of sweaty feet and chlorine whacked the back of my throat.

'Why here?' I said, covering my mouth with my hand.

'I'm friends with the manager and he says we can use the space for free.'

'Yeah but... a swimming pool?'

'Yes, to tighten that footwork of yours,' he said, opening another door and leading me out to the impossibly turquoise pool.

'I'm not dancing underwater,' I said as we stood on the edge, looking into the pool. There were no lights above, but the pool was lit from inside which gave it a beautiful but eerie quality – all we could hear was a dripping sound.

'We aren't going in the water, Lola, you only need to put your trainers on. If we were going in I'd have told you to bring your tiny, fluorescent bikini.' We both laughed hard at that... Tony laughed a little too hard for my liking, so I whacked him with one of my trainers, then wandered to the edge of the water and peeped in.

'It's quite ghostly, like a scene from a TV drama,' I said, peering down into the aqua depths. I hadn't watched TV for ages - not even Silent Witness, and Strictly wasn't back until the Autumn - I made a mental note to tell Sophie how I'd been too busy to watch TV.

'Yeah, it's good though, isn't it? I was down here with Peter the other night and it struck me that it's the perfect place to dance.'

'Peter?'

He smiled. 'The manager, I told you we're friends.'

I didn't ask how friendly, but I could guess.

'Anyway, see this,' he was pointing at the fairly narrow strip around the pool, the way the blue on white tiles formed a line.

'We dance between the pool and the line,' he explained. 'It's only a couple of feet wide and it will keep your footwork tight. The flamenco is about using a small area and if your feet go over that line you know you're dancing too wide. And if your feet go over the other side – then it's woman overboard,' he laughed.

'I'm not a great swimmer,' I warned him.

'Even more reason to keep your feet tight,' he pulled me to him and we danced, me keeping my feet very close together as I was petrified of landing in the water.

As we danced around the flickering turquoise light I began to feel a little more relaxed, allowing the dance to take me somewhere else. The only music was in our heads and we had complete solitude. The radiance from the pool reflected back in turquoise, a cool ripple moving gently across the water, luminous in the dim setting. The light cast ghostly shadows on the tiled wall as we moved in the strange blue glow, like we were dancing in another time and place.

Suddenly there was a gentle clapping from above and someone stepped out of the shadows.

Tony looked up, his hand over his brow to see the shadow, who stepped nearer, still clapping. I could see he was handsome and smiling – Peter I presumed?

'It's a ten from me!' the voice said.

'Oh no you've been watching us?' Tony was pretending to be embarrassed, but I could tell he was secretly pleased.

As Peter joined us by the pool and introductions were made, Tony congratulated me on my footwork. 'It works doesn't it? Much better, Lola... very tight footwork... but you're still not letting go, love.'

'Yeah, perhaps tonight wasn't the best time to try and let go,' I smiled, 'but it made me feel so much better.' It was just what I needed after the news about bloody Cameron, mind you I felt even more sorry for his poor wife who hadn't a clue what he got up to on Facebook.'

I thanked Peter for allowing us to dance by the pool and they both walked me to the door. Tony said he had a lift back… and I knew what that meant. I was pleased for him. I drove home that night feeling like I'd had a very magical experience dancing by the pool, it reminded me again of my dad's dream to dance under the Spanish sun and I felt so sad and happy I cried.

The following morning I was having a scintillating conversation with a customer about the virtues of breaded pollock when Carole's voice emerged from behind the baked bean pyramid; 'Laura – have you heard from Tony this morning?'

'No,' I said and leaned forward to continue my 'conversation' with the baked beans. 'Why?'

'I think something's happened,' the voice said.

'What do you mean?'

'It's Tony... he's been hurt.'

'But I was only with him last night... oh for God's sake, Carole, come out from behind the beans,' I said abruptly.

She shuffled towards me. 'It's all right for you; I'm on my third written warning,' she said crossly.

'What's happened? What makes you think he's hurt?'

'Well, there was something on the radio this morning about someone being beaten up by thugs. Then I go online just now and the headlines are 'Leisure centre manager and local dance teacher Tony Hernandez beaten in suspected homophobic attack.''

My legs collapsed from under me. 'And... what's ... how is... he? Does it say?'

'No, it says one of them is in the local hospital with serious injuries but it doesn't say who.'

'I have to go,' I said, throwing my green nylon overall at Carole. 'Cover for me will you?' I asked, abandoning Mrs Breaded Pollock and her shopping and running through the store. All I could think was poor Tony, poor lovely, kind Tony – how could anyone do something like this?

'What on earth is going on?' I heard Julie's voice, harsh and shrill in front of me, blocking my exit, where the bloody hell had she come from?

'I'm sorry, Julie – I've just heard my friend's in hospital... he...'

'I'm sorry but you can't just leave your checkout.'

'No. I haven't, I've left it with Carole. Look I have to go.'

'Hang on a minute, lady,' she said, coming over all aggressive. 'Your friend, you say? Is this a family member, friend or a boyfriend?'

'What difference does it make?'

'It makes a lot of difference, because if you think you can just run out of the building because some "friend" is in hospital, forget it. You might be allowed to go at my discretion – for family care or bereavement purposes, but not for one of your mates.'

'But he's been hurt... I think... he doesn't have much family, only a sister – I don't even know if she knows yet.'

'Not my problem – take him a bunch of flowers when you've finished,' she snapped.

'No. I'm going,' I said, adamantly.

I went to push past her and she pushed her face into mine, 'If you go now, don't even think about coming back.'

'Oh, shove it, Julie, you ridiculous woman! How dare you speak to me like that. You strut around here thinking you're better than everyone else just because you earn an extra 20p an hour. Well I've got news for you, love – in that big world outside, this green overall and your sad little supervisor's badge are nothing... *you* are nothing. I've left someone on my till and I am now going to see my friend who's in hospital, whether *you* like it or not.' I didn't wait for her response, her open mouth said it all, and I ran straight past her and into the car park, grabbing my keys from my bag and leaping into the car. Driving to the hospital all I could think about was Tony and just kept saying over and over in my head, please be okay, please be okay.

Arriving in reception I explained I'd come to see Tony Hernandez and the lady behind the desk nodded and looked at me with pity, then ushered me into a room. 'The doctor will be with you shortly. There are a few magazines and a coffee machine just outside,' she said, trying to be helpful.

'I don't want to be rude, but I don't want coffee and magazines I want to see my friend... how is he?'

'A doctor is coming to talk to you,' she smiled sympathetically and left. I wanted to call after her, rugby tackle her to the ground and make her tell me he was okay, but I just sat there in the square room with white walls covered in leaflets about syphilis and breastfeeding.

My heart was in my mouth – why had the woman put me in here? Was this where they gave bad news? I stood up and walked around, sat down, and then stood up again, I couldn't rest, I was so anxious. Tony was so talented and funny and clever... and so young. All kinds of horrors were whirling through my head – perhaps the worst was 'if he lives – will he ever dance again?' A life without dancing wouldn't be a life for Tony.

After what seemed like an eternity a doctor appeared clutching a sheaf of paperwork, she nodded, quietly closed the door and pulled up a chair. Sitting down gently, she looked into my face.

'His friend said his name is Tony Hernandez, but we can't find him on the system.'

'No... no his name's Griffiths, Tony Griffiths. Hernandez is his stage name. How is he?'

'It's too soon to tell... his address?' she was writing his details on a form. She looked at me, my mind was blank, all I could think was, is he dead?

I was so upset and frustrated I said, 'Just please tell me how he is... how is my friend?'

She didn't flinch, she was obviously used to this frantic, brisk behaviour from worried family and friends.

'He's comfortable. He took quite a beating, he was protecting his friend who escaped with cuts and bruises, but I'm afraid Tony has some severe injuries.'

'How... bad? His brain?'

'Not as far as we can tell. He's under heavy sedation at the moment, and it may be a few hours before we can establish his injuries. At the moment we can't confirm anything more than broken bones.'

'Bones? Broken? But he's a dancer...'

'His left leg has been injured, his left arm is fractured – it seems his arm was stamped on by one of the people who attacked him. There's a lot of bruising and he needed stitches over his eye.'

'Did they hurt him... because he was gay?'

She half nodded. 'We can't confirm anything at this stage – but the police suggest it would seem to be the case... I have to warn you, he's in a bad way.'

Chapter Fifteen

Fat Octogenarians and Flamenco Dreams

It was two days before Tony finally came round and was moved out of Intensive Care. I'd been visiting him for two days, sitting by his bed with his sister Rita, we were both distressed by his injuries, not knowing what the outcome would be until he woke up. And when he finally opened his eyes Rita and I were sitting by his bedside. The nurse had been in and done some checks, arranged for the doctor to come and see him and gave him some water. Apart from his physical injuries he seemed to be his old self, he was smiling and when he said 'Lola what are you doing hanging around here? You should be practising,' I knew he was fine.

'You're the one hanging around. If you didn't want to be my partner anymore why didn't you say instead of getting yourself beaten up,' I joked.

'Don't make me laugh it hurts,' he winced. I felt terrible for him, unable to move, his face and body covered in bruises.

'They got the men that did this to you, love,' Rita said, holding his hand. 'They're in Police Custody and it's just as well because me and Laura were going to find them – and we'd have been on a murder charge,' she laughed.

'Oh well, Laura watches enough detective dramas to commit the perfect murder and even if she was caught she'd conduct her own defence.'

'It's true,' I laughed. 'On another note, I brought you these – and I want one,',' I said, holding up a box of his favourite cupcakes from the local bakery.

'Oh, brought those for yourself, did you Lola,' he smiled, and reached out to squeeze my hand. 'I was thinking – we'll need to cancel my classes, we don't want students turning up on Monday night and no Tony Hernandez.'

'Don't worry, I'll put a notice up on the dance centre door and I can call your students too if you have their numbers.'

'Thanks babe. The doctor's coming round later to give me some idea of my treatment and when I'll be able to go home, but the nurse said it could be weeks, and even then I'll need someone to give me a hand.'

'I can look after you,' Rita and I said at the same time.

'It will mean wiping my arse,' he smiled angelically.

'In that case Rita can do it,' I said.

'I think Laura would be very good at that,' Rita laughed.

'Have you seen Peter?' I asked, after we had finished laughing. He nodded.

'How is he?'

'Not too bad. He popped in this morning. He just had a few cuts and feels awful about me getting the brunt of it, but he ran for help in the bar and when the big heavies came out the cowards ran off. He saved me...'

His eyes were filled with tears and despite all the joking and the upbeat approach I knew Tony was hurting at the memory. I couldn't get my head round what had happened, how could anyone physically attack someone for just being who they are?

At nine p.m. Rita and I were told by one of the nurses that we had to go, so we hugged Tony goodbye. He was tired from his injuries and from our visit, but managed to give us a list of his requirements for our next visit: 'Sushi, pink lemonade, proper coffee... don't forget the chocolate... 70% cocoa solids. Oh, and I need my brows doing, I can't sit here with brows like this,' he said. His brows looked fine to me, what you could see of them with the bruising, but he had them 'done' every fortnight by Mandy at 'Curl Up and Dye'. And it seemed it would take more than a few broken bones to stop him making his regular beauty appointments.

'Ask Mandy if she does hospital visits,' he said.

'Mandy? By your bed with tweezers. Telling a graphic story about her latest conquest? You're incapacitated, she'll have all the power – anything could happen.'

He nodded slowly and took my hand, 'Sometimes one has to think of the greater good and suffer for their brows. And if that means enduring physical agony while listening to a long and detailed description of Mandy's latest shag then so be it. That girl can take ten years off my face with her HD brow treatment.'

I laughed, said I'd call her and was just heading to the door behind Rita when he said, 'Lola... there's something else.'

'What? You've just given us a list that will keep you in face cream and eye treatments for ten years. And if it's anything to do with Grindr, forget it – you are not capable, and I'm certainly not "Grinding" anyone for you, if that's the expression.'

'No, I wanted to ask you about something else.'

'Tone... what else could you possibly need?' Rita said, laughing. 'Over to you, Laura, I've got kids to feed,' she announced, waving and promising to come back the next day.

'Lola...it's the flamenco course...' he said, when she'd left.

'What about it?'

'I can't go now,' he said, sadly.

'Oh Tony – you're due to go in a couple of weeks aren't you?' In all the madness I hadn't really had chance to think about his trip. I'd been so worried that he might not wake up everything else had been pushed to the back of my mind.

'Yep, I was due to go on Madonna's Birthday, 16th August,' He said. 'I don't know how long I'm going to be in here, but I won't be fit to go away. With a broken arm, I couldn't even get on a plane let alone do a stompy tango when I got there.'

I felt so sorry for him, this was his dream and now he wouldn't be able to go – he'd been saving up for so long. 'I'll ring them. You might not get a full refund, but...' I took out a notebook. 'Give me the number and I'll cancel it.'

'No. You can't do that, the flight's booked and everything – it's too late – I won't get any money back now.'

'Tony, don't just give up on this – it would break my heart if you didn't make it and I'm sure you can just rebook it.'

'No, I've read the small print. But I've had an idea – why don't you go in my place? You can change the name on the flight and the course, I'll phone them and explain.'

'Tony, I can't do that, it's your holiday, let's see what we can salvage money-wise and perhaps you can go next year?'

'Lola – I love you to bits but you can be a silly mare. My injuries will take weeks to heal. I want you to go – I want you to learn if for both of us and bring it back here, to me.'

The nurse came in and told me I really had to leave.

'Look, just say yes. Tell me you'll go…'

Something started to fizz inside me. Why not? Was it fate that this was my father's dream and it was being handed to me on a plate?

'I want you to do this… if not for yourself, do it for me,' he said.

'Oh Tony…' I looked at him and he was looking straight at me like he was daring me to say yes. I paced around the bed, going through the possibilities in my head. I'd need time off work – if Julie hadn't sacked me – and I'd have to get a holiday wardrobe together. I didn't have time to save for this, but could use some of Sophie's wedding money to take with me. Then there was Mum… would she be okay while I was away? And then I thought about Dad's dream to dance flamenco and how he'd put it off until it was too late, and my decision was made.

'Yes,' I heard myself say.

'Oh Lola, that's wonderful, you won't regret it girl.'

'Oh yes, yes, yes,' I just kept saying it and hugging him tightly.

'Ow, that hurts,' he squealed as I squeezed his face and kissed him on the cheek.

'Thank you, thank you, thank you. I'll ask work if I can get the time off... if you're really sure?'

'I've never been more sure of anything,' he said. 'Now fuck off and pack that tiny fluorescent bikini... or whatever fat octogenarians wear these days.'

I was about to slap him playfully, but decided against it.

'Oh and you need to learn a few Spanish words or you won't know what the bloody hell's going on – you daft cow.'

The nurse appeared again, so I left, waving and blowing him kisses before running down the corridor, my parking ticket had probably run out, but that was the least of my problems. I was heading unexpectedly to Spain in a couple of weeks... I'd never been to another country, and never travelled alone before. I wish it had been under different circumstances, but it looked like I was going to dance flamenco under that Spanish sun after all.

'It looks like we're going Dad... you and me, Flamenco under the stars,' I said under my breath.

Chapter Sixteen

Blurred Pixels and Overplucked Brows

The next two weeks were a whirlwind of organising things for my upcoming trip. Because of this, my FaceTime sessions with Sophie had been sporadic, so that night I made an effort to call her and fill her in on my news.

I told her all about Tony and was dying to tell her about Spain but wanted to know how she was first.

'So how are you, sweetie?'

'Well, actually, Mum, I'm thinking of coming home soon.'

It was music to my ears, I couldn't wait to see her.

'That's great news, love – when?' I was wondering how this would work with me being in Spain.

'Probably in a couple of weeks... I'll have to see what happens here.'

'Okay. Good. If you can let me know...'

'Mum, I'm in South America – I can't give you a time and a date, anything could happen between now and then.'

'I appreciate that, my love, but I do need to know because...'

'God mum, don't pin me down! Things might change and if I decide to stay you'll be worrying at an airport somewhere waiting to pick me up and then I'll feel bad.'

'I won't be waiting at an airport for you...'

'Yes you will it's what you do... and you'll be phoning and texting and panicking...'

Sophie was seeing the overprotective mother, but I was about to surprise her with 'Cosmopolitan Mother.'

'If you come home in the next couple of weeks you'll have to make your own arrangements from the airport because I won't even be in the UK.'

'What? Why? Where will you be?'

'Spain.'

'Spain? You can't just go off to Spain like that! What are you going to do there?'

I had to smile at the irony, Sophie was the one who'd told me I had to be random and live life and when I did she was completely thrown.

'I'm going to live my life, Sophie. Despite what you might think, I don't sit by the TV every night with a bag of Revels,' I said. 'That's the past, and I'm going to Spain to learn flamenco.'

I told her about Tony's course and I could see by the blurred pixels she wasn't pleased.

'But what if I decide to come home when you're away?'

'Then I'll make sure there's food in the freezer and someone has a key and I'll see you when I get back.'

I wanted to be there for Sophie, but just as she had her own life I now had mine.

'So when exactly is this trip taking place... you can't just say "in a couple of weeks".'

'Sorry, but you did... 'I said pointedly, but with a smile. I gave her the dates and told her a bit more about the course and she seemed okay with that.

'I might wait until you're back then Mum.'

'Okay, that would be good. Sophie you were right - you told me I had no life and made me realise I needed something else other than work, worry and watching TV.'

There was silence as she took it in; 'Mum, when I said that... I didn't mean to upset you... I just felt that you needed to live a bit.'

'I know darling, and that's what I'm doing. I had to learn to let go, find my own path so I can leave you to take yours. I've watched you grow wings and fly and I'm so bloody proud of you Sophie – but it's time now for me take the ride ... and see what happens.'

There was silence for seventeen seconds, which is a long time on FaceTime, but Sophie needed to process what I'd said.

'I understand, Mum... I just worry about you, in another country.'

I gave her a look which was meant to say 'welcome to my world,' but was probably lost among the pixels. 'I know, love, and there will be no one happier than me when you're back home safe, but I won't clip your wings – and you mustn't clip mine.'

During that call I think Sophie realised that things had changed for me. Hopefully she wasn't too worried – I hope she felt empowered by it – I was finally becoming the role model I wanted to be.

❃ ❃ ❃

On the night before I went away, I'd popped in to see Mum who was about to enjoy a seventies night with the other residents. As Mum explained, some of 'the more showbizzy guys and gals' were putting on a concert, featuring various pop stars and bands from the era. Mum was Agnetha, the beautiful Swedish blonde in ABBA, and compared to some of the other residents in their costumes she looked good. Dressed as Alice Cooper, Stanley was in full make-up looking like something from a Wes Craven horror movie. And when eighty-nine–year-old Betty sashayed into the communal area wearing a Madonna wig and suspenders, several of us gasped – and it wasn't in admiration. The gentrified atmosphere of Wisteria Lodge was quickly morphing into a very dark geriatric version of The Rocky Horror Show.

'I thought this was Seventies Night? Madonna wasn't around in the seventies,' I said to Mum, trying to keep my voice down.

'She is – Madonna's in her seventies. She lies about her age... she was at school with Cher, you know.'

My mother called Betty over and they started giggling like two teenagers. It was wonderful to see Mum so happy and involved, but I wasn't ready for another OAP fancy dress show, I was still getting flashbacks from the last one. I wished her luck and told her I had an early start so would get off. I gave her my flight times

on a notepad along with the airline and the address where I'd be
staying. She took the notepaper off me and nodded, but I could
see she had half a mind on Betty's dance routine, which she was
now practising in front of us.

'So this time tomorrow I'll be in Spain, Mum,' I said, hoping for a chance to explain my reasons for going. We still hadn't
talked about the letter I'd found, or about my rediscovered love of
dancing. I suspected Mum knew, but she never raised the subject
with me.

She hadn't heard me, so I repeated, 'Mum, I'll be in Spain.'

'You're in pain... oh whatever's the matter?'

'No... Spain, Mum, I told you.'

'Lovely... lovely.'

I was so excited about the trip and the dancing and Mum seemed
happy so it felt like a good time to tell her I was going to learn flamenco while I was there. I wanted her blessing, to know it was okay
with her that I was dancing. The timing was also good because I
was about to leave anyway so could would throw the hand grenade
into the middle of the room then make a run for it, 'Mum. I'm
going to learn flamenco... while I'm in Spain...' I started.

'Betty did that, didn't you Betty?' she said, without missing a
beat.

'Yes I can do the flamenco...' Betty said and started stomping
and clicking her fingers, which was surreal and quite disturbing in
the Madonna basque.

'So... what time are you on?' I heard myself asking, and in that
split second I realised that it wasn't just Mum who couldn't talk

about the past – it was me too. I'd been moulded by both my parents only to look at the pretty stuff, the easy conversations and anything confrontational or difficult was avoided. I could now see as an adult that they were good people, but naive, both dreamers with delusions of grandeur, living in a fantasy world of faded chintz and afternoon tea dances. Mum was like a fragile film star with her pale skin and long fair hair while Dad was tall, dark and handsome. He never let their financial problems dampen his enthusiasm for life or dancing, his only desire was to make Mum happy, but having read the letter I wondered now if he behaved this way towards her to stop her leaving him for someone else? A veil was pulled over everything and no-one really spoke about money or whatever it was that had made Mum unhappy throughout my childhood. We'd almost had a breakthrough and I had just pushed it away, Mum had heard me, acknowledged what I'd said and finally began a dialogue, but this time it was me who shied away from it. Sometimes we surprise ourselves, don't we? I realised that I didn't want to see her face when I told her I was going to follow in her and Dad's footsteps. I wanted her approval, I had wanted it all my life, but wondered if I'd ever make her proud.

She'd been pleased for me and encouraging about my trip, which wasn't like her. In the past she'd been keen to tell me how lonely she'd be if I so much as talked about going on holiday without her. But she was now so busy with her own life she'd stopped trying to police mine... and me hers. She touched my arm, like she was telling me it was okay, she was okay... and so was I. Mum had never been so easy, so warm and for the first time in my life I didn't feel guilt about leaving her.

'I'm sorry, love, but I have to go – Bjorn wants to do a sound check.' I turned to see Mr Roberts in a blonde wig, an open-neck shirt and flairs.

'Oh I'll push off then Mum,' I smiled, kissing her on the cheek.

'What did you tell me to do?'

'I said I'll push off...' I shouted.

'Charming, the Kardashians don't speak to their mother like that.'

'No Mum, but their mother isn't deaf as a post and too vain to wear a hearing aid,' I laughed. She didn't hear me.

As I drove away from Wisteria Lodge I had a warm feeling about Mum and her new friends – despite seeing at least ten things in black leather and lace that I needed to unsee.

❅ ❅ ❅

A little later I went to say goodbye to Tony, who was mid brow treatment at the hospital when I arrived. Mandy was straddling him and her bedside manner was as I'd feared, not unlike her Beauty Therapist manner – the results were always good but pain wasn't something she ever acknowledged. I'd heard her vajazzles were a work of art but so painful they could put a woman off sex for life.

'Oh you are so going to get shagged,' was her opening line as I walked in.

'Is that because I'm so gorgeous?' I joked. I'd been 'fitted' if that's the term for contact lenses and this was my first day trying them out and I was amazed at how much better I looked without my glasses on. I'd never properly seen myself without my glasses ... because I couldn't.

'Tony's telling me you're off to Spain, and the first thing you have to do when you get there is a Porn Star Martini, they are lush,' Mandy was saying, holding her tweezers in the air. 'Oh and if it's anything like Kavos you had better have plenty of condoms and smuggle a bloody big bottle of vodka in your bag.'

'That sounds like good advice,' I lied, 'but it's not really that kind of trip... I'm going to learn to dance flamenco,' I said brightly, doing a little stomp.

'Well, you might be going to do that, but when you get there and see all those gorgeous Spanish lads you'll be doing flamenco on their faces.' She roared, laughing.

Here was something else for me to unsee – I was still recovering from Mum's seventies night and Mandy was on overload. I had to sit down.

Poor Tony was lying down with his eyes closed while she tweezered vigorously at his brows, her guffawing causing the bed to rock and him to twitch violently.

'Feeling any better, Tony?' I asked, trying to get Mandy off topic and pulling my chair up to the bed for a better view of the torture. Hadn't he been through enough? Did he really need the Guantanamo Bay eyebrow technique?

'Oh love, I could be better... and this daft cow sitting on my smashed arm and ripping at my brows isn't helping.'

'Oh shut up. He's got the hots for one of the nurses,' Mandy added, applying thick brown dye to his brows.

'Really? A male nurse?'

'No... after being beaten up I have seen the error of my ways,' he said sarcastically.

'Sorry. I mean is the nurse gay?' I asked, worried he may get his heart broken by falling for a straight man.

'How do I know if he's gay or not? He isn't carrying a sign,' he sighed. 'I've told you before it's one of the great tragedies of being gay, you never know until you've got their penis in your hand.'

'It's the same when you're straight,' Mandy sympathised with a knowing nod.

I nodded too, not quite sure what I was agreeing to.

'Well, either way, it's giving me something to take my mind off things,' Tony said. 'You know me – I will overanalyse and obsess over everything a cute guy does, just to see if he's gay or not. Even when he brings me the water jug I'm thinking is he making eye contact? Is that a rainbow in his trousers or is he just pleased to see me?'

'Or is he playing with his dick?' Mandy offered in all seriousness. She wasn't one for subtleties or euphemisms.

I tried to change the subject several times but they were as bad as each other and when the conversation turned to sex toys I decided to make my excuses and leave.

I leaned in between Tony and Mandy, who was still sitting astride him, 'Tony... thanks so much for Spain. You've given me your dream and I'll never forget that.'

'Babe, you look fabulous. You got the new lenses then?'

I nodded; 'Yes and it feels great not to have face furniture on.'

'You have changed so much babe – and all for the better. So I want you to go out there and show them what you can do – you'll be fabulous. And when you get back you can teach me.'

He had tears in his eyes and I couldn't tell if it was the fact I was going – or the pain Mandy was inflicting on him.

'Ooh I have something for you. Mand, just reach into that drawer will you?'

Mandy yanked the drawer open from her position on top of Tony and brought out a small package wrapped in pretty paper with a bow and handed it to me.

I took the parcel and started opening it.

'Our Rita got it for me and wrapped it too – I've been a bit stuck,' he laughed, pulling his mouth downwards.

It was a Spanish phrase book. With everything going on, I hadn't even thought about learning any Spanish so was really grateful.

'Oh Tony, thank you,' I said opening the book. He'd written something in Spanish – I had no idea what it meant.

Bailar como si nadie estuviera mirando, Tony x

'What does it mean?' I said, puzzled.

'It means ... dance like nobody's watching,' he said.

I felt tears spring to my eyes and I hugged him goodbye, unable to say very much. But as I left the hospital, I swung those double doors open and strode out into the sunlight. I'm about to shoot for the moon, I thought – so look out world, here I come.

Chapter Seventeen

A Room with a View and a Woman on a Mission

Going to Spain was a big deal for me on so many levels. I was living my life as my daughter had told me to and I was going so I could bring back the flamenco for Tony – I didn't know if he'd ever dance it, but I would do it for him. Then there was my dad, whose dearest wish was to learn the Flamenco in the place where it was born. I packed Dad's letter in my suitcase, I kept it in a transparent plastic wallet now to preserve it forever.

Early the following morning I took my flight. I'd never travelled alone before and it felt exciting and scary. It sounds silly, but I felt like Dad was with me, keeping an eye on things and making sure I was safe. There seemed to be so many possibilities just getting on a plane to another country – I could be anyone I wanted to be, there was no one to tell me how I should behave or the sort of person I was. My mum had said I was overweight, my daughter had said I had no life, and most of my colleagues saw me as a quiet member of staff who did very little other than her job. I was now a woman on a mission, keen to prove to myself and those around me I was about so much more than a green nylon overall, big knickers and a little life.

I looked through the plane window, thinking about how much our identity and sense of self is tied up with our friends and family. I felt so different and free being completely alone... I didn't have to be me, I could be anyone while here in Spain... I could be Lola.

The only person who really saw my potential was Tony... in the same way my dad wanted me to learn to dance, they both knew I could do it. They both loved me in their different ways, saw my imperfections and my doubts and yet they still believed in me.

Tony had given me that belief in myself and the means to fly and I loved him for it.

Arriving at Granada airport, I was immediately hit by the heat and colour and a sense of wonderful strangeness. I was a little scared, my mouth was dry as I walked towards what looked like a beaten up old bus. I showed my leaflet from Escuela Carmen de las Cuevas Flamenco, the school where I would be attending classes, and the driver nodded. I assumed that meant he was going my way and managed to get myself and my large suitcase on just before he set off.

Dropping me off on the narrow, winding streets of the Albayzín, a district of Granada, the driver offered vague directions to the Flamenco School, but I felt quite unsure of where I was going. After a short, but hot and uphill walk, I reached the top of the steep slope and the edge of the Sacramonte Hill, which was a relief because according to the directions I had arrived. The school was built around the gypsy cave complex – a maze of whitewashed caves, staircases, terraces and rooms. And there it was, the entrance – an ancient gateway with a sign 'Carmen de las Cuevas, School of Spanish for foreigners; Flamenco School'.

I couldn't believe it; I was standing on sacred ground, in the throbbing sunshine in Granada at the birthplace of flamenco. With my heart in my mouth and tears in my eyes, I took it all in. 'We made it, Dad,' I said under my breath and stood for a while, lost in my thoughts, before walking slowly towards the entrance.

I opened the door leading into a beautiful whitewashed court-yard filled with sunshine and greenery. Several small trees were breaking through the terracotta floor and little tables for two or three were waiting. Once inside I was amazed that this tiny sugar-cube exterior cut into the side of the mountain held the unexpected secret of a warren of modern studios, grotto-like cave classrooms and vine-covered terraces. I was mesmerised by the portraits of famous flamenco artists that lined the walls along with brightly coloured ceramic plates. This wasn't the Spain of package tours and manicured pools, it was like the postcards we'd received from Spain in the early seventies. When I was a child, anyone who'd been abroad was spoken of in the same breath as an astronaut who'd been to the moon. In the days before package tours a place called 'abroad' might as well have been on the moon for families like mine with little money. And this was the Spain we imagined back then – the Spain of flamenco dolls and women with dark eyes, black hair and swirling scarlet dresses. This was a place of Mediterranean mystery and magic. I stood in the hallway feeling like that little girl holding my flamenco doll in wonder and imagining what the world was like.

I wandered into the reception area to be greeted by one of the teachers, who was Spanish, and after a mumbled 'hola' from me, gave me a short tour of the school. Peeping into classrooms where fourteen or fifteen women were all stomping and shouting and sweating, I immediately felt revitalised after my journey, and wanted to join in straight away. But she lead me away from the dancing through the caves and the echoes of flamenco guitars and up onto a beautiful sunny terrace. The views looked out onto Granada took my breath away. The woman must have thought I was mad, I just kept smiling and staring like I was walking through a wonderful dream – it was everything I'd hoped it would be and I couldn't wait to dance. Finally she gave me all the class details, directions to my accommodation and said she'd see me tomorrow.

Leaving the school, I could still hear distant strains from a flamenco guitar, a voice singing in Spanish and the percussion-like sound of stomping, clapping dancers. My heart did a little skip – I was excited like a child, and despite the intense heat wanted to dance through the streets. Fortunately I managed to resist and walked carefully, following the directions, and headed to the apartment. It was set in the hills further down the road and I found it easily. It took a few minutes to work the key in the lock but once inside I felt pure relief from the blistering afternoon heat. The apartment was a cool stone with shiny white floors and walls. Consisting of just one room with a tiny kitchen off to the side, a bathroom and a little sofa bed, this was all I needed. The place was light and airy, but at the same time made cosy with ceramic plates, more brasses and pictures on the walls and traditional tapestry throws and cushions on the sofa. I walked towards the window to get a sense of where I was and realised they opened out on to a tiny, but lovely patio with the most spectacular views, just like the terrace at the school – looking down onto Granada. My throat swelled at the magnificent sight before me. Hundreds of higgledy-piggledy ancient buildings scattered and piled up in the sunshine, and there in the middle The Alhambra Palace. I'd read all about the palace before I came, and it was described by Moorish poets as 'a pearl set in emeralds'. I could see now that the palace was the colour of pearls and the emeralds were the surrounding forests.

It was majestic – described in the guidebook as 'part fort, part palace, part garden', I stood in awe at the view – like a huge feast laid before me, I longed to eat it all up and savour every moment while I was here. Gazing at the palace, I decided it had to be one of my first sightseeing stops and I ran to grab the phrase book so I could work out what to ask for in Spanish when I visited.

Opening the book, I saw Tony's message and suddenly missed him terribly, so I called him.

'Hi Tony? I'm here! I wish I could say you're not missing anything and it's terrible. But it's amazing! I have a patio and a fabulous view and the school is brilliant and... I am so grateful. I am loving this so much already, I've only just got here and I never want to leave!'

'Oh Lola, it sounds as fabulous as I hoped it would be...'

'I just feel so bad...'

'Why?'

'Because you're stuck in hospital and I'm here and ...'

'Right. I knew this would happen. Now listen to me "Laura can't", I do not want to hear any stupid talk about you feeling guilty because you're having a good time. You are not responsible for my happiness. And while I'm on the subject, you're not responsible for your mother's or your daughter's either...' he said. 'They have their own lives, as do I – and I have to tell you that a very cute nurse is tending to my every need at the moment. So believe it or not I'm very happy to be "stuck in hospital" as you put it.'

'I know but...'

'Shut up and let me speak. Guess what, sweetcakes? You will never find your own happiness until you stop fretting about everyone else's.'

'Is that from a book?'

'Yeah. It's from "Find the fear and jump in the fucking fire"... or something like that. Forget everyone else. Find yourself a hot Spanish guy. I will be so furious with you if you come back a virgin.'

I started to laugh and with that he turned his phone off – which was either for dramatic impact or because the male nurse was 'tending' to him. I felt better after that call and as he'd made me feel so positive, I decided to leave Mum and Sophie until later.

I unpacked, showered and made myself a cup of tea (observing Tony's mantra which was 'you'll always be okay if you carry lip balm and tea bags') and sat on my patio just gazing at the white-washed buildings slowly turn to pale gold. No endless loop of musak playing in the background, no 'do you have a loyalty card?' no

Julie around to tell me how to behave, how to feel. Best of all – no bloody conveyor belt of people's whole lives in consumer goods flashing before me.

Later I dressed in a kaftan and jeans and marvelled at my spectacle-less face and the length of my hair. I'd never had long hair in my life but recently I'd felt confident enough to let it grow and I liked how it felt. So checking myself one last time in the ornate mirror in the bathroom, I wandered down into the town. I had no plans to trawl the vicinity for available Spanish men as Tony had instructed and sought only sangria and supper.

It was early evening and pleasantly warm after the blistering afternoon heat I'd arrived in. I walked down narrow roads lined with dust and prickly pear trees, stopping at a clearing that looked right across the city just as the sun was dipping behind the mountains on the South East slopes. Arriving in Albayzín, the city's Moorish quarter, I spotted a young girl twirling and flapping her dress at a guy leaning against a restaurant wall. He was playing an accordion and diners sitting outside the restaurants were clapping along. Flamenco was in the streets here, in the blood of the locals, in the caves and the vines. And I felt it was in me too. The rhythm fizzed through my blood, the fiery stomping punctuating my walk as I wandered past the diners on the Plaza de San Miguel Bajo. The music chased me on clouds of orange and jasmine along narrow, whitewashed streets to a little tapas bar, an arched doorway in a wall, where I decided to eat.

Like most of the buildings in the Albayzín, the bar was Moorish in style, with decorated arches, carved wooden ceilings, scalloped stucco, and patterned ceramic tiles. I took a table by one of the filigreed windows looking out onto the busy street. It was so different to the streets at home, the view from my checkout, the people I saw every day in green nylon. If we could choose our birthplace, I would choose this, a place of warmth and vibrant life, I thought as I gazed through the window. Oh if only I could have shared this with my father - together we would hear the heartbeat of this place of exotic splendour and heat like I'd never known.

I was so excited I didn't think I was hungry, but I enjoyed a delicious plate of tapas, crunching on fried, garlicky shrimps and a caramel-rich manchego cheese accompanied by crusty bread and a crisp Rioja. I'd waited so long for something like this and now here it was, and here I was drinking wine in paradise. 'Life can sometimes take you by surprise,' I thought – but only if you let it.

❊ ❊ ❊

The next day I set off up the hill to the school. I had been quite nervous, but once inside was overwhelmed by the friendliness of the teachers and all the other dancers. There were fourteen of us learning to dance for those two weeks and as Tony had chosen the 'intermediate' classes, I just hoped they wouldn't be too tough on me.

We put on our shoes and some of the other dancers changed, but I was wearing a T-shirt and skirt that I'd felt would work for the dance. The teacher told us we would be learning the 'tangos' element of flamenco. Pronounced 'tangoss', this involved a more familiar rhythm than some flamenco dancing so we could acclimatise. We all trooped into the classroom and began an hour and a half of fabulous, fiery foot-stamping and clapping. The joy was immeasurable, as was the stress-relief – I felt like I was in another world, completely taken away by the music and the rhythm. We also did compás classes which were all about the rhythm, the beat – a vital part of flamenco as it brings together the guitar, the voice and the dance.

I made friends with a couple of other women in the group around my own age, but as one was German and the other French, we communicated with smiles and nods. Somewhere in the jumble of flamenco and foreign language we all established that we'd like to attend a few Spanish language classes also held at the school. My Spanish phrasebook from Tony would be useful but this was a chance to get to know other students, so signed up for the 'Spanish for beginners' course. I was glad I had because according to our dance teacher it was 'muy importante' to learn some Spanish, if only to understand which particular flamenco style we were supposed to be clapping.

The first day was intense, we were surrounded by mirrors, forced to watch ourselves stumble through the machine-gun beats, the sweat, the endurance. I hadn't comprehended the physical stamina and the mental agility required to grasp the complexity of rhythm and movement. I watched the teacher's feet, almost too fast for my eyes, and tried desperately to copy what she was doing, but her feet were speaking a foreign language to mine. That first night I was completely exhausted, stiff and unable to contemplate any kind of movement – fit only to fall into bed. I lay there just imagining the next day, the heat, the wonderful views from the patios at Carmen de las Cuevas. I thought about how, just a year before I could never have imagined myself here, alone in another country learning Flamenco.

The next day, after another hour and a half of arduous stomping and clapping, I staggered out to a vine-clad, sun-drenched terrace with my new friends. Here in the midday sunshine we began a rather confused conversation with their schoolgirl English and my very scant knowledge of French (which consisted of reciting a list of French cheeses available at Bilton's and didn't really work as a language on its own). We all clutched our notebooks where we wrote down the steps in number order, all loving the dance, the place – but complaining through mime about our stiff joints. We were laughing hysterically at one point as Bette, the German lady, attempted to tell us what her job was by getting down on all fours and snorting like a pig. Eva, the Parisian woman, was laughing so much she was running around the terrace clutching her tummy as I wondered what the French was for pelvic floor. Not surprisingly, the three of us (well the two of them) were attracting some attention and a guy wandered over to our table and said, 'I translate? I speak the French and the English and... little bit German?' He held his thumb and forefinger almost together to show how little German he knew – but compared to me he was probably fluent. Gratefully we nodded, inviting him to our table, where he introduced himself as Juan. He was Spanish, a bit Antonio Banderas with longish hair and dark eyes, and he told us he lived in Granada and was attending the school to learn flamenco guitar. With a few questions he was able to reveal that Bette was a pig farmer, Eva worked in a bank and I worked in a big shop. It was basic, but it saved me from miming a day at the checkout, and it helped to bond us all – albeit slightly. Being here in this wonderful place steeped in the dance and the culture and the sunshine, it depressed me to even think of Bilton's, so I was glad when the conversation moved back to my favourite subject, dancing.

'You dance the flamenco?' Juan asked and we all nodded enthusiastically and Eva mimed a little with her hands and stamped her feet and we all laughed politely. As lovely as these ladies were it was going to be a tough week trying to communicate in three languages, and once his task was complete, Juan said his goodbyes and told us he was attending the school for three weeks. 'If you need me in translation just to stamp your feet and click of your fingers,' he laughed. 'And I will be there.' He said this three times in three different languages. I didn't know the words for 'wonderful' or 'take me, I'm yours,' but as he wandered away, every woman at the table was glowing.

Chapter Eighteen

Hot Chorizo and a Spicy Spanish Poet

I was determined to make the most of my time here and really explore. Two weeks wouldn't be long to capture this beautiful city and I wanted to start straightaway, so later that afternoon I decided to visit the Alhambra, the place that had really captured my imagination in the guide book

I headed into Granada on foot, as I had the first night I arrived. It was late afternoon, and I hadn't expected it to be so incredibly hot. Walking along the dusty road, exposed to the arid heat was soon sucking my bones dry and I hadn't brought a bottle of water with me or any kind of cover apart from my sunglasses and hat. It wasn't like me to be so disorganised and I blamed the Mediterranean for messing with my head. I looked behind me, I'd come too far to go back, so stopped by the side of the road and sheltered under a prickly pear tree.

I wasn't there long when a motorbike pulled up at the side of the road. 'Hola guapa!' I heard and my heart lifted slightly. I knew from my phrase book that meant 'hello gorgeous,' which was a bit unexpected but not unpleasant.

'You don't be sitting here by the road, it's too hot – midday, Laura?' and the admirer knew my name too... how weird.

I looked up to see a man taking off his helmet and though it took a couple of seconds to realise – it was Juan. My heart did a little jump.

'Hi... I'm okay,' I smiled. 'I just needed a few minutes sit down in the shade. My mouth is dry,' I said.

'No, no, no. You mustn't – too hot, dangerous. I take you, on the bike.'

'Oh really?' I said straightening up. I reckoned it was more dangerous to get on Juan's bike than stay in the boiling heat, he might take me off to the mountains and try to seduce me... with any luck.

'Your mouth? She is dry? I have something for you to put in for the wetness.' I heard from behind me. Oh God, did I even dare turn round for this?

'Water?' I heard him say, to my deep relief as he brandished a frosty-looking bottle and sat down next to me. He pushed it at me gently and as I took the bottle from him our eyes met and I felt a shock go through me. My mouth was crisp and dusty and the cold water soothed my insides as it went down. I was aware he was watching me quite intensely. To me, the very act of sharing this bottle, putting my mouth where his had been, was escalating our intimacy. Or was it just the heat and my imagination? I didn't think for one minute that Juan saw a shared water bottle in those terms, I was just another tourist to him... and a middle-aged one at that.

'You were dry?' he said.

'Thirsty,' I nodded, looking at him properly, taking in his tanned skin and curly dark hair. Juan was about the same age as me, perhaps a little older judging by the silver strands around his face. His eyes were dark and his smile was devastating.

'You going into the city, Laura?'

'Yes... I wanted to see the palace...'

'Ah Alhambra?' He nodded. 'I can take you now?' He was looking straight at me and I knew I was going to say yes.

Thanking him, I tried to climb on his bike in the most ladylike way possible. All I could think was I hoped Sophie would never do such a stupid thing and get on the back of a motorbike with a handsome stranger on foreign soil.

After several attempts, Juan had to help me onto the leather seat which was so hot it made my mouth water (but not in a good way). He handed me a helmet which I put on, but couldn't work out how to fasten it and he didn't wait to be asked. Within seconds, he was up close and personal and we were nose to nose as he secured it for me, his smoky breath in my face, his big hands at my chin. I looked away, feeling quite invaded by his eyes and his smell, a rather exotic sandalwood and smoke combination that made my head say 'be careful,' but my body rebelled, wanting to sniff his neck. I resisted, that would have been weird, so he started up the engine and I clutched at the seat trying not to lean on him or make too much upper body contact, after all I didn't know this man and I already had my legs around him. But as he set off at 100 miles an hour downhill I found it necessary to grip harder with my thighs, wrap my arms around his waist and scream in his ear until we rode like Hell's Angels into the city centre.

I'd never been on a motorbike before and apart from the pet-rifying speed and the fact we nearly killed several pedestrians, the whole thing was very intimate to be doing with someone I didn't know. Even after we stopped, my thighs were rock hard, clinging to his, and I was so tightly wrapped around him, with fear, excite-ment and exhilaration, I felt like a teenager again and whooped uncharacteristically as I tried to get off – not pretty or seductive. I looked and felt like rigor mortis had set in and I could see him smiling to himself as he peeled me off his own back. I was breath-less, and suddenly ready for anything.

'You like the ride?' he asked, helping me down. I tried to smile but the flesh of my inner thigh was coming off on scalding leather and the expression on my face showed everything.

'You enjoy?'

'Yes, it was wonderful,' I said, trying not to put my legs to-gether now for fear of deep, post-motorbike chafing.

'Laura. Can I ask to take you for drink?' he said, putting his hand to my forehead like I was ill. I must have been very red and sweaty, but I didn't care – this was a date where I came from.

'That would be lovely,' I said, as my legs crumbled underneath me. I tried to laugh it off as I staggered around insisting I was great but not convincing anyone. And when a crowd formed around me, I asked if we could sit in the shade and have a drink.

We'd parked the bike in a huge tree-lined square with a foun-tain and several restaurants and cafes, so when Juan pointed at the nearest one I was happy to head for it.

'I think it's all the dancing and walking uphill and the heat and... the motorbike. And I haven't eaten much today,' I explained as we sat down at a small table covered in white linen and glasses. I had been so excited and so busy I hadn't even thought about food, which was a first for me.

'Let's eat,' he nodded, beckoning the waiter. I was very hungry but as my Spanish was still very basic and I wanted to taste 'real' Spanish food, I asked Juan to order for both of us.

'Where are we?' I said, as the waiter brought a welcome jug of iced water and a bottle of Rioja, accompanied by a dish of olives and almonds.

'Where are we?' he asked. I notice the people here did this a lot, repeated the question, I found it quite endearing, along with his smile. 'We are in the Paseo de los Tristes.' He poured the water for both of us and offered me an olive from the terracotta dish. 'It means in English... erm... walk, erm, promenade of the sad.'

'Oh dear... why?' I tasted the oily, salty olive and my jaw ached with joy.

'Because funerals passed through here on their way to the... do you say cemetery?' he said, now pouring the red wine into our glasses without taking his eyes from mine.

'Oh I see... yes cemetery that makes sense.' I was interested in what he was saying of course, but I was struggling to take it in due to the intensity of his eyes.

He was very attentive and as I took a sip, I looked at him over my glass and he was looking straight back. What the hell,

I thought, he's good-looking and he can speak Spanish, it will be fun to spend some time with him. Besides, he knew his wine – it was rich and comforting, a perfect complement to the gentle crunch of the smoky, spicy almonds and the savoury olives.

We talked about everything over that first bottle of wine and it transpired that Juan danced too.

'I love the dance, the flamenco she is in your blood when you are from here,' he said, gesturing around him. 'She is something you feel, something that itches at your skin and to move is the only way she is sated.'

'I think I understand that feeling,' I smiled, sipping on the delicious wine. 'Dancing, she is what you say... my mistress,' he smiled wickedly, 'I try to leave her but she drags me back.'

I tried not to look for too long into his dark eyes. The wine was making me very relaxed and I loved his accent, the way he talked conjured up late nights in faraway cities. I imagined us dancing close, his hand on the small of my back, my face in his neck, tango music floating through us. And as I drank more, I imagined lying naked next to him and I knew if the food didn't arrive soon I would be informing him of this.

So when the nibbles were but a distant memory and the wine was almost gone, I was glad when a huge steaming platter of paella was placed before us, smelling of Spain, the colour of sunshine, with splashes of red and green, spicy chorizo, hot scarlet peppers jumbled up with every type of seafood imaginable. The flavours were rich and soft, smoky and salty – each mouthful seemed to trigger the need for another and I ate far more than I intended, washed down with a second bottle of the robust red wine.

We chatted about Granada, flamenco, our real lives – and when everything in our glasses and on our plates was gone, we ordered coffee and Juan lit a cigarette and we talked some more. He explained that flamenco is a very old gypsy dance and to dance like a gypsy you have to be free.

'They had nothing... so they dance. And while they dance on the tiny patch of land, they can say, as long as I dance here this land is mine.'

I was enchanted by this thought, that the dance could empower a whole culture. And it gave me goose bumps as he talked about how flamenco can be deeply sad and at the same time happy. 'You hear songs so full of grief... they speak about the grief of a nation. And you think how can I compare my own sadness to this?'

His words really spoke to me. About how there are life is so much bigger, and grief so much deeper than our own individual sorrows. And I thought about my mum and her grief when she lost Dad. She gave up after he'd gone and I was filled with sadness for how much life she'd missed, by choice. She'd allowed her grief to become bigger than her – it swallowed her up and took over her life. Perhaps mine too? But not anymore.

In between flamenco stories he told me he worked in a bar in the Sacramento district, quite near the school. 'I am a musician... and a poet... but poets they don't make so much money,' he shrugged. I watched him talk, drinking in his words, his eyes, his lovely Spanish voice. 'I ate paella in the square with a Spanish poet,' I heard myself telling Tony and Sophie. And all I could think was... is this really me? Laura from Bilton's?

It was peaceful here, the low hum of chatter, the trickle of the fountain. We talked and talked and the soundtrack of the afternoon turned seamlessly from heat and ice cream and families, to a golden dusk of couples and wine. Glasses clinked, the children had all gone, and in their place cigarette smoke and the promise of sex hung over the Paseo de los Tristes like a delicious cloud.

I'd smile across at Juan, sip my wine and wait for the familiar wave of guilt to wash over me. I momentarily wondered if Sophie and Mum were okay, I thought about Tony and then Carole too. What if one of them needed me and I was sat here flirting and drinking? Then I remembered no one needed me to call them, visit them, FaceTime them, or worry about them in any way. For the first time in my life all I had to worry about was me. I lifted my head, feeling the final flickers of light on my face as the orange sun dropped slowly in the cobalt blue sky... this was living.

The feeling of liberation was so intoxicating that when Juan asked if I would like some sherry, despite feeling quite tipsy, I said, 'Why not?'

So we sat a while, sipping the dry, buttery Manzanilla sherry and taking in the view as it dimmed, like house lights being turned down in the theatre. And when the moon came up behind the Moorish palaces, the effect was hypnotic... the evening performance had begun. I'd never seen anything so beautiful, but it may have been the two bottles of wine, the sherry and the fact that a very handsome Spanish poet's knee was touching mine under the table.

Looking at him over the empty glasses and the prawn shells, the unmade bed of our afternoon, I knew I wanted to sleep with him. I'd never ever slept with anyone I didn't know, never had a one-night stand with a man I might never see again. I'd never done anything I shouldn't really do – which is why I had to do it.

He was looking at me with eyes like liquid chocolate, a sprinkling of desire, a vague dimple in his smile, turning his broody look into pure wickedness. He may be the wrong man, but the time was right.

'Will you take me home?' I heard myself say. He didn't answer, he just asked for the bill, and as we left the restaurant he caught my arm and slipped his hand into mine. It felt good, firm and strong, and a little further on we let go of each other's hands and he put his arm around my shoulder, firmly massaging my flesh through cotton, and my arm went about his waist, my hand pushed under his T-shirt, freeing it from his tight jeans and making contact with his warm back. It was like my body had gone on ahead before my mind could even decide what was going to happen next. This wasn't like me – I didn't act on instinct, I planned everything – but not tonight, not here, with the sound of flamenco guitar on the air and a throbbing in my chest. The ride back was better, more exciting and I felt no fear. I loved the feeling of my body next to his and clung tightly to him my cheek now resting snugly on his broad back as we wound uphill fast through the narrow streets. Swerving to avoid dogs and people, I heard myself shouting to go faster – and when we arrived at my apartment I was breathless with anticipation.

The evening was hot and it was a relief to be inside the cool apartment. I went straight to my bed and lay there, tired, wanton, feeling very bohemian and exotic. He followed and lay down next to me, kissing my neck, gently tugging at my clothes, and I began to undress him. In the moonlight I unveiled his body – it was perfect for me – not too muscular, but strong and manly. It had been so long for me I wanted to wrap my arms around him and kiss him madly, passionately. I'd almost forgotten what it was like this 'bedroom dance,' and wasn't sure what was expected of me, so held back a little waiting for my cue. And he turned to me, gently lifting the kaftan over my head, unhooking my bra and pulling down my jeans. I lay back on the bed, and for the first time in my life I felt good about my naked body. I felt shapely and confident now with my dancer's physique and flexibility. I wrapped my legs around his waist and he lifted me up, and pushing into me, we both gasped with pleasure. This had been building all afternoon as we'd talked and gazed into each other's eyes over olives and wine, and when we came it was an explosion of pent-up lust and heat. That night we slept deeply, heady with sex and alcohol.

Over the past few months I'd changed, my life had changed and it was all about dancing. But here on a hot summer night in a magical place I could feel myself changing even more. The final stage of my metamorphosis had begun and I was a different woman. No more subdued, anxious checkout girl whose journey had stopped halfway, never chasing her dreams, never believing in herself. She had such low self-esteem she thought she was only worthy of an online flirtation with someone from her past, who she knew would never be her present.

But here, in Spain was Lola – the flamenco dancer, filled with heat and fire. And when, the following day, my flamenco teacher complimented me on my passion, I smiled, thinking back to the night and how the moonlight reflected on the sheen of Juan's chest as I sat astride him, uninhibited, finally free.

Chapter Nineteen
The Princess Awakes

The following evening I joined Bette and Eva to see a real flamenco show. We went straight from the school into the local bars, where we ordered jugs of sangria and laughed about our communication problems. Later we went to the flamenco clubs in the caves, sitting in high-backed Andalusian chairs, large oak wine barrels lined the wall and an array of copperware hung from the wooden beams. It felt like old Spain, and when the dancers came on I was transported back to the past, Mum and Dad dancing at home, trying out their own brand of flamenco. Dad had a record of Engelbert Humperdinck singing 'Spanish eyes' – I could almost hear it in the flamenco guitar, and Dad's voice, singing to Mum, 'Please say si si... say you and your Spanish eyes will wait for me.'

My eyes filled with tears but I swallowed them back down and smiled – I was beginning to understand my mother's reaction to her loss. Mum had always had her problems whatever they might be, and those problems took her physically and emotionally. Whether her stays in hospital were connected to the difficulties in their marriage that Dad alluded to in his letter I didn't know, but she could barely go on after losing my dad. I'd blamed her for not following Dad's last wish, to bring me into their world of dance and teach me everything she knew... but without him, how could she ever dance again?

I'd never really wanted to meet Cameron, I was happy to keep him at a distance, just chat online, text now and then, because that way he couldn't hurt me. I'd only asked him to meet me because Sophie said I should and I wanted to impress her. Even if he'd been single it would never have worked, we were different people now from the kids we'd been. I'd just needed to revisit my own, teen-age past and put it to rest. And as Engelbert sang his last refrain, I knew I'd stopped looking for forever, I was only looking for now.

❋ ❋ ❋

Later, the flamenco guitarist began to play, and the pace quick-ened, the dance beat grew louder, stronger, as the fiery feet hit the floor, fingers clicked castanets, and I was lost. Dramatic wrist curls, sudden head movements, very straight bodies – how I en-vied them their craft, their performance. To the onlooker there is little movement, but I knew now that to dance flamenco, every single muscle and every single emotion is wrung out.

My friends and I were engrossed, pointing out the dancing, the dresses, and In spite of our language issues and the noise, we also managed to pass on snippets of information about ourselves and our lives. Eva was divorced, her children grown and she wanted to get her old self back, the one before she became Mrs and Mum...

or as she would say Madame and Maman. Bette had spent her life on the farm and wanted to feel less like a pig farmer and more like a woman again. We were all from different countries with different lives, but we'd been brought together by flamenco. And it seemed each one of us had a reason to dance.

I thought about it later as we watched an older Spanish woman dance – her flamenco was intimate yet open, powerful emotions, thunderous steps, her dance reaching out to the audience, but always, always, keeping a little bit back for herself. And I thought – yes that's the woman we all want to be, she's inside all of us – we just need the key to unlock her.

Dancing had freed me and forced me to express emotions I'd buried deep for a long time and to begin to understand myself, why I was here and what I was really looking for in life. Sitting in the flamenco club until dawn, we laughed and we drank and we joined in the dancing. I had never felt so free, so happy – and I realised I wasn't relying on a man to provide that happiness, it was coming from inside me. I thought about Dad and how he would be so proud of me being here, finally, after all these years, achieving his last wishes... and finding my own dream along the way.

✻ ✻ ✻

The next day, I whirled and clapped and stomped my way through class and at midday I wandered out into the sunshine, exhausted and emotional. Standing on one of the many terraces overlooking stunning views of Granada, I breathed in, the sun warming my face, recharging me. I felt strong and positive, like my life had some direction, some meaning – and to add to my joy, when I walked out of the gate, Juan was unexpectedly waiting for me by the vine-clad caves.

The sun was beating down on his tanned face, his black hair tied back, he looked like a handsome Spanish gypsy and I felt a surge of pride and excitement that this guy was actually waiting for me. Here was someone who could probably have any woman he wanted, but he had chosen to be with me. And today, I was choosing to be with him. He'd brought wine and fresh bread and cheese and we went straight back to my apartment and made love all afternoon like young lovers.

'How old are you?' I said, lying naked in a tangle of cotton sheets, both of us shimmering with sweat in the aftermath of lust and hot weather.

'I am forty-six, but you are only thirty-four, thirty-five?' he said, a twinkle in his eye.

'Mmmm, I wish. But you are being kind – you know I'm nearer to your age,' I said.

'Age, she doesn't matter when love is nearby,' he sighed, then he got out of bed and took out a bundle of papers from his bag.

'I write this for you... and for me,' he put his glasses on and began reading from the handwritten notes. A poem. He had written. For me. I was so touched, it was like a scene from a film, the Spanish lover so intoxicated by me he couldn't help but write about it. No one wrote Spanish poetry for check-out girls from the West Midlands – did they? But apparently they did.

It was called 'Amor', and sounded so beautiful in Spanish I cried.

'That's just beautiful,' I said, gently taking the well-worn piece of paper from his hands. He'd obviously toiled over this, writing out each word, folding and refolding the paper, probably wondering whether or not he should share it with me. 'Read it to me again,' I sighed, laying back on the pillows listening to the sensual way he spoke while looking into his Spanish eyes. I could hear the music in my head, Engelbert's sincere, pleading voice, 'please say si si...'

'El amor, a qué huele? Parece, cuando se ama,' Juan said softly, his eyes melting as he looked at me. He might have been reading his shopping list and it would still have sounded like the most wonderful love poem I'd ever heard. 'Que el mundo entero tiene rumor de primavera,' he went on, still looking at me, he didn't need to read it he knew it so well. I suppose when you write your own poetry it's written on your soul, I thought to myself, looking at his beautiful hands, wanting them all over my naked body – again. 'Las hojas secas tornan y las ramas con nieve.'

'What does it mean?' I asked, hoarse with desire.

'That our love is like spring... like a new rose – "y él sigue ardiente y joven, oliendo a la rosa eterna..." – and it will live for eternity, no matter how old we are.'

This man was baring his soul to me and I felt so moved, no one had ever done anything so caring, so romantic.

'Y él sigue ardiente y joven, oliendo a la rosa eterna...' I sighed, saying the words after him. Reaching out, I pulled him towards me, kissing him full on the lips. He threw the paper on the floor and within seconds we were making love again.

My muscles ached from the dancing but it was a good feeling, to be aware of every part of me, every sinew, every muscle being worked... awoken after years of sleep. I felt like a princess in a fairy tale, my body had been frozen for years and a handsome Spanish Prince had woken me with his kisses. I climbed on top of him, my hands on his chest, my new, firm, dancers' hips on his. I heard the thrash of flamenco, the beat of his poem and felt the movement of our bodies, together, like dancers. And when the dance ended, we collapsed together in an exhausted heap.

I lay in the afterglow, the sun slanting through the window, casting warm rectangles of light onto the bed. Who would have thought at the age of forty-four – just when you think you're life's mapped out on a conveyor belt of soap powder and yoghurts and 'what's the weather like?' – that this would happen? Juan had come into my life at a time of such significance, a time of huge change for me. Was it more than just a holiday romance? Perhaps he really had fallen for me? After all, when did a holiday romance involve writing love poetry?

Later, when Juan had left to go to work, I FaceTimed Sophie; 'So I've met this lovely guy,' I started.

'Oh God, mother, you've only been there three days,' she said, looking alarmed. 'Have you been out with him?'

'Yes... we've been ... for drinks and dinner and...'

'You haven't been alone with him, have you?' She sounded worried.

'What do you mean?'

'Mum, you have to be careful, you know what these Spanish guys are like, make sure you meet him in the day in a public place.'

'Well that wouldn't be appropriate, I mean you can't have sex in a ...'

'Oh my God, Mum! You haven't...?'

'Oh yes. More than once... and oh Sophie, he's so good,' I smiled.

'Mum, I hope you're being careful. You've turned into some kind of man-eating nympho...' she was mortified, but I swear I saw a glimmer of respect in her eyes.

'Yes – I think I have. But the dancing uses up most of my energy, so sadly I can only manage sex a couple of times a day...' I laughed. It was nice to enjoy a bit of role reversal, I felt like a rebellious daughter for once.

'Mum, can you stop please...'

'He wrote me a love poem and read it to me in bed. In the afterglow.' I was enjoying teasing my daughter, I felt like I'd finally joined the human race and I wasn't going to hide away any more.

'That's enough, Mum,' she snapped.

'I'm only having fun with you, Sophie. We're both women of the world, I'm sorry if it's uncomfortable for you to know your mother's having amazing sex with a Spanish Gypsy but...'

'It's pretty uncomfortable for me too, Mrs Watkins,' came a male voice.

'Oh... hi Carl?' I said.

Chapter Twenty
Chocolate Churros on Plaza Nueva

As lovely as it was to have a man around, being in Spain was about my freedom and enjoying some time alone. I wanted to experience this place through my own eyes without anyone else's input or opinions, to see how I felt, how I reacted – it was a holiday with myself. And I was finding out so much about me – I liked to get up very early before anyone else, and taking long walks before the sun was too warm. I loved the feeling of being truly alone, wandering through the Albayzín, with its geranium-filled balconies and glimpses of the Alhambra between every building. Most of all I loved the quiet, I loved that I didn't have to hear the looped music I was force-fed every day in the supermarket – here I could choose what I listened to. Life for me was finally about choices and on those early mornings all I chose to hear was bird song and the delicious swishing sound of running water from the fountains dotted throughout the squares.

Drinking strong coffee on pavement cafes and watching as the world woke up was another favourite pastime for me. On the way to class I would sometimes stop for chocolate and churros at a bar on Plaza Nueva, dipping the doughy sticks into the warm, pudding-like chocolate was pure therapy. On other days I'd stroll into town and breakfast on crisp tostados drenched in olive-oily tomatoes, sweet and ripe in Plaza Larga. And there were days when a warm and golden tortilla was the only companion I needed to share the stunning views of Granada. I just ate when I wanted where I wanted, and wandering alone through the early morning Spanish streets seeking my breakfast of choice still unable to believe I was really here.

I grew to love the stalls and markets overflowing onto pavements, stuffing the narrow streets with even more noise and heat and colour. I loved the food, served on the street in paper, or just in bread, the wine from dusty bottles, the children out late playing in squares while their parents sat nearby with a coffee, a glass of wine. Life was so different here and I imagined what my father would think walking these streets, dancing in class, just letting go to the music and the movement.

With Juan I saw a different Granada. He'd take me to quiet little bars in the back streets, the restaurants the Spaniards kept secret from the hordes of tourists. In these hidden, little places, we'd eat tapas and drink red wine. We'd talk about everything and I learned so much from him about the place and its culture. I couldn't imagine how Granada with its permanent sunshine and Moroccan-style buildings in rainbow colours was on the same planet as Bilton's 'where quality counts' and the car park was vandalised.

I'd asked Juan early on why he was single and he'd told me he was recently divorced. 'She broke my heart and left me for another man. She lives in Madrid now, it's all over.' There were no children involved and though he said he'd been alone since she left the previous year, I suspected he'd enjoyed the company of a few women before meeting me. He was suave, charming and good-looking. I doubted he would ever be on his own for long.

As we sat on my little patio outside, we fantasised vaguely about a future in the same place and I told him how I would one day love to live in Granada there.

'I would love to live in England,' he said. 'See the Queen's palace, the Houses of Parliament... the great Wayne Rooney... '

I smiled as he went on to list more famous people, monuments and buildings.

'My England is a little different from yours,' I said; 'I live near Birmingham, in the Midlands, with no sea and not much sunshine. We don't have any palaces or many celebrity footballers... and unlike here, the night isn't filled with the sounds of flamenco guitar...' It's filled with the sound of cars and arguments and people puking up on the way home from the pub.'

One evening I was with Juan and we passed a shop selling Arabic lamps. It was just a hole in the wall, but once inside it opened out into a gold-lit fairy-tale setting of jewel colours twinkling everywhere. It was an Aladdin's cave of light and I took it all in, looking above and around me, entranced by the lights and shadows dancing on the walls, lifting the windowless room. It was like something from a Disney cartoon, impossible colours, and illusory beauty – so captivating it couldn't possibly be real.

'You like this lamp?' Juan asked holding a pretty lamp in silver and blue. It reminded me of a Tiffany lamp my parents had in the hall at home. 'Let me buy this for you,' he said, and though I said no out of politeness, I wanted it desperately.

'I love it – I could put it by my bed at home,' I sighed. I wasn't ready to think about home yet, I wanted to wonder about what life would be like living here under sunny skies, dancing all day. I played around with the idea of waking up to the views of Granada, the daily thrill and frill of flamenco instead of loyalty cards and green nylon. And though I knew in my heart I could never leave my home and the people I loved – there were alternative lives to the one I'd been living.

❊ ❊ ❊

The flamenco school was wonderful, and how I wished my dad could be there with me. It sounds crazy, but there were times I was convinced he was – like when I was lost in the Albayzín and I almost felt his hand on my elbow, guiding me back to my apartment. And while dancing, feeling exhausted, dripping in sweat and my muscles screaming for me to stop, I would feel a gentle breeze on my face – Dad saying, 'Go on Laura, just a few more minutes, girl.'

By the second week I wondered if I could ever live another life but the one here – dancing by day, practising at night, and spending precious time alone with Juan or with my lovely 'international' friends, drinking coffee and talking about flamenco. The teaching at the school was brilliant and I couldn't wait to get into class. I was the fiery, passionate flamenco dancer, learning that flamenco is not just a dance in Spain, but a way of life, I understood how it crept inside you. Flamenco steals into your bed in the night when you're awake and makes you count steps and practise arm movements in the dark. It visits you in the shower and lifts your arms and stomps your bare feet, hot water lashing down, soap suds everywhere. It is everything.

Late one afternoon after classes, I sat with Juan on my sun-drenched patio, he was playing notes on his guitar, gently talking me through the sounds, the rhythm. Then he began slowly tapping out a rhythm on the concrete floor with his foot and playing a tune, which always sounded sad to me, like listing a lifetime of regrets. I couldn't help it, I stood up and started slowly dancing, thinking of my own list of regrets and I danced for the lost years, for all the times I'd locked myself away, saying no to life, and pretending everything would be okay.

But as the rhythm became faster, I thought about how I'd come to Spain and was learning to dance flamenco under the stars, just as Dad had dreamed of doing. And here I was, finally carrying that baton and living his dream along with my own. And as Juan began to build the steady beat with his weeping guitar I raised my arms in the air, a sign of strength and pride. I stamped to the beat as I'd been taught while Juan increased the speed until it was almost too fast for my feet and I was whisked away on a tide of music, I stopped thinking about my own emotions and tried to master the complex flamenco footwork. I couldn't, and I almost fell to the floor, defeated by the dance.

Juan caught me, grabbing me by the waist and kissing me passionately on the mouth then letting me go, like we were dancing.

'There is a phrase, which says, *"When you learn to dance, you must also learn how to forget it",*' *he said, gazing out onto the dusk.*

I looked at him, puzzled.

'How to explain... all that you have been taught must at times be ignored, the dancer must rely on the wisdom that flows in his blood. You must feel the rhythm of your own heartbeat and let that guide you.'

I nodded, I understood what he meant and wondered if that's what Tony meant when he said I had to 'perform' and stop worrying about the steps?

'Flamenco is not a technical art performed with ... how you say, the precision,' he explained. 'It is passed down from father to son, mother to daughter – there are no "rules". To dance flamenco you have to have the *duende*... the passion. I have met the British women afraid to show how they feel, you too – but with Flamenco it is okay to feel, Laura. Good to express anger, sorrow, loss, loneliness... and of course, love.'

He held my gaze for a while and took my hand, walking me through the steps, and I let him lead until he led me into the apartment.

Gently pushing me back on the bed, he made love to me, passionately, moving as fast as the flamenco, until I gasped, hearing myself scream with pleasure. I'd never done that before, I was always worried someone might hear, but that night with him, I didn't care about anyone but me. Afterwards he slept, and I lay entwined with him and the sheets and my abandoned dance skirt, just looking at his face and thinking how lucky I was.

Later, when the sun had dropped behind the mountains and little lights appeared in the city below, we went back out on to the patio. We drank wine and as the moon appeared, he played his guitar again. The sound filled the air, reminding me of the dark caves, the gypsy dancers from the past and how I would love to dance with their spirit, no inhibitions. I stood up, gently tapping my feet on the floor, reaching my arms in the air and moving my hips to the music, then I started dancing slowly, hitching my skirt a few inches from the floor and stamping out the rhythm. The tempo increased and I moved with it, and this time I felt different, magical, and almost unaware of my feet, the rhythm rushed through me, drawing inspiration from the sediment in my blood. Years of hang-ups, anxiety and feeling uptight were being unleashed, like toxins, stomping out of me onto the floor in a dazzling swirl of fabric and footwork. It was as though my mind had disconnected from my body – I felt free and strong and I danced like I'd never danced before. I was that Spanish gypsy girl with nothing but the ground she stood on. I whirled and clapped and stomped and shook my hair loose and threw myself into the music, the rhythm, with no thought for anything just the dance. I danced like I was alone and as the music ended I collapsed into a chair, exhausted.

'*Now* you can dance,' Juan smiled, and his Spanish eyes twinkled.

So that was duende. The thrill of flamenco, the feeling that ran from the tips of my toes and came out somewhere through my head and shook my whole body. Now it all made sense – believing in myself wasn't a technical aspect to be taught or learned; it had to be felt – something I'd never quite comprehended before. Now I understood my father's phrase in his letter because I finally knew – I had to 'feel' the passion to dance.

As a child who'd stood on the sidelines watching and who lost a parent only to gain responsibility for another at a very early age, I had never really been able to let go. I'd never truly grieved for my father because I'd been too preoccupied dealing with my mother's grief. I'd rarely shared my real feelings with anyone, especially not my mother or daughter because I was the one who looked after them. As for my relationships, Sophie's Dad and Cameron had never encouraged or coaxed me to talk, but then along came Tony, and now Juan, who not only asked me how I felt, but told me how he felt in poetry... but most of all showed me.

And that night I discovered the strong, passionate woman I had always wanted to be was there all the time, she just needed coaxing – her name was Lola.

Chapter Twenty-one

A Gypsy Wedding and a Long Goodbye

I woke each morning and pinched myself – I was so very lucky to have the experience here, and for that I had to thank Tony. I had discovered while at the school that Tony could have easily postponed his holiday and had his money back. In the same way my dad had known all those years before that I had to dance, Tony knew I had to come to Spain, to dance and be me, the real me that had hidden inside all those years. Tony had given me back my life.

To say I could dance the flamenco after two weeks sounds rather arrogant – it's a dance that takes years to learn, but I had made a good start. I'd also learned some Spanish, which helped with the compás and gave me confidence while I was there and made me determined to return one day. I'd also met a wonderful man who seemed to be more caring, more attentive as the days (and nights!) went on. Juan made me feel special, confident – and most of all, beautiful.

With just two days left in Granada, Juan said he wanted to take me somewhere special. 'I don't ever want you to forget,' he said mysteriously as he held my hand and we walked through the Sacramento. I was tired, but keen to squeeze every last ounce out of what was left of my stay.

I was wearing a white vest and ankle-length skirt, a little lipstick and mascara and I'd left my hair down. When I was in my thirties I'd read in a magazine that a woman shouldn't bare her arms or grow her hair long after the age of twenty-five. At the time I didn't question this but blindly adhered to the 'wisdom'. I thought about this now, walking through the dusk, enjoying the swing of my hair and the warmth of early evening on my arms. I questioned things much more these days, I didn't just accept what others told me, or what I read in magazines. Juan held my hand as we walked through the streets and I smiled at this new sense of liberation in my life – and I wanted to punch that bitch of a beauty editor whose comment about women in their forties being too old to wear their hair long had made me, and doubtless many other women like me, feel inadequate, unworthy. Not any more though.

Juan led me into a small, intimate cave bar where he said a jeurga – a private party – was being held. Once inside the whitewashed crumbly walls, I heard the now familiar sound of the flamenco guitar. I studied the photos of flamenco artists and famous dancers that performed there and felt privileged to be in a place steeped in dance history.

We sat at a table and Juan ordered sangria.

'This is real flamenco,' he smiled and took my hand on the table. I was excited to be here, the place was tiny, but the air was thick with anticipation.

Within minutes the sound of castanets could be heard over the guitar and several women strutted onto the floor. It was thrilling to watch the music and dance come to life in front of us with whirling, whipping skirts, clicking feet and fingers. Shouts of 'olé' filled the air as we clapped along, and I couldn't help it, my feet, unable to stay still despite being tired from the day's dancing, tapped out the rhythm from my seat.

'The dancers are performing the zambra,' Juan explained in my ear, 'a bit like a gypsy wedding.'

I nodded, unable to take my eyes off the flamboyant, energetic dancing, both thrilling and exhausting to watch. They were all good, but as a flamenco connoisseur I could now see the most talented dancer was in fact the one who looked the oldest and the biggest. That made me feel good – you don't have to be young and skinny and beautiful to be the best. She didn't just dance the zambra, she embodied it, the emotion showing in her pained, contorted expressions, the elaborate stomping of her feet. By the time she finished, her eyeliner was running down her cheeks. And it occurred to me that you have to be a certain age, to live through pain, love and disappointment, to dance like that.

Later, Juan invited some of the dancers and the singer to our table, they were old friends of his and he introduced me as 'the British Flamenco dancer'.

After a few drinks they invited us to join them all outside in the moonlight. They chatted and I tried to join in, what little bit of Spanish I'd learned helped, but Juan translated – as he had on the first day we met. Soon the flamenco guitar strains started up and Juan asked me to dance by holding out his hand dramatically, his eyes smouldering. I looked up and took his hand and strutted onto the floor.

'You're good,' I shouted, impressed with his dramatic moves, his meaningful stare.

'I am Andalusian... my blood runs with flamenco,' he said his hands clapping in the air, his feet stomping to the music. When I whirled around him, he caught me by the waist and hissed into my ear, 'You dance like a gypsy.'

I laughed, threw back my head and flapped my skirts as he stood back clapping.

The singer's voice was wonderful, and though I wasn't sure of the words, the sound was raw with emotion. Then the women joined me – supporting me in my dance, not outshining me as they could, so easily, have done. It was amazing to me that with such little language we could form such understanding through a voice, a guitar and the dance, moving in the moonlight. Of all the memories I will keep the one I will treasure is dancing with new friends, at midnight somewhere in the South of Spain.

❀ ❀ ❀

After the flamenco party – Juan and I returned to my apartment and he stayed with me until morning. We talked about dancing and how the music made us feel.

'What are the songs about?' I asked him.

'Don't ask the meanings – it's like asking why the sun sets. They are of everything – they sing of love, loss, war politics, family... being human.'

I could see that was why we didn't need language when we had dance – the movements and the sound spoke to my heart in a way nothing else did. I couldn't believe my time there was almost over and I was due to leave the following day. Juan said he'd miss me and I really felt he meant it – I'd miss him too, along with the heat, the wonderful sights and the amazing dancing.

After a few hours sleep Juan and I exchanged phone numbers and emails.

We were sitting at the little table in the tiny kitchenette in my apartment facing each other, the sun streaming through the windows. My eyes filled with tears, I knew this was only a holiday fling, a few nights of passion, but it had meant so much to me, Juan had awoken something inside me and made me feel so free, so happy.

'Don't be sad, I'll be back one day,' I said as he gazed longingly into my eyes. 'I promise,' I said, reaching for his hand across the table.

'I can't live without you, Laura,' he sighed. 'I think I am a little bit in love.'

'Ah, me too.' I heard my voice croaking with emotion, I hadn't come to Granada to find love, I'd come here to dance – what a wonderful surprise all this had been. But now it was time to say our final goodbyes, he was working that evening and my flight was early and though he'd wanted to meet up during my last few hours, I'd said no. I didn't want rushed, painful goodbyes before the airport. I wanted to remember him, my beautiful dark-haired Spanish lover, smiling in the morning sunshine.

I stood up from the table, leaned over and kissed him full on the lips, then pulled him towards me, my back against the tiny sink. And I was in Buenos Aires, I was hot, the heat from the sun licking at my face, and I wanted him now, against the wall. I pulled him towards me, kissing him passionately, then pushing him away just like the dance, teasing him, making him want me more. Then, when I knew I had his full attention, I unzipped him as we kissed more fervently, his breath in my neck, his hands on my breasts as he lifted me onto the sink, raising my nightdress he pulled my legs around him. His hands and mouth were all over me and I had to put my face in his neck to stifle the sounds of ecstasy, and my tears - our dance was over.

Chapter Twenty-two

Spanish Eyes... Telling Lies?

My last day at dance class was bittersweet. I had come so far in such a short time, the classes were high-calibre and challenging and I'd come through with flying colours. Along with Juan, the dancing classes had released me, unpacking the complicated code of flamenco - and of freeing myself to dance. 'You have the actitude, Laura,' my teacher said; 'In English it means attitude...you came without it, but found it here.'

I was so proud of myself. Here at the Escuela le Carmen School of Flamenco not only had I found Juan, but I had found my duende, my passion for flamenco – and Lola was here to stay.

✳ ✳ ✳

Despite fervent plans for packing and a nun-like early night that the old Laura would have relished and adhered to, I rebelled. Sitting on my patio at eight p.m., the sound of flamenco guitar drifting through the air, I couldn't resist a final wander into the Albayzín.

I walked through the streets, memories of earlier in my stay, the restaurant where we ate paella and drank until the sun dropped in the sky. The little tapas bars, Juan waiting for me by the school, the sun beating down, my heart dancing with happiness. I It seemed so long ago that first night when I'd sat alone in a tapas bar enjoying garlicky battered prawns and Rioja. I imagined that woman in her kaftan, white skin, hair tied up, nervous, wondering what the next two weeks might bring.. She felt like someone else.

I thought it would be fitting to end my journey where I began, to compare the woman who arrived here and the one who would be leaving at dawn. Sitting down, I asked for a sherry. It was the dry, buttery Manzanilla sherry I'd enjoyed on that first night with Juan and with it, I ate simple tapas – a slice of crusty bread topped with local cheese, fiery red chorizo that tingled on my tongue, and a savoury sliver of meltingly salty jamon. With my hair down, my shoulders bare and brown, enjoying this Spanish feast, I felt like a native.

After I'd eaten, I wandered the lanes and there I bought Sophie a mantilla, Mum a brooch of a flamenco dancer and Tony a pair of castanets. Then, in Barrio, I found an artisan shop selling flamenco practice skirts that some of the other students had told me about. Local girls made the skirts and each one was different. They were available in every colour, every design, from black to bright orange to plain to floral. I immediately alighted on a black skirt with bright pink frills at the bottom and rushing behind the little curtain, I unfurled it. There was hardly room for both of us in that tiny cubicle, but when I put her on, I was Lola. I had to stop myself from foot stomping and swirling – I couldn't wait to dance in my new gypsy flamenco skirt.

Delighted with all my purchases, I decided to have a coffee and perhaps something to eat before heading back uphill with my shopping and chose the terrace bar overlooking the city.

There is an old saying in Granada, '... there is nothing worse in this life than to be blind in Granada.' But watching the moon on the fountains cascading, swishing over secret conversations, the smell of tapas and jasmine carried on the evening breeze, caressing my bare shoulders – the way the music wound through the streets, the flamenco rhythm beating a constant pulse through the city. Granada wasn't just a feast for the eyes. This city sated all the senses and a warm evening in Granada is one of the best experiences in the world.

❊ ❊ ❊

I ordered coffee in a little cafe near the palace and as it was my last night I tried the famous Piononos de Santa Fe. According to my guidebook this cake was made for Pope Pius IX when he visited Granada in 1897... and I bet he loved it. A sweet, sticky cake flavoured with lemon and rum, the delicious, dense mixture stuck to the roof of my mouth. The lemon brought it all alive, adding a zesty lift to the sugar and the kick of the rum. I ate this jaw-achingly sweet confection with bitter black coffee – and took my time, enjoying the moment, living for the 'now' and just being.

After a second coffee, it was almost 11 and I really did have to head back if I was going to rise early in the morning for my flight. So I gathered my bags and began the long walk uphill to my apartment.

Stopping briefly to put my bags down and take a moment, I gazed at some beautiful flamenco posters on an orange wall. I thought it would make a good photo so I took out my phone. I was just standing back, holding the phone up in front of the poster when something caught my eye in the corner of the frame. It was a couple, heads close, and when I zoomed in I could see they were sharing a moment. The man was reading something from a piece of paper – it reminded me of Juan and his poetry. I zoomed in further so I could get a closer look and my heart did a little bounce. For there he was, the one who'd fallen so much in love with me it hurt, the man who said he couldn't survive without me – Juan was with another woman, and he was reading her one of his poems.

It took me a few seconds to register what was going on and in my rush to get the hell out of there, I started to run. Of course these things never go smoothly and within seconds a voice was calling, 'Senorita... senorita...' I'd left one of the bags behind on the floor and although I just wanted to go, I knew if I didn't go back, the woman would just keep shouting and drawing attention to me.

So I quickly ran back to where my carrier bag stood, with the old woman like a bloody sentinel standing over it, announcing both my departure and now my re-entrance. There was no way Juan wouldn't see me now, I thought, and as I quietly and quickly thanked the woman and made a grab for the bag, I turned to see him watching me. For a moment time stood still, our eyes met and I waited for the glimmer of recognition, the sudden smile to light his face. But nothing. He looked straight through me – and in that moment I realised – for him I was already gone. I was his yesterday and he'd already moved on. He looked back at his companion, continuing their intimate conversation. His eyes and his smile were for her now, and I noted – so were his hands, which now held one of hers in both of his, just like he had with me.

Tears sprung to my eyes as I picked up my bags and started walking away. I had fallen for the oldest trick in the book… again. First Cameron and now Juan. I know we'd never promised each other anything and we'd said goodbye but I was hurt and angry by the speed with which he'd found a replacement. Was I so forgettable? As I walked away I thought about how the old Laura would have just put her head down and walked on… like I was doing now. She found it hard to stand up for herself, to face things head on – but this wasn't the old Laura, this was Lola. I slowed down and glanced back, they were still deep in conversation and I was suddenly filled with a surge of anger and slowly turning around I went back to the bar. I was strong, I could hold my own on the dance floor, and now it was time to hold my own in life. I strode through the tables, unable to believe this was me, almost strutting, my head held high Lola style. Juan looked up at the ruckus I was causing as I sashayed past chairs and tables towards him. Arriving at his table our eyes met, he couldn't turn away from me now. I was the gypsy, the wild woman who wouldn't be tamed and he couldn't read me, had no idea what I would do next – and scarily, neither did I. His face was a combination of horror and confusion and I saw my hand reach for the large bottle of olive oil on their table. I took it, unscrewed the cork, held it high and slowly poured it all over his head. He just sat there in horrified silence as it glooped down through his hair, onto his face and seeped into his T shirt, hopefully ruining it forever. A hush had descended, as the other diners sat, open-mouthed, watching the show. I glanced at his companion, whose hand was over her mouth in shock, she was looking from me to him for a clue, but I would leave it to Juan to explain.

'Adios mi sole,' I said, a line from his poem which in Spanish means 'you are my sun.' I saw a look of guilt, sadness even - flash across his face as I carefully placed the empty bottle on the table in front of him, took his napkin and wiped my hands. With that, I picked up my bags - and left.

I walked away, leaving Juan and his new love behind. It had felt wonderful to show my feelings like that, and I could hear Tony's voice in my head; 'very Joan Crawford dear.' I'd never done anything like that before, I'd always accepted it when men dumped me or didn't call, never wanted to make a fuss didn't want confrontation and always keeping my feelings to myself – well not anymore. I was still tinged with anger and hurt as I marched back to my apartment. Then the evening breeze brushed over me, filling me with calm and a strange happiness and the rustling trees said, shhhhhh it's okay... it's all okay. And it was.

I found my way back in the darkness, I heard a flamenco guitar in the distance and my heart sand thinking about the wonderful nights we'd spent together. For me it hadn't just been about sex, it had been about the idea of romance, the dancing and feeling desired, like a woman again. It hurt that I hadn't apparently made any impact on him. I had been so unmemorable he'd found another 'tourist' before I'd even left the country, but that was life. I was able to rationalise everything because I'd taken back control and made myself heard... okay it was through the medium of olive oil, but I'd said my piece in my own way I don't know why I cried all the way back to my apartment, probably because I wished he'd meant just a few of all the lovely things he'd said, but he probably didn't. Later that night I sat on my balcony in the darkness overlooking the starry lights sprinkled through the city. I counted my blessings, I had just had the most wonderful two weeks in this amazing place and I was grateful and happy. I reminded myself that Juan had never promised me his forever– and I was ready now to make my own forevers, on my own terms.

Chapter Twenty-three

Goodbye Granada and Hello Dreamboys

Before I went to bed I called Tony and gave him a quick rundown on the latest episode in my love life. It was funny, because even if it had ended, I was proud of the fact that I even had a love life – before I'd just listened to stories about everyone else's. I felt like I was finally part of something.

Tony was, of course, furious on my behalf when I told him I'd seen Juan with another woman, but calmed down when I told him what I'd done.

'Whoa girl! Didn't think you had it in you but she's one feisty bitch that Lola.'

'Yes and she doesn't give a toss, but Laura's rather pissed off that he hadn't even waited until she was on the bloody plane,' I sighed.

'Ooh olive oil was too good for him,' Tony started. 'I'd have given him a piece of my mind, torn his bloody poem up, said something fabulous from my Joan Crawford collection and stomped off.'

I laughed. 'Yes, I could just imagine *that* scenario. But seeing him with someone else so soon reminded me that you can't rely on other people to make you happy. I'm responsible for my own happiness, and I will have it - I'm not hanging around waiting for some man to tell me how good I am how beautiful I am and 'validating' me with his love... I don't need it.'

'Oh how very Bette Davis!' he said, in his Joan Crawford voice. I laughed, realising how much I'd missed him; his dancing, his old Hollywood films, his eyebrow dramas, and his Grindr scandals – but most of all I missed his friendship.

'Sounds like you have had quite a time, girl,' he was saying.

'Yeah... the best, the very best, but I'm ready to come home now.'

Hanging up, I took the beautiful flamenco skirt from the bag and tried it on. I strutted around the place, sweeping out onto the balcony and gazing out onto the city lit with a million twinkling lights. The stars were out and the moon had reached its fullness and that night the city was all mine.

'I'll be back Granada,' I sighed, knowing in my heart this was the first of a million visits.

✳ ✳ ✳

The next morning I woke early and hearing the beep of the taxi I'd ordered to take me to the airport I picked up my suitcase and put the rucksack on my back. I felt good, my body was firmer, my legs and feet stronger, and I was wearing shorts, something I hadn't done for years. I had one last look in the mirror – my hair was down, my arms were bare but here in Granada I'd learned that Laura could do anything she wanted to. She could sleep with a man she hardly knew – and she could dance flamenco with strangers until dawn. 'I am one shameless, forty-four-year-old hussy,' I said into the mirror, and blowing myself a kiss, said goodbye to the place where I'd found duende and come across some 'actitude'.

❅ ❅ ❅

Arriving back in the UK, I couldn't believe how cold it was, and Tony, who was waiting for me, confirmed it in his own inimitable way.

'My testicles have been shrivelled up for a week with this chill,' he announced. 'My love, I want to hear EVERYTHING.' Mandy, eyebrow specialist to the stars, was with him, nodding vigorously at this. She had apparently passed her driving test only the week before and had brought him to the airport to meet me because he was still unable to drive. There were as usual lots of colourful adjectives directed at Tony from Mandy as he made us all detour to the nearest newsagent to pick up for the latest 'Dreamboys' magazine.

'So what about your holiday?' Mandy was saying as we headed out to the car. Bloody hell Laura, Tone's been telling me all about you rubbing olive oil into a Spanish guy's willy on a pavement. Outside a restaurant!'

'Well it wasn't quite like...'

'Babe - even I wouldn't do that... like ... get a room girl!' She said this like I was the most sexually outrageous woman she'd ever met, which was saying something for Mandy. I didn't disillusion or disappoint her with the truth, she wouldn't believe me anyway, she liked her own version better. So I just squeezed myself and my bags into the back of Mandy's little car and prayed her driving was less aggressive than her eyebrow styling.

'I need a blindfold, I can't look,' Tony screamed, covering his eyes as she pulled away, just missing a whole family walking through the car park.

'Jesus, Mandy, did you actually see them?' he squealed. She hit him and told him to shut his 'gob'.

'She nearly killed me on the way here, as if I haven't been through enough. I need something to take my mind off her bloody driving...' Tony said, covering his face with his magazine. 'If I'm gonna die a horrible death in a twisted car wreck, I want to die with guys like this.' He opened 'Dreamboys' and gasped with sheer joy at the naked spectacle before him. 'What about that spread-eagled on your king-sized, love?' he shouted to me in the back waving a glossy centrefold of muscular male. Mandy roared and grappled the magazine off him... still driving... well I use the term loosely. I almost lost my lunch.

✳ ✳ ✳

The following morning I woke, remembered I wasn't in Spain and my heart did a little dip. My only consolation was that on the last day at the school we'd been allowed to film the teacher dancing. This meant I would be able to show Tony everything I'd learned, so I took my flamenco shoes and practice skirt and headed off to meet him at the dance centre as we'd arranged the night before. When I arrived he was doing some stretching exercises and I was impressed at how his leg had improved. Apparently once the swellings and bruising had gone down his injuries hadn't been quite as bad as we'd thought.

I put my shoes on and in between torrid tales of sex with Juan and the flamenco caves, we watched my short film and Tony said he would modify some of the footwork so it would be more suitable for a man, but essentially copied my moves.

'The idea is to keep the footwork tight, stay on the smallest space,' I explained, feeling like the teacher for once as I watched him move, shouting, 'golpe, golpe,' a word I'd heard a million times at the school, meaning stamp. After we'd been dancing for a couple of hours (which we took steadily to accommodate Tony's recovery) we sat down on the floor to rest a while and I popped into the cake shop down the road and brought us both coffee, sandwiches and cupcakes.

'Ooh I missed this chocolate velvet,' I said, biting into my cupcake.

'Yeah... love em.... oooh. Oh. My. God, I'm having an orgasm,' he announced.

I nodded. It was good to be back home, dancing with Tony and eating my favourite cupcakes, I just dreaded going back to work on Monday.

'I feel I've changed so much,' I sighed. 'It will be like walking back into my old life.'

'Don't... just leave.'

'If only – I have the matter of a small thing called a mortgage.'

'I thought your mum's house had sold?' he said, licking cream from his fingers.

'It has – and I might buy a new pair of dancing shoes, even a dress when it's all signed and the cheque arrives – but until then we need the money to pay for Mum's care.'

'Mmmm... about the dress?'

'I don't need one – not until we do a competition next year...'

He was nodding frantically and looking guilty at the same time. 'You do need one ... you need a flamenco dress for November.'

'Why? What's happening then?'

He looked down, I always knew when he had done something he shouldn't.

'It's erm... well, there's a Dance Festival... in Blackpool.'

'Next November?'

'This November.'

'But that's only three months away. We can't do it this year, I'm not ready and...'

'Oh love, you'll never be ready, if we wait for you we'll both be dragging our arses onto that Blackpool dance floor in zimmer frames. It's not a competition, just a display, but it will be your first public performance and the beginning of our glittering career together. So while you were off enjoying tapas and tangos I booked our places.'

'But apart from anything else, are you sure you're ready after all you've been through?'

He stood up and started walking around and in his Joan Crawford voice said, 'Darling ... they beat me. But they didn't knock me down... the show must go on. You see, my love, that night was meant to happen... it's made me realise I need to grasp at everything before it's too late. No one knows how many tomorrows we have, and no, I didn't get that from a self-help book, I made that up myself.'

'Oh Tony, I feel the same. After being in Spain and dancing every day and... well, being with Juan... I feel so... different. I feel like Lola came out in Spain and she won't be pushed back inside... Lola's going to Blackpool!'

'She is, darling. And I bet flamenco lessons, warm weather and a few "goes" on Juan has made the world of difference to Lola's dancing,' he winked.

'Yes... I can really feel it now.'

'I bet you can, love,' he smirked.

'You know what I mean. But, Tony, are you feeling strong enough mentally to cope with the pressure – after everything?'

'After all the publicity about "Local Dance Teacher Being Beaten", I thought I will turn this into a silver lining and get the local press on board too. It will be good for us, good for my dance lessons... and it's good for the charity I'm working for.'

'Charity?'

'Yes, it's against homophobia, and I've been invited to give talks in local schools. I'm a cause célèbre, darling. It's an issue we need to make everyone aware of – homophobia gets them young, let's try and nip it in the bud.'

'Brilliant.' I was impressed. Then he did what Tony always does and overegged the pudding.

'Because, my love...' he started singing, 'I believe the children are the future... teach them well and let them lead the way...'

'Yes, I get it – and I think what you're doing is wonderful. But please don't sing.'

'Darling, just because some haters say I can't sing... doesn't mean I can't. I sing perfectly when I'm alone at home in front of the mirror with a Coke-bottle mic.'

'Yes, well, it's the world's loss that any singing talent you may have when you're alone seems to disappear when anyone's present.'

'Oh you've gone all feisty since you learned flamenco,' he laughed.

'Oh yes, honey,' I laughed, 'I'm one shady bitch, as Mandy would say.'

He was right. My time in Spain had given me more confidence in myself, it wasn't just about the dancing, it was also about meeting Juan. We'd both enjoyed spending time together no-strings, just a wonderful, wonderful time – and that had released something inside me.

'So go on, let's get going, I want you to share everything you learned with me,' Tony said, rubbing his hands together excitedly.

'Yes... we will. But first can we try the Argentine Tango one more time?' I said. 'I think I might just be ready to let go.'

'Oh girl, yess... let's see what Juan did that I couldn't.'

He was smiling to himself as he put the music on, and we listened for a while. After a few minutes, I had to move. 'Let's go for it,' I said. Tony stood behind me and pushed his leg into mine, lifting my leg up, and then we moved together slowly, winding around each other to the music. Then he lifted me and as the music reached a crescendo, I was suddenly there, in the streets of Buenos Aires, the rhythm running through me. We were moving, hip to hip, our upper bodies leading the dance, our legs working through the intricate, complex movements. Our foreheads were touching as we moved as one across the floor. The tango and the music had taken me over. I was the lady of the night, strutting around the man, teasing him, moving into a tight hold, then pulling away, flirting, flouncing, and together making a figure of eight on the floor. Tony lifted me and I was euphoric landing perfectly, leading naturally into a final scene entwined together on the floor.

We stayed in our prone position for a few seconds, recovering, just coming up gently, it was like being woken from an amazing sleep.

'Wow! Lola that was amazing – Oh my God you are a total prostitute!' he screamed.

'Thank you,' I curtseyed, never thinking I would be so pleased to be called that.

'Lola, you are on fire. You really let go, you were rampant, I almost fancied you myself, but of course that would never happen... no offence.'

'None taken,' I smiled, glowing in his praise. He'd just told me I was a prostitute and he could never really fancy me. And I was delighted.

'I told you all you needed was a hot night of passion with a gorgeous man and it would come flooding...'

'Yeah, he can take *some* of the credit,' I smiled, 'but that girl on the floor was all me, baby,' I said in my 'Tony' voice, shaking my finger from side to side. 'And ain't no man taking no credit!'

❋ ❋ ❋

Later I talked Tony through the basic flamenco steps, blocking them through as I talked about the culture, the history, the whole fabulous stuff around the dance. Then I put on some music on and danced for him. I stomped until my legs reverberated and the room shook, I whipped around and flounced my skirts and raised my arms high. My whole body pulsed with the dance, the emotions of the past few months all simmering inside me, and bubbling through my veins, and when I finished I threw myself onto the floor, holding the pose, my whole body trembling. After what felt like several minutes, I got my breath and looked up from my final position waiting for Tony's reaction. But he just stared ahead.

'Is that what you learned in Spain?' he asked, eventually.

I nodded. 'Do you like it? Have I improved?'

'Improved? Oh. My. God. I am in a catsuit of emotions right now... you have bloody transformed yourself, Lola. I have never seen you dance like that, what the fuck have you been doing until now? You've been hiding all that talent, all that passion and emotion, and *that*, my love, was a performance. Lola the gypsy girl just landed in the UK and she isn't leaving any time soon.'

Chapter Twenty-four

Weetabix, Weather and the Wrong Juan

Going back to work was awful. It wasn't just the 'post-holiday blues', it was more than that. I was already growing out of the job before I'd gone away, but this change in me had made it even more difficult to get through a day behind the checkout.

'I hate Bilton's so much I think it would be preferable to have stayed in Granada with cheating Juan,' I said to Tony one night, after another long day at work.

'Oh no love, I'm glad you came back. I was missing you... I don't know what I'd do without you. Besides he was a bad un.'

'Was he? Perhaps I overreacted? I've had time this week, sitting on my checkout to wonder if Juan really was "with" that woman.'

'What? Like the woman he was holding hands with and reading love poetry to was... his sister?' Tony huffed, sarcastically.

'Not exactly. But when a man writes a poem for you... that's special.'

'Mmmm I suppose so... but I wasn't going to tell you this. But he didn't.'

'He did... I told you "my life, my faith, my ..."'

'Juan Ramón Jiménez.'

'No his name's Juan...'

'No, Juan Ramón Jiménez wrote the poem... I was so bloody furious with him I googled "Amor" the poem, and there it was.'

'Oh...' I blushed, feeling a little foolish. I thought the poem was just for me, but it wasn't even written by my Juan, it was another one...I don't know who I thought 'my Juan' even was. 'You'd think I'd learn wouldn't you?' I sighed.

'No, you and I will never learn, because we are dreamers, and we always expect the best of a man and we're usually disappointed. But another Joel or Juan will be along soon and you and I will fall in love all over again – cos that's what life's about, falling in love, learning lessons, then boiling a few bunnies. And one day, who knows, we might even fall for someone who doesn't take us for a ride and live happily ever after with the man of our dreams. We've got to hope, if we didn't, we'd shrivel up.'

I nodded, he was right – whatever happens you have to have hope.

'Meanwhile we can keep dancing and make do with each other. Just don't get any ideas about us having sex… eww,' he joked. 'The best relationships are left unconsummated.'

I laughed, knowing I could move on without looking backwards and just remember Juan as a lovely summer fling.

❄ ❄ ❄

Over the next few weeks Tony and I trained every night and every weekend. By day he was a discreet shop assistant dressing foot-ballers' wives and local businesswomen in cocktail and cruise wear. But by night he was Tony Hernandez, fiery Latin dancer, squiring Lola the gypsy girl around the floor. Meanwhile Lola spent her days as Laura, at the checkout, pushing through the Weetabix, talking about the bloody weather and dreaming of another life.

Most people live quite ordinary lives in ordinary homes doing boring jobs. Like them I'd always accepted my lot – but now I'd changed, I felt special, and l had a dream that might just lift me out of this life into another one day. Meanwhile, I had a reason to get up in the morning, a reason to go to work – to earn the money to dance. For the next couple of years I would put some money away and in the meantime I could dance and dream... like my parents had.

Dad's letter was filled with sadness, but also with hope, it float-ed under the text, flew off the page, filling my head with sunshine and Cha Cha. Sadly my dad's hopes and dreams were meaningless because he'd never pursued them. But dreams won't come to you, they have to be chased and nurtured. And it might be next week or next year – but I wasn't going to let mine die.

I knew it was hard to step out of your comfort zone and all too easy to lose sight of your dreams in the debris of everyday life. Here I was, dressed in green nylon doing just that – wasting every day behind my checkout. I couldn't tell anyone at Bilton's I wanted to dance for a living, they'd laugh and think I was foolish. I could hear them now; 'Who does she think she is?' So as I rung the till and filled shelves with tampons and tea I made a promise to myself, that I wouldn't do this forever. And all the time I kept my dreams to myself, like a secret little bud growing inside me, giving me hope and keeping me sane.

❄ ❄ ❄

By October, Tony and I had decided we would be ready to dance the flamenco in Blackpool the following month.

'It's the first time they've ever allowed flamenco on the floor there,' he said, with a catch of excitement in his voice. It was contagious, I felt a shimmer of anticipation as he said it and grabbed his arm. 'Lola, I can't wait to get there and show them what we're made of... your flamenco will floor them.'

'Oh I am so excited, but I'm nervous and I... oh I'm all over the place. But – bring it on,' I said.

'That's it, girl... what's that saying, do something every day that scares you?'

'Ooh yes, I like that.'

'Yes, but take my advice and don't apply it to one-night stands... I met up with a scary bald guy in the Red Lion last Wednesday. Cute face, but... let's put it this way, he *will* kill again.'

I laughed. 'I've told you, stop looking for love in all the wrong places, Tony... and polite request – would you not turn our Blackpool trip into a Grindr special? And DON'T arrange to meet unsuitable men under the pier.'

I was thinking about Blackpool and wondering how I would feel going back there after all these years. After what happened to dad, I never thought I'd have the strength to return, but things were changing for me now. I tried to focus on the positive aspects – the beautiful Winter Gardens where we would dance, the candy floss...

'I won't meet anyone under the pier,' Tony was saying. 'The sea's horrendous in November, big, rough and grey... and that's just how I like my men,' he smiled.

'Forget men, Blackpool has the best fish and chips in the world, all salt and vinegary and hot and crispy. And they have to be eaten out of newspaper on the sea front, regardless of the weather,' I said, pushing away dark thoughts, trying not to think of The Empress Ballrooms, my mother's screams when the music stopped.

'Do they still sell Kiss me Quick hats and candy floss?' I asked, one half of me still there, the other forcing the juggernaut of my feelings into something lighter, more trivial.

'Of course they still have Kiss me Quick hats... and pink rock with Blackpool written all the way through it. Blackpool's full of queens not Quakers. We love the seaside like anyone else – riding on donkeys and getting sand in our spandex, as for candy floss, I can't get enough. Mind you, last time I had some it played havoc with my lip gloss,' he laughed.

I would need a flamenco dress and a decent pair of dance shoes, so we decided to spend the evening planning our outfits. Within minutes, we were on Tony's laptop surfing dance shoes and dresses. Tony said the sooner I had my stagewear the better. 'You have to get used to practising in your outfits – especially the shoes, it's like an athlete and their trainers,' he was saying.

Tony and I had gone through Mum's shoes and dresses together when I'd moved them from Mum's to his garage a few days previously.

He'd kindly offered to store them for me as there was no room at mine. I was convinced he was trying them on late at night – he talked about them often, referring to 'the pink chiffon waltz' and 'the aqua silk foxtrot' like they were old friends. Tony had discovered Mum's lovely dance shoes in various shades and though I'd said they were several sizes too small, he insisted they would fit me. But after much painful shouting and pushing, he conceded, 'Yeah, you're no Cinderella, love, more Ugly Sister.' So we'd gone back to the drawing board.

'For the American Smooth a woman should wear pastel pink and net with matching shoes, hashtag Grace Kelly!' he was now sighing, clicking the mouse excitedly as he cruised the luscious satins and feathers and fringes.

If there was one thing Tony loved almost as much as ballroom dancing, it was ballroom dresses. He was smiling at the computer screen, lost in sparkle and tulle.

Ballroom porn he called it and whooped every time he saw something 'orgasmic'.

'I want long, I don't want one that will show my cellulite,' I said anxiously.

'Darling, what do you think American Tan tights were made for? They were designed for cottage cheese thighs just like yours.'

'Stop, you're making me big-headed,' I said sarcastically.

'Oooh, ooh. You would look gorgeous doing the Argentine Tango in that little number, Lola,' he was pointing to a lovely black dress with a hint of glitter and a slash up the thigh.

I sighed, agreeing it would look spectacular under the disco ball, even on my lumpy thighs. But looking at the price just made me want to cry. 'They are hundreds of pounds, I can't possibly afford that – if I start entering competitions next year and need a new dress every time, it's going to be impossible... I can't.'

But he was like a magpie and soon chasing something else glittery on screen. 'Ooh come to daddy,' he sighed, peering at a glamorous pink-feathered jumpsuit.

'I'm not sure about feathers,' I said.

'Who said it's for you?' he looked at me. 'I could carry that off, couldn't I?'

I wasn't sure if he was joking or not, so I gave him a doubtful look and continued to complain about the prices. 'I don't need a tango dress yet, but I need something to wear to dance flamenco,' I pointed out. 'I'd love to wear a real flamenco dress, but these are just eye-wateringly expensive.'

'I know, you'd have to be a trust-fund chick or the wife of a Russian oligarch to own one of those – and sadly, my love, you're neither.'

'No,' I sighed. 'Thanks for reminding me.' Even if I had the money, I couldn't justify spending so much on one item of clothing. Sophie's wedding money was still sitting in the bank but I'd already used some to pay my spending money in Spain and I wasn't taking any more. Besides, the way things seemed to be going with Carl I wondered if we might need that money soon for another wedding.

'No... we're not going to be able to buy a flamenco dress,' Tony was saying. I know it's only a dancing display, but those East German lesbians are very competitive when it comes to dancing frocks, love. They are ballroom Olympians... big burly girls with a million sequins, fierce ambition and even fiercer eyebrows.'

'I have my practice skirt... it's frilly and I could buy a new shawl?'

'Yeah that sounds good, let's see if our Rita can add an extra frill here and there – we can work with that.'

It was disappointing not to be able to wear the real thing for the display, but there were other, more important things to worry about – like the dance itself.

Later we practised our flamenco in his garden, it was bloody freezing but the stomping on his wooden floor after 10 p.m. alarmed the neighbours. I practised in my swirling skirt, my shoes and my shawl with roses in my hair and hoops in my ears.

'You look lovely, Lola... let me do your make-up,' he said.

He drew sweeping black eyeliner on my eyes and brows, pulled down my hair and applied a scarlet lipstick he found in my bag that I hadn't worn in years.

'Is that a bit young for me?' I asked.

'No... you look like a dark and glamorous gypsy, only a little bit drag queen with those earrings...'

'Oh!'

'I'm teasing you – you stupid mare, you look bloody fabulous... even *with* the earrings.'

❀ ❀ ❀

After Spain I wanted to make a fresh start with everything, 'wipe away the cobwebs' as my dad used to say. And the thing I needed to do most was talk to Mum. I wanted to clear the air and finally talk to her about Dad's letter. I had to ask her who Dad meant when he wrote, *'I know you're thinking of him.'* I also wanted to ask her why she'd never encouraged me to dance as Dad had wanted. It was time to tell her about mine and Tony's plans – and if she'd let me, I wanted to share my dancing with her. I wanted to talk to her about moves and steps, ask her advice – she'd been a wonderful dancer in her time and I wanted to learn more from her. So I headed to Wisteria Lodge with a bunch of red roses – the flowers my dad always bought for her.

We sat outside in the late Autumn sunshine, drinking tea and I decided it was time to talk.

'Mum, I've started dancing... like you and Dad.'

There was silence while she fiddled with her saucer, I wasn't sure if she'd heard, so I spoke more loudly.

'I started classes almost a year ago. And when I went to Spain I was learning Flamenco,' I offered into the silence.

'Yes, I remember you said... your dad always wanted to learn the flamenco.'

I was relieved she acknowledged this – perhaps we were finally getting somewhere;

'Yes... I know. It doesn't hurt you, does it? That I'm doing it now?'

She shook her head and smiled; 'I remember him shouting olé,' she said, lifting her arms and clicking her fingers.

I smiled. 'I remember us dancing on the table.' I looked at her. 'I didn't want to tell you I was dancing – in case it upset you... reminded you of the past, what happened.'

'Oh I've messed everything up haven't I, Laura?' she looked crumpled, like she might cry.

'No, Mum, you haven't, but we should have talked – about Dad, about the past.'

She nodded, I wasn't sure if she'd heard me but I ploughed on. 'I'm sorry, I don't want to hurt you and you can tell me to mind my own business... it's just... I found a letter. I know I shouldn't have, it was private, but I'm sorry, I read it...' I opened my handbag and, carefully taking the letter out of its laminated sheet, I handed it to her. She took it from me silently.

'I'm sorry, Mum, I've kept it for a while, I wasn't sure how to ask you...'

'I remember this,' she said, nodding, putting on her glasses and holding the letter right up to her face. 'I thought I'd lost it,' she said, continuing to read it.

'He wrote it before Blackpool,' she was still looking at it. 'Who'd have thought it?'

I let her read it to the end, she half-smiled a little here and there, but I could see she was upset. When she finished, she folded the letter and stared ahead. If I didn't ask now, I never would...and I finally felt strong enough to hear what she had to say, whatever it might be.

'Mum... in the letter Dad talks about a man?'

She didn't respond, just kept staring ahead.

'Dad say she changed everything... this other man, and he couldn't bear to say his name.'

She wiped her eyes with a handkerchief, but fat tears sat in the crinkles of flesh on her cheek. I took the hankie and wiped her face gently, she had that same faraway look Dad spoke of in his letter –

the one we both knew so well. What was she thinking about? Who was it that made her look this way?

'Did something happen Mum... between you and Dad? Did you meet someone else? Were you going to leave him... us?' There I'd said it and as hard as it was for me to say, it must have been harder for her to hear. She didn't respond, she was staring into space and for a few moments I thought she might ignore me, pretend she hadn't heard, when I knew she had.

Then she reached for my hand.

'No, love. I talked about it, but I'd never have left,' her voice faltered.

'Why... who?'

'It was only ever your dad for me – I never looked at another man.'

'Why were you going to leave Dad? Who is he talking about in the letter, Mum?'

'David... he's talking about David,' she said, her voice breaking, more tears emerging.

'Who's David?'

'He was your little brother, love.'

Chapter Twenty-five

Answers, Questions and Tears

My head filled with questions and confusion. I'd always been an only child, like it or not I had always defined myself as such, this news shifted my world on its axis.

'Me and your dad should have talked, but we never did. It was my fault, I found it all too painful and I wanted to run away from everything. That's why he wrote this letter – he didn't want me to go,' she started to cry.

'Tell me... about David,' I begged, my heart was hammering in my chest.

'When you were four, I got pregnant... we'd wanted another baby for such a long time – a little brother or sister for you. Oh, your dad was delighted, we were so happy, but I'd had a difficult time carrying you, so we decided not to tell anyone until we knew it would all be fine. You probably don't remember, but for a few months we didn't do any competitions and your dad treated me like I was made of glass, wrapped me in cotton wool, he did,' she was smiling at the memory. 'He'd always wanted a house full of children, but I didn't get pregnant easily and when I did, well I'd already had two miscarriages before you.'

'I had no idea, Mum.'

'Miscarriages weren't something you spoke about then, you just got on with it. I'd sometimes have to go into hospital afterwards, the loss of a baby at any stage is terrible... just terrible. Each blow knocked me further, but in those days there weren't these therapist people to talk to, you just carried on.'

The jigsaw was slowly coming together: Mum's stays in hospital when I was a child were about depression, about her grieving for the babies she lost. This also explained my father's desperate need to make her happy all the time, regardless of the cost.

'When I got pregnant with David, it seemed like everything was fine,' she was saying. 'We bought you a Tiny Tears doll so you could get used to a new baby in the house. It was our way of introducing the idea, a way of telling you, so it wouldn't be such a surprise when the baby came. Then... at eight months, it was a Friday night and we were eating sponge cake, your dad always brought one home on a Friday... do you remember?'

I nodded.

'Anyway, I suddenly knew something was wrong, and your dad called the doctor and David was born that night. I'm sure he would have been fine if that had happened now, with all the technology... but he was a month early and in distress... There was nothing anyone could do.'

She blew her nose, she was shaking and I reached out to hold her hand. She squeezed mine. 'The midwife said he looked like your dad, a perfect little boy she said.' Then that faraway look came in her eyes. 'A perfect little boy... except he wasn't breathing.'

I rested my eyes on the smooth, green lawn with pale yellow edges, I was desperately looking for some order, some calm. But I felt like there'd been an explosion in my head. All this heartbreak and pain had happened in my own family, in my home, and I'd had no idea. I gave Mum some time, it was clear that in telling me all this, the emotion she'd packed down for so long had overwhelmed her.

'Of course I understand why you didn't tell me at the time...' I said after a few minutes. 'I remember the Tiny Tears, and I remember you crying. I was too young to comprehend what was going on.'

'We never intended to keep it from you, but when we buried David we buried everything else. From the day he died we never talked about it. I think we were protecting each other, but it wasn't the answer. Your dad adored you and was able to pour all his love and all his hopes into you, which helped him to move on, but I couldn't escape, I found it so hard to live again. Then when your dad... went... I was swallowed up in a sinking sand of grief and loss and my heart broke completely. I sometimes wonder if the clock started ticking for your dad the day David died – the stress must have weighed him down so much. And I was helpless, he must have felt so alone, carrying the burden, looking after you and me and keeping life on track. He couldn't opt out, he had to keep on going for all of us.'

'Oh Mum, all those years, you never talked to me... you never talked to anyone.'

'I couldn't burden you. There were times I wondered if it would be kinder to you if I just ended it all, but I couldn't leave you, your dad had already left and you only had me.'

'Oh Mum, you should have talked to someone after Dad,' I sighed.

'Yes, but you didn't in those days, young people today talk more to each other. I sometimes hear you and Sophie arguing or talking about how you feel – it's not easy to listen to – but it's healthier. You can't keep stuff locked up inside – it rots away, poisons you. I've been talking to Mrs Brown, the matron here, she says it helps to talk about things, she lost her mother last winter and she said she'd have gone mad if she hadn't talked about it. That's why I'm able to talk to you now... a year ago, I couldn't have had this conversation. Your dad was right when he said in his letter that we weren't good at talking, so we just kept on, lying to ourselves, lying to each other and covering everything in sequins.'

I was seeing Mum through new eyes, she'd had such a difficult life, yet she'd done what she thought was right and protected me, keeping me from her pain. My Mum was a lot stronger than I'd ever given her credit for.

'Thanks for telling me, Mum, I can imagine it must hurt, trawling through the past like that. I wish I'd known and could have helped...or at least listened.'

'The thought of you kept me going, love... so you did help me. I'd been with your dad since I was eighteen,' Mum started, smiling at the memory. 'Oh he was handsome, all my friends fancied their chances with him, but he only had eyes for me. My mother, your grandmother, used to say we lit up the room when we were together. He looked after me, especially after David...he wanted to leave the country, live in Spain where we could dance and forget. But I knew we could never forget, and leaving here would mean leaving David... his memory at least. But then I lost your dad and I felt like I'd lost everything... '

'Is that why you gave up dancing?'

'Yes, your dad was all part of that, he brought it into my life, taught me everything. Ken was my dancing, my memories, my music. Sometimes, when you were at school and I was all alone at home, I would steal myself and put a record on. I'd do what he used to – I'd move that big mahogany table and make some space to dance, but when it came to actually doing the steps... I couldn't, I always ended up crying. Dancing is for two people, and when you find the right partner it's for life.'

We sat for a long time in silence while I took everything in and we both cried a little and hugged a lot.

'I think I was meant to find that letter, it gave me direction, something to aim for,' I said. 'That's when I started dancing – it's why I went to Spain. A year ago if Tony had offered me that trip I'd have turned it down, but something, someone, was behind me urging me on... you know?'

'Yes. I've felt that too recently... I can't quite put my finger on it, but I know he's around. It feels nice.'

'Good. I'm glad you feel like that. Perhaps we're both letting him back in, Mum? He never really left us, but we were too closed up.'

She nodded. 'And now look at you. You're dancing and you've even been to Spain, and learned flamenco, he'd be so pleased. I'm sorry I never encouraged you to dance, I could have taught you, but I would have got upset, and that would have upset you. I decided it was best just to leave it... too painful, too many memories of him in the music and the dances.'

'Yes, I understand Mum. But I got there in the end and I danced under the stars – just like he talked about.'

'It's something he always wanted... for all of us. He even bought me a flamenco dress, you know? Red it was. I never wore it.'

'Really? I didn't know.' Then I said, 'Mum, why don't I take you to Spain? Next year, we can watch the flamenco dancing together.'

'Dreams are for young people, Laura. I'm too old now for any of that.'

'Mum, the young don't have the monopoly on dreams – none of us know how long we've got, but we have to make the most of that time. I'm in my forties, does that mean I'm too old to dream? I don't think so, and neither are you.'

She patted my knee. 'You're more like your dad these days, full of hope. "Always believe in a better tomorrow," he'd say. I see him in you now.'

I smiled; 'Thank you. '

'All I want, and all your dad would have wanted is for you to be happy.'

'I am.'

'Those dresses, in the attic,' she suddenly said, 'I'm sure that's where that flamenco dress is...the one your dad bought me. Why don't you have a look, you could wear it?'

'I'd love to wear your dress, Mum, but it's probably too small for me.'

'You could get it widened?'

'Yes, I'd have to, you were a slip of a thing, remember?'

'I do,' she said, getting that faraway look in her eyes again.

'Mum, you're not cold are you?' She shook her head, she liked sitting outside these days, after being locked in the house for so many years. But it was getting chilly and I knew it would soon be time to go in, I just had one last question.

'Mum?' I said, breaking into the thick silence. 'Do you think Dad would be proud of me?'

'Do you want to know what I think?'

My heart sank, it had been an emotional afternoon and I wasn't sure I was ready for one of mother's brutally honest answers. I braced myself.

'I think... yes. He would be very proud of you – and so am I.' She put her hand over mine in a protective gesture and I wanted to cry with happiness. My mum had never been demonstrative, never told me she was proud, and I knew it wasn't easy for her to say that. Mum and I had both been battle-scarred by the past – and we were both scared of loving too much because it meant losing too much.

'Laura,' she said, 'if I'm still here this time next year I might come with you, see Spain, the dancing...'

I nodded, and took hold of her hand, determined to take her there.

❄ ❄ ❄

As soon as I got back, I called Tony and told him all about mine and Mum's conversation.

'Oh I'm so pleased for you, love,' he said. 'I've always thought it so sad that you both love dancing yet couldn't share it. We need Margaret's top tips on tango now,' he said.

'Yes – I just wish I could fit in her dresses too. Mum mentioned that Dad had bought her a flamenco dress... a red one... I'm probably too fat for it, but I was thinking, perhaps your Rita might be able to alter it? You haven't seen it in the bin liners in your garage have you?'

'No, love – I'd remember that. I've been through them all.'

'Never mind, I've been worried about what I'm going to wear for the flamenco dance and I thought my prayers might have been answered.'

'Look, I think your practice skirt will be fine... nice fitted black T-shirt with it... lovely.'

'Yes, I suppose,' I sighed. Blackpool was a big deal for me, it was a place of my dreams and my nightmares and it was important to me that everything was done right, because if Dad was anywhere, he'd be watching me dance at The Winter Gardens. It would have been wonderful to dance in a proper dress, but even if we found Mum's it would be far too small. I wasn't going to let it get me down, I'd come too far for that.

Chapter Twenty-six

Film Stars, Flamenco and a Very Special Dress

By early November we were ready. Our flamenco was passionate and fiery and our Argentine Tango was fast, exciting and sensual – according to Mandy it was like 'shagging, standing up... in a posh frock,' which I took as a compliment. We were training so hard I worried Tony had put too much strain on his injured leg, but he wouldn't let that stop him. After the assault, Tony had called up all the local and regional newspapers and did several interviews on local radio about his ordeal. As awful as it all had been for him, he was certainly enjoying his new-found fame – and milking it. He was such a funny, colourful character the radio stations had asked him back and his recovery had become a regular feature in the local paper. So for the Blackpool festival he'd even managed to drum up some national coverage about how 'Tony WILL Dance Again.' A local college had offered to film our performance and put it on the internet too which was all good news for Tony's dream of building his classes so one day he could leave the day job. He'd talked of 'Tony's Dance School' and had even suggested I go in with him as a partner, but it felt like a big leap too soon.

'One day perhaps, but I'm not good enough to teach yet,' I'd said.

'I told you... even if Laura can't... Lola can.'

❄ ❄ ❄

It was just a week before the Blackpool Festival and Tony had been keen to take 'full creative control, darling' where our 'dancing look' was concerned. Rita had taken my measurements but hadn't been able to make any frilly additions to my practice skirt because one of her kids was sick and her dog had puppies and ... well the last thing on the poor woman's mind was my skirt. So I had bought a black T shirt and would wear my flamenco practice skirt and a shawl, which wasn't ideal, but would have to do.

I wasn't just worried about my outfit – I was also nervous because Tony had asked Mandy to come to the festival as 'chief brow manager'. She was delighted and had also offered (threatened?) to do my hair and make-up. I felt like I was losing control and was at the mercy of a crazed beauty therapist and a mad queen.

'Sorry the skirt enhancement didn't work out, our Rita's up to her neck in puppies and sick kids,' Tony said as we watched a 'Joan Retrospective', - his whole collection of Joan Crawford movies - with a large bowl of popcorn on his sofa.

'Poor Rita. My practice skirt's fine and I have a shawl. I *will* be okay in my practice skirt won't I?'

'Yeah, great,' he nodded absently, gripped with the drama on screen.

'Christ, Tony, you're supposed to be my gay best friend – it's like being in a relationship with a straight man sitting here with you half-listening, your eyes glued to the telly.'

He turned it off. 'Sorry, love, but I adore that bit when Joan says, "There is a name for you, ladies, but it isn't used in high society... outside of a kennel." Classic Joan!' he was smiling and shaking his head in awe.

'I love Joan too, but Tony, we need to talk about our outfits and our hair... are you sure Mandy's the right person to do our styling?'

'Er hello? A beauty therapist who does hair? She's a one-stop shop.'

'Mmm, I believe that's what they call her in Kavos,' I smiled.

He laughed. 'I wouldn't let anyone else near this hair or these brows. It has been said that a brow shape from Mandy Johnson is more painful than childbirth, but darling, it's brow art and we have to suffer for it. What that girl can do with a Brazilian blow-dry beggars belief,' he said.

'I don't doubt it.'

'I've told her that if I died... she would have to do my hair for the funeral. Oh God, touch wood I don't, but that poor grieving girl has promised to do a Brazilian blow-dry on my corpse.'

It conjured up quite a disturbing image. Tony reminded me of my mum when she was younger, all about the clothes, the make-up and the drama. I think that's why I took to him so quickly, it was like I'd known him all my life.

'You and my mother both think you're forties film stars, sipping on your gin cocktails and bitching through tight lips about everyone.'

Tony laughed. 'Yes but Margaret's more Bette Davis with her delusions of grandeur and intolerance of anyone less than perfect. I'm more Joan Crawford... a clairvoyant once told me I was Joanie in a previous life.'

'Well you've got the walk, and the eyebrows,' I said. He took this as a compliment and was curtseying when the doorbell went.

'I know who that will be,' he said, mysteriously but all excited and ran to get it. I heard some talking then Rita came in carrying a large plastic bag on a clothes hanger.

'Hope it's okay,' she said, laying the plastic across the dining table.

Tony clapped his hands together.

'Thanks so much, Rita,' he said. 'Now you stroppy old cow, we have a little surprise for you.'

I was intrigued and a little excited, suddenly felt like I was nine years old and it was my birthday.

Tony clutched my arm. 'I can't look, you open it, Rita, I'll just faint... brace yourself, Lola,' he turned away theatrically with the back of his hand on his forehead as Rita slowly, carefully opened the plastic. I saw scarlet fabric and tears sprang to my eyes as a million scarlet satin ruffles were unleashed.

I looked from brother to sister. 'It's a flamenco dress?'

'Yes love, that's right...

'It's red...'

'It is, love... and the sofa's blue, aren't you good with your colours?' Tony was talking to me like a nursery school teacher.

'But how did you get this? I can't afford a real one... and this is
real,' I said, holding the weighty dress, still on the verge of tears.

'It's your mum's, you daft mare, she wanted you to have it,'
Tony laughed.

'Oh?' I was now in tears.

'I took your measurements so I could do something with your
skirt and in the meantime Tony tells me he's found the dress in the
garage. Anyway when I measured your Mum's dress it turns out
you're now the same size your mum was when she was dancing,'
Rita explained.

'Yeah, so I said forget about the practice skirt Rita we've got the
real thing here so let's just tidy it up... and she worked her magic,
made a few minor alterations and it's even better. We wanted to
surprise you - it's fabulous isn't it?' Tony sighed, gazing at it.

'Oh thank you, thank you so much. But Mum was a size ten.'

'A small size 12, love, and don't let Margaret tell you any different,' Tony laughed. 'That woman lies about her age and her
dress size – talk about giving her daughter impossible standards,'
he huffed, 'but she loves you to bits, make no mistake about that.'

'I know,' I smiled.

'And, you've lost a lot of weight in the last twelve months, babe.
As Margaret said when I told her, "She's not as fat as we thought,"'
he roared laughing at this and I had to join in.

'Classic Mum,' I laughed, caressing the smooth satin bodice.
'I've only ever seen it in a photo,' I sighed. 'When Mum men-

tioned it to me, and neither you nor I had come across it, I assumed it had been lost.'

'It was in the bottom of one of the bags. I almost died of excitement that night when you phoned and asked if I'd seen it... I rushed out to the garage and after about two hours I found it. Then the next day I popped over to see Margaret and asked her if she'd mind if we gave it a bit of a refresh and an iron and she was almost as excited as me. It was a bit crumpled but now Rita's done her bit it's as beautiful as the day your dad bought it for her,' Tony said.

'Oh Rita, and you had all those puppies and sick children...'

She looked at me blankly.

'Oh you silly mare I just told you that so you wouldn't wonder why she wasn't tarting up your practice skirt.'

I stood there, clutching the dress, my chin wobbling.

'Now try it on, you daft cow.'

I looked at Rita and smiled a thank you then lifted the dress, which was heavy with frills, and tried it on in Tony's little pink bathroom. My only slight concern was that the dress might be a little tight – I wasn't convinced I was the same size as Mum had been, she always seemed so slim. I watched myself in the mirror as I stepped into the scarlet flamenco dress and, pulling it gently up past my hips, my breasts filled the cups and my body fit into it like a glove, the ruffles, like a scarlet waterfall began at the thigh and swished to the floor. I couldn't believe how good I looked. And for the first time in my life, at the age of forty-four, I felt beautiful. I looked at myself in the mirror and saw my mother – my lovely slim, attractive mother, something I'd never thought possible. I believed it was life's cruel joke that I was made clumsy and plain next to my beautiful mother. But with confidence, a little make-up and the right clothes anyone can be beautiful. It had been up to me all the time. I had to believe in myself, surround myself with the people and things that made me happy and everything now fit into place. Happiness doesn't land on your doorstep, sometimes you have to fight for it. My Mum's happiness had been drowned and she was never strong enough to fight her way to the surface. But here I was wearing her dress and walking in her footsteps, with everything my father had wanted for me. Dancing had saved me from my little life and I was now ready to take on anything. Walking downstairs, I felt like a bride, gliding carefully down each step, anticipating the reaction of my friends. I couldn't wait for my mum to see me, to see her beautiful dress resurrected and brought to life, by her own flesh and blood.

I entered the room and as soon as he saw me Tony burst into tears. Rita and I were laughing at him, but I had tears in my eyes too because the dress symbolised so much. It wasn't just about the way I looked and the way my body had changed, but how far I'd moved forward with my life. I'd also made peace with the past, my Mum and all my parent's dreams.

Tony held out his hand and I took it and we danced across the carpet.

'I have a little something else for you,' he said, letting me go for a moment and wiping his tears on a lavender-scented hankie.

Rita was smiling, and when he came back in the room she had her hands clasped together expectantly.

Tony handed me a beautiful oblong box, it was black with a huge silk bow tied around it. I stood in the middle of the room holding it. 'Oh it's too pretty to open,' I sighed.

'Open it, you daft cow, or I'll have a coronary,' Tony hissed. He always got overexcited about presents, especially if he was the one giving them.

I untied the bow, carefully opened the lid and delved gently into the tissue paper, where my hands alighted on something leather. I lifted up a pair of perfect flamenco shoes, the exact scarlet of my dress and I just stood holding them, speechless.

'Go on, Lola, put them on, I felt so sorry for you when you couldn't get into your mum's size fours. I thought, "She might look like an ugly sister but that poor cow has to have her Cinderella moment."'

And I did – as they slipped on easily. 'They are so, so beautiful,' I sighed, my eyes filling with tears again. I was sitting on the edge of the sofa with my feet out, just admiring them like a little girl.

'From me to you, Lola.'

I hugged him and Rita, unable to find the words to truly thank them.

'And guess what? They have a name – you'll love it - they are called 'Leona Freed.' It made me think of you. You're freed now, aren't you, Lola?'

I nodded. I was.

Chapter Twenty-seven

Lip Balm, Tea Bags and a Pussycat Doll

The following day I went straight to Wisteria Lodge to see Mum. Tony had taken some pictures of me on his phone so I could show her how I looked. I would have tried the dress on there and then for her, but the residents were all so theatrically rampant I was worried they might make me part of a Wisteria Lodge show. There had been vague talk about an 'Our Kids Have Got Talent' show and I knew mother was dropping hints for me to do a reprieve of my Celine Dion Titanic number. I'd received a standing ovation the previous year, but there wasn't much competition, just Doris's sixty-two-year-old daughter, dressed as a Pussycat Doll demanding to know if everyone wished their girlfriend was hot like her. I'm the last person to stop an older woman doing her thing... but as Mum had loudly observed, 'Ripped stockings, and a mini skirt are just not right on a woman in her sixties.'

So instead of trying the dress on and risking an impromptu audition for 'Our Kids Have Got Talent', I decided to just tell Mum about the dress. 'Mum, thank you, it actually fits,' I said, hugging her as I walked in. She was in the communal area with 'the girls' and they all smiled and nodded.

'Your mum's been showing off all morning about you,' one of the ladies said.

I looked puzzled.

'Yes... I thought it was an alarm when my phone went off, but Mrs Rawlins got these photos up,' Mum said, like it was magic.

I took her phone off her and smiled. Tony had already sent the pictures over.

'Ah, do you like it, Mum, the dress?'

'I was never sure of that dress,' Mum started, addressing the assembled throng. My heart sank, I thought it had been too good to be true, Mum 'showing off' about me. 'Yes I never really suited red... but our Laura looks smashing.'

'She's got that lovely Mediterranean colouring,' Mrs Rawlins piped up.

'Yes, she's like her father,' Mum smiled, looking fondly at the photos. 'She's quite beautiful.'

I almost choked on tears, Mum had never said anything so lovely about me.

'Will you excuse me ladies, Laura and I are just going to pop to my room. She's very busy with her dancing career and I don't want to keep her too long.'

I had to smile as I walked back to her room with her. 'Mum I don't have a career as such. I'm still at Bilton's.'

'Oh I know, but you're not a checkout girl – you're a dancer, it's in your blood. Besides, it shut those shady bitches up.'

'Mum... you can't say that.'

'I can, the girl that comes to do my nails is always saying it.'

'Really? Her name isn't Mandy by any chance is it?'

'That's right... lovely looking girl. You want to get yourself some eyebrows like hers.'

'Mmmm,' I said, still smiling to myself and wondering just how hilarious it would be to watch Mandy's encounter with my mother, who probably didn't understand half of what she was saying – but repeated it loudly.

'Here, I've got something for you,' she said. 'I got it on that day trip to Birmingham last week... it's from Selfridges, I hope you like it.' She handed me a gift bag stuffed with tissue and when I put my hand inside, I brought out the most beautiful silk rose in scarlet.

'Mum it's gorgeous, but you shouldn't...'

'Nonsense. I haven't given you enough pretty things in your life. Sometimes I think I've only given you sadness and worry.'

I didn't answer, I couldn't because I might cry and I wanted this to be a happy visit. I just studied the lovely rose and realising it had a clip put it in my hair.

'Every flamenco dancer needs a rose in her hair,' she smiled, hugging me. 'It looks beautiful on you – especially now you don't wear those glasses any more and we can see your lovely eyes.'

I glowed, my Mum had always been proud of me, always loved me, but through the years life and heartache had got in the way. I stayed for longer than usual that day. We talked about the dancing and the dresses and I suggested next time we go out for lunch together. We'd never ever done anything like that – mother-and-daughter shopping trips and meals out had never been on the agenda for us.

'I'd like that,' she said. 'I'd really like that.'

'Me too,' I said, hugging her before I left. 'There's a new restaurant in town, they do tapas – we could practice for our trip to Spain.'

'Yes... and Laura?'

'Yes, Mum.'

'There's a new drink they have now – supposed to be delicious. We could have one of those. I think it's called a Porn Star Martini.'

❄ ❄ ❄

'One day, when I'm starring in my own TV dance show I think I'll write a book,' Tony was saying. We were finally heading for Blackpool and the Dance festival. I was driving so I could take my mind off what was to come. I was really nervous about the dancing – it was the first time I'd ever performed in public and I felt sick every time I thought about it. But for me there was the added dread of returning to the place my father died, and all the horrific memories associated with that.

'Yep, I'm going to write my own self-help book: "Tony Hernandez Sez", see what I did there with the Z?'

'Yes, I'm sure it will be a bestseller,' I said sarcastically. I didn't mind him going on, I knew he was only doing it to take my mind off everything. And I knew he was nervous too, he'd organised a lot of publicity and if we did well he might be able to start thinking about opening his own dance business and teaching full-time. So Blackpool was a big deal for both of us.

'I want to inspire people everywhere with my thoughts, like lip balm and tea bags are all one needs in life.'

'Oh the world will be waiting for that one.'

He laughed. 'You've inspired me you know, Lola.'

'Really?'

'Yes. Believe it or not, when we met on that cold dark night after you'd shown yourself up in the Zumba class I was about to give up.'

'Give up dancing?' I was shocked.

'Well, teaching. I will always dance, darling – but I was about to give up the teaching and the dream to dance professionally one day. I know it will surprise you because I never tell my age because I look twenty-two...'

'Forty-two.'

'Twenty-two... but I am in fact almost thirty-five.'

'You are at least forty, Tony,' I laughed.

'Okay, but I felt like I'd left it too late and didn't feel like it was leading anywhere. Then when I saw you dance I just knew you had it in you, and I don't know why, but I liked you straightaway. I felt we were going through the same stuff – we both needed to road-test our emerging inner butterflies,' he pushed in a travel sweet with a puff of icing sugar.

'Ooh I like that, did you read it somewhere?'

'Yeah... in one of our Rita's magazines. I knew it would be useful for something. I'll put it in my book,' he said as we pulled up at the Blackpool guest house which was pink and owned by lovely Robin and Gary, Tony and I dumped our bags in our shared room and headed out to the promenade. The wind was whipping up the sea but that didn't stop us heading out to see the sights.

Walking along the windy promenade was like walking back into my childhood. The little girl inside me was skipping along holding Dad's hand, anticipating the chips and the dancing later.

The salty sea air took my breath away with its sheer vigour, and the cold was laced with memories. Mum would walk on one side, Dad on the other – and I'd be holding both their hands as they swung me in the air. I looked at Tony – and even though I'd lost weight, I doubted he'd be up for swinging me around the promenade.

'I'll beat you to that lamp post,' I called after him, running along the front, the wind in my hair, my strong legs taking me further and faster than ever before.

He was soon grabbing me by the waist, pulling me back, the sibling I never had trying to beat me to the winning post. I didn't stand a chance – he was over six feet with long legs, and apart from cheating by trying to push me out of the way – he won.

I 'landed' at his side, panting, holding onto him after my sprint.

'As your partner and mentor, I should have said, there will be no running, no jumping and no sex before the performance,' he announced, arms folded at the lamp post pretending it hadn't been an effort to run.

'You mean like footballers before a match,' I was still trying to get my breath.

'Yeah. And I don't care how much you pester me, Lola, I am not finding you a toyboy on the pier to satisfy your lust.'

'One wouldn't be enough – what's the collective term for toy-boys.'

'A warehouse,' he giggled.

We laughed and then he took my hand and we ran together, me skipping alongside him like a little girl as we crossed the road from the seafront to the shops.

Despite it being the middle of winter, there was a flavour of Blackpool summers hanging in the air. It was early evening, the sea was a vast expanse of sequinned blackness.

In the distance was The Pleasure Beach, the rides were lit and moving, the screams carried on the wind – pure fear and exhilaration for just a couple of quid. I could see the lights on the little trains swirling through the air, the slow, trundling ride upwards, followed by the whoosh and the accompanying screams as the roller coaster plunged to its depths. I could taste the candy floss, feel the remembered thrill of my tummy rising and falling as we swept through the air.

When I was a kid it was just the Big Dipper, but now it was 'The Big One', over two hundred feet of metal that dwarfed all the other rides. Even The Pleasure Beach isn't immune to change, I thought, everything moves on. I'd held on to my dad's arm and screamed on the Big Dipper as we lurched from sky to ground in seconds. I remember Dad laughing loudly. 'Wave to Mum,' he'd shout and we'd both wave frantically at the tiny figure down below waiting for us.

'I'm starving, we have to have fish and chips,' I demanded, so we bought takeaway fish and chips from a cafe and walked along the road eating them straight out of the paper. The wooden fork was reassuringly rough on my tongue, the chips hot and vinegary, and the gold battered fish tasted just like the sea. We tried on hats and scarves and fell into each other laughing at the sight while holding each other up.

Later, we sat with a couple of beers outside a gay bar and took in the sights – and I don't mean the seascape. It was chilly, but we were wrapped up in the warm, both enjoying the handsome young men coming and going in the pink paradise. I looked over at Tony as two drag queens walked by dressed from head to toe in glitz and feathers. He caught my eye and we smiled at the madness and colour of it all, both enjoying the spectacle. 'You know, it's funny – because you're everything I've ever wanted in a partner. You're handsome, funny... caring...' I started.

'I am, aren't I? I'd make a lovely husband but I just don't think it's ever going to happen. We'll both be in our sixties, still single, sitting outside bars in the dark drinking pink cocktails and lusting after young men.'

'Oh, *dahling*, I do hope so,' I said, in my best Bette Davis voice.

❄ ❄ ❄

The following morning at dawn we awoke and I prepared myself for the day ahead. The dancing itself was a huge challenge, but going back there, to the place it happened was terrifying.

My dress was hanging on the back of the door, a reminder of what was to come, I looked at it and a thrill of fear danced through me. I packed some toiletries and make-up into a big bag with Dad's letter. I also had with me some old photos of Mum and Dad dancing, posing, laughing. I took them out and looked at them again, remembering how things had been before that terrible night and the last time they ever danced together. I was doing this for them too.

Chapter Twenty-eight

Ghosts and Glitterballs

Every detail was vivid, it had been raining and the air was fresh and damp when we arrived at The Winter Gardens in Blackpool on the evening of May 12th 1980. The atmosphere was electric, excited chatter competing with Doris Day's voice singing 'Perhaps, Perhaps'. We'd been to the competition before, but Mum and Dad had never won anything and finally were in with a chance with their rumba. People had called it 'show-stopping', I wasn't quite sure what that meant, but it sounded good and I was carried along on the fever of winning. I remember sticking my thumbs up to them both as the dance started and saying a little prayer asking God to let them win as the competing couples flooded onto the dance floor in a wave of colour and glitter. A young couple flew onto the floor, they had such verve and energy – looking back, I imagine it was simply their youth, but I couldn't take my eyes off them. Despite Mum and Dad being on the floor, I was compelled to watch this couple, and I have wondered so many times since if Dad had waved to me and I hadn't waved back. The girl was wearing sparkly, fluorescent green like a refreshing splash of Corona limeade, their fire and passion fizzed onto the dance floor. They were called John and Francesca, but I knew Mum didn't like them – perhaps she was jealous, the new hot talent, taking over when her own star was fading, her passion barely cooled? I've always felt guilty because I was so mesmerised by John and Francesca it was a while before I realised something was happening at the other side of the dance floor. By then it was too late – the music stopped and all I remember is hearing the word 'ambulance'.

Within minutes everyone had stopped dancing. The organisers were calling for all dancers to clear the floor until the entire area was empty except for Mum and Dad. They were directly under the glitterball, Mum was slumped over Dad just like at the end of their dance, but there was panic in her eyes and Dad lay there, motionless. I was ten years old and my greatest fear was my father dying. And here it was, pure horror laid before me surrounded by sequins and spangles under the disco ball.

The shock was so strong, so physical, that I couldn't move my feet to go to them and the next thing I saw was my dad being lowered onto a stretcher as Mum howled like an animal at his side.

It was a massive heart attack.

❋ ❋ ❋

Arriving at the hallowed portals of The Winter Gardens started my stomach churning. The sight of that big, majestic arched building brought everything back and walking inside I was overcome with memories, ghosts from the past danced through me in ballroom gowns. I tasted the sugary lemonade I always drank while watching Mum and Dad. I particularly loved watching their paso doble. He was her matador, swirling her around the dance floor, she his submissive scarlet cloak. She relied on him, trusted him and with him she moved with such grace and elegance. Their dance partnership was, like their life partnership, based on love, mutual respect and trust. The intensity and happiness of their love revealed every time they danced.

Now it was my turn to dance here, the place where my father took his last steps. I'd often wondered if I should come here to exorcise the ghosts, but I hadn't been ready until now.

I must have gone very quiet, as Tony took me gently by the elbow and guided me in. 'Come on, Lola, you can do it,' he said from the side of his mouth. For all his flamboyance and drama, Tony was astute – he could always sense my mood, my feelings and he treated me with such gentleness.

The entrance hall was busy and I looked up into the dome of the rotunda and lost myself as I had all those years ago. 'I used to twirl around here until I was dizzy,' I said to Tony.

'Mmm that's nice, dear, but we don't want you going all dizzy now, do we? It's okay to do that when you're five, but at forty-five it looks just a little bit creepy.'

'I'm forty-four,' I said.

'Whatever you say, Lola.'

People were walking quickly, some running, late dancers, I thought, recalling the stress of the last-minute arrivals, my mother's panicked voice, 'Do you have the paperwork? Are you sure you locked the car, Ken?'

Music was vibrating through the Victorian stone and I could sense the build-up as we walked into the Empress Ballroom. A cold waft of air greeted me as I went through the doors into the huge, shiny-floored space. I took in the barrel-vaulted ceiling, the ornate balconies and the sheer lavishness of the surroundings. 'I used to pretend I was a princess and this was where I lived,' I smiled.

Tony squeezed my arm. 'You okay – your highness?'

I wasn't sure, but nodded and put my arm through his as he led me to the dancers' changing area.

Hearing the music and watching the dancers glide onto the floor made me feel sick. With each step, each rustle of silk, each turn of the head, I was thrust back in time, reliving every moment of my last visit here.

❊ ❊ ❊

In all the madness and hysteria I was aware of Dad's body being taken out on a stretcher – I knew he was dead because his face was covered and I'd seen that on TV. He was taken to a local hospital and Mum and I were ferried to the morgue there by taxi – organised by the competition sponsors. It was all such a mess, such a confusing time – I felt like I'd been put in a washing machine and it was just going round and round, I heard sound, saw colours, but none of it made any sense. A post-mortem was carried out (Dad died so suddenly it was apparently a legal requirement) and as Mum couldn't bear to leave him, the dance organisers put us up in a guest house for a couple of days. Throughout this time Mum lay on her bed holding one of his shirts, reeking of his aftershave and sobbing. Whenever I smell Paco Rabanne I think of that time and it takes me straight back In the weeks after his death. I'd walk into the house and smell the warm, aromatic scent, convinced he'd returned, only to have my hopes dashed every time.

I remember a woman coming to our room to ask if there was anyone she could call for us. Mum couldn't speak to anyone so it was left to me to answer and I said, 'No... there's no-one else... just us, the three musketeers.' Except now, there were just two musketeers.

❋ ❋ ❋

I felt a tear spring to my eye. 'I wish my Dad was here,' I said.

'Mmm I meant to talk to you about that.'

'What, my dad being here?' I said.

'No love... I'm not Psychic Sally in drag... though I would love that woman's gift. No, the good news is your mum's coming. I invited her, she's bringing her friend. Mandy's driving them... '

'Mum? Driving with Mandy for the dancing... oh no.'

'I know... but I figured it was worth it for her to see you dance. If Mandy ends up driving into a wall, they've had a good life.'

'I didn't mean that – I just mean, oh thank you, but I wish you hadn't told me – I'll be even more nervous knowing Mum's out there.'

I was delighted and scared that Mum would be in the audience. In some ways she was my harshest critic in life but she was the woman I wanted most to impress. To make her proud was everything to me. I just hoped that being back here wouldn't be too distressing for her. It had been the worst night of our lives and I hoped Mum was now strong enough to face the ghosts of our past.

※ ※ ※

I was just coming off the phone to Sophie who'd called to wish me good luck all the way from Chile when Tony announced our stylist's imminent arrival.

'Oh just get your arse moving girl, Mandy's left your mum and her friend in the cafe and she's on her way backstage ready to transform us. She's brought three-hundred cans of hairspray, a ton of body glitter and eighty gallons of fake tan. And that's just for me,' Tony was saying.

I laughed. Too much. I was very fragile, close to tears, trembling and more scared and nervous than I'd ever been in my life. And now Mandy 'Guantanamo' Johnson was here with her beauty 'weapons' to waterboard me and my hair before backcombing it into oblivion, turning me orange and slathering me in glitter. I had faced one of the biggest traumas of my life head on and was about to dance in front of hundreds of people for the first time. I felt physically sick with nerves and a pummelling from Mandy would probably just about finish me off.

The festival was due to start mid-afternoon and Tony and I were on the running order at the very end to do the flamenco. Tony was pleased, 'They've given us the finale, Lola, they have high hopes!'

I wished I could share his joy, but I just wanted to vomit. I'd never been so nervous and my only consolation was that if we were last on everyone might have gone home by then.

We stayed backstage and tried to practise in the little spaces we could find, but eventually gave up when Mandy arrived to 'transform' us. She was brandishing what looked like surgical equipment and threatening Tony with a 'manscape' – my eyes watered at the mere thought.

'You should have seen me last night,' was her opening gambit, 'I was off my tits on Porn Star Martinis.'

'I hope you've sobered up enough to do my brows,' Tony said, clutching his forehead.

'Shut up and lie back,' she commanded, almost mounting him to get at his precious brows.

Within seconds she was on him and had whipped out her weapons of choice from a huge holdall.

After half an hour of screaming, Tony's brows were done and he was released from Mandy's grip to go and live his life.

'Your turn,' Mandy said coming at me with big tweezers. I don't remember much after that, I think my body shut down to protect me from the horror. I came round looking like I'd been dropped in a vat of orange dye, everything glittered, and my eye make-up. I worried I'd end up resembling a 'glittering drag queen', but as I looked in the mirror, I could see what Tony meant about Mandy's talent. Her contouring had made my face look younger and slimmer and under ballroom lights I would look pretty damn good. And I thought to myself – how many women my age get to dress up and wear glamorous make-up like this? I'd felt like a child in the dressing-up box – it was the first time I'd ever worn a long dress and the first time I'd ever worn body glitter – and do you know what, it felt fabulous.

'You will cop tonight,' was Mandy's prediction as she jammed a final set of fake lashes onto my eyelids.

'Thanks Mandy,' I coughed as she 'finished me off' with a truckload of hairspray. I just hoped there weren't any candles or smokers within a twenty mile radius of me – one sniff of a naked flame and I'd go up like bonfire night.

'No prob, Laura.' Then she leaned in, 'Just a bit of advice, take those eyelashes off before you snog anyone or get really pissed,' she said this with a serious face and a wink, like she was imparting a long-hidden beauty secret.

'Er... thanks, I will.'

Then I climbed into that scarlet gown. I caught myself in the mirror and realised with a jolt that I looked like the dancers in the gypsy caves. I might have been Spanish with my long, dark hair coiled up, adorned with a scarlet flower. My body looked shapely but slim and my scarlet lips and loop earrings added even more drama. I loved myself, and as we heard our names called to say we were on next, I walked trance-like to the dance floor – I was Lola, and even though my eyebrows throbbed and my heart was beating so hard I thought it might leap from my chest – I felt amazing. I was still in a trance-like state as Tony led me out onto the floor. I was taut with nerves and scared that Mum was in the audience and worried how she'd feel seeing me dance for the first time. I hoped she would love me in her never-worn dress.

I stood on the floor, light facets from the glitterball shining in my face, Tony holding my hand, he was trembling and so was I. Then the music started and despite Tony going into our opening positions, I couldn't move, I was stiff with nerves and worry and all the old fears were flooding back, clouding my head and my feet. My upper lip was dripping in sweat and I really thought I was going to be sick.

Then a sound like rolling thunder, feet stomping on the ground, applause and Tony in my ear; 'Lola… you can do this. Just dance like nobody's watching.'

I felt the throb coming from the darkness, beyond the sea outside, and the gypsy in me awoke – 'Come on Lola, it's show time.'

And we danced to the tears of the flamenco guitar telling stories of lost love, hot nights and all the pain and joy of being human.

I danced for Mum and Dad, for everything they'd been through, the joy of their love and the pain of their loss. I danced for the brother I never knew, the fun we never had, the bond we never shared. And as the flamenco guitar spilled my tears onto the dance floor, I mourned for the true love I'd never found, the bride I would never be, but the joy of being a mother, of being loved and finally loving myself.

At the final stomp, Tony was on his knees at my feet looking up, we had both danced the dance of our lives and all I could think was, I want to do it again. The music stopped, we both stood in our final positions like a tableau, the dust particles rising like tiny stars, the glitterball refracting light through the ballroom and the deep silence. I looked ahead, I couldn't look at Tony, I didn't know what to do next. We kept our pose, my scarlet dress ruffling around me, my heart beating out of my chest.

I glanced over my shoulder, smiling at the audience now on their feet clapping, whistling, shouting, and I spotted, at the back of the ballroom, an elderly lady and gentleman dancing to the closing strains of the flamenco guitar. Mum and Mr Roberts. Tony had seen them too and began clapping and shouting, 'Mags, you go girl!' All eyes turned to watch them and when she wiggled her bottom, clicked her fingers, stomped her feet and shouted 'Olé,' I wanted to weep. I felt so sad for the lost years, the grief that had overwhelmed us and stopped us both from dancing, from sharing something special to losing ourselves – and finding ourselves again. The whole room was clapping along with their dance and my feisty mother was dancing flamenco, just as she and Dad had dreamed of doing so many years ago.

I thought the roof would come off the building. The roars of approval, the screams of expectation and delight were so loud I couldn't believe how many people must be there shouting for 'more, more, more.' As the stomping flamenco feet in the audience got louder and louder, I looked at Tony.

He stepped forward, I could see this had really taken it out of him.

'Can someone turn the lights up,' he said out into the black abyss and within seconds the house lights were on and we could see our audience.

'I want to thank my partner... Laura. In the past year she has learned to dance, and in August she headed out to Granada in Spain where she learned the Flamenco. She left the UK as an ordinary woman with an extra ordinary talent – and she returned with Flamenco in her blood and a fiery gypsy girl in her steps... I give you Lola!'

He handed me the mic, started to clap me and walked away, the audience followed suit, roaring and stomping. Tears sprung to my eyes and I smiled and nodded, I was standing in front of hundreds of people and they were clapping me... us. I dragged Tony back and waited for the audience to fall into silence.

'Thank you all so much, I can't believe all that clapping was just for me!' I started, and everyone laughed. 'I may have learned Flamenco in Spain, but Tony was the one who started my journey,' I said looking at him seriously. 'He is the most talented dancer, teacher and partner - when I say 'I can't,' Tony always tells me I can,' and in doing so he has freed Lola...' I looked at him; 'thank you from the depths of her fiery heart.' He smiled at me, and unable to make a quip or a comedy remark was unable to hide the tears in his eyes. I turned from Tony to look out at the audience where I knew Mum would be; 'I'd like to also say a special thank you, to the woman I watched dancing through my childhood, the dancer who glided across this ballroom, under this glitterball,' I looked up at the twinkly orb. 'This is the woman who gave me the gift of the dance. Thank you Mum.' I clapped my mum and the audience clapped her and the nice lighting man shone a spotlight on her and she stood up and did a few little steps and took a great, big sweeping bow.

'Love you Mum,' I shouted and enunciated from the stage and amazingly she seemed to have heard, 'Love you too, Laura... encore!'

With this, the crowd roared again and Tony and I stepped up to give them one last dance. He pushed me forward, 'This one's just you – go girl,' and he left me alone and headed off into the audience. 'Keep the lights up,' he shouted. 'In Granada everyone dances Flamenco together... so get on your feet.' I looked out helplessly, trying to see Tony, to make him come back and dance with me, and when I saw him I gestured with my hand for him to return to the floor. But he shook his head, several people got to their feet and I stood alone, for the first time without Tony, wondering if I could do this on my own in front of so many people.

Then the guitar started, and I felt the rhythm in my chest, moving up through my body, filling my veins with duende. The passion rose in me like a huge, crashing wave and I raised both my arms and started to dance. And I was suddenly on the kitchen table dancing, I was holding my mother's hands in that first foxtrot in the living room. And I was riding the Big Dipper, next to my dad, the night before he danced his last dance on this floor. Then I was in the gypsy caves in Granada, dancing under the moon and stars. And despite there being hundreds of people around – it was just me and the dance. Like no one was watching.

At the end, I stood proud, arms in the air, I had given everything and was exhausted, but still holding my pose. I did that final, solo flamenco for me, proving to myself how independent, strong, and beautiful I could be on my own. And I hoped with all my heart that in the audience there might be a woman like I used to be – a supermarket checkout girl of a certain age, who thought it was too late to change her life, until tonight.

And I looked out into the darkness, lit by a sea of faces, and saw my mother, tiny, frail, tears running down her cheeks. And there in Blackpool Winter Gardens, home of international ball-room dancing where my world had once stopped – I knew my life had begun again.

❋ ❋ ❋

Later that night, exhausted and happy I lay in bed going over and over the night, like the steps of a dance, each moment charged with emotion – some good, some bad. Dancing with Tony had been a revelation. From that first moment he took me in his arms on that cold evening, he'd made me feel like that little girl again, dancing in Mum's too big, strappy shoes with my dad. I'd step forward, feeling like a princess and he'd place one arm on my back, the other holding my hand in the air and he would lead. It was the perfect moment crystallised in my mind and my heart – it had always been there pulling me through bad days and offering me a glimmer of light at the end of a dark tunnel. It's what I'd been searching for all my life, the safety and happiness of that moment. And I'd never found it, until now.

I had found what I needed in dance, in the applause, the emotional challenge and the satisfaction – and me. I also had Tony, who was in some ways my soul mate and the man I'd been looking for all my life.

The following day I told Tony, I wanted him to know how important he was to me and what an impact he'd made on my life.

'Aah, you've made me go all teary,' he sighed, putting his arm round me. 'I feel the same way, but don't get any ideas... I'm still not coming over to the dark side, Lola, let's keep things firmly above the waist.'

Chapter Twenty-Nine

The Sizzling Senorita from Birmingham

The Monday morning after the festival was pure hell. It had been bad enough going back to the checkout and the chatter after two weeks in Spain, but after that Saturday night in Blackpool it was almost impossible. Arriving back at work, I was greeted in the staff room by cheers, so many of my friends had watched me online. 'Who'd have thought you could move like that? At your age?' One of the younger team members remarked.

'Yeah you're no spring chicken, but bloody hell, you can move,' Security Mike added, he was never one to mince his words.

But once the congratulations and speculations about my age (just forty-five) and weight (none of your business!) had been aired, it was time to take my position on my checkout. It felt like such an anti-climax and I sat there all morning in a daze. My head was still in Blackpool, my feet were dancing flamenco and I couldn't go back to this. But what choice did I have?

At lunchtime I put a gloopy, neon-orange ready meal in the canteen microwave and ate it dreaming of tapas and a crisp Rioja overlooking the Alhambra. Then I wallowed in the sheer joy of the previous Saturday night, hearing the applause, mentally taking my bows... seeing Mum's face, glowing with pride. The sound of clapping morphed into something else and I realised my phone was buzzing, so I abandoned the gloopy lunch and answered it.

'Lola... I've been trying to reach you...' It was Tony.

'Oh I'm sorry. I had my phone off, I'm at work, it's not allowed at the checkout. I was going to call you later, I've had a hell of a morning.'

'Me too.'

'Oh are you okay?' he sounded out of breath.

'Yeah... you have to come to the dance centre, you should see the...'

At that point another call came through.

'Oh Tony, hang on I have to answer it – it's Sophie.'

'Mum? What the hell is going on?'

'Oh ... Oh God, I haven't sexted Carl again have I?' Earlier Carole had texted me a photo of David Beckham with no top on and I'd texted back; 'Oh what I'd give for half an hour with that firm taut body – naked!' Carole and Carl began with C – I went cold... once was a mistake, but twice would be creepy.

'Mum, you're all over the internet.'

'But it was Carole's photo, honestly, I wasn't asking for half an hour with Carl's naked body.'

'Mum, I don't know what you're talking about. And I'm not sure I want to, but what *I'm* talking about is you, on YouTube doing the flamenco. Mum, it's wild... I had no idea. You are fabulous.'

'You Tube? Me? I'll have to get off, Sophie, I'll call you back... Oh – you're okay, aren't you?'

'There are a couple of masked gunmen here threatening me, but other than that and the man-eating leopards I'm fine.'

'Good, glad you're okay.'

I got straight back on to Tony.

'YouTube?' I shouted.

'That's what I've been trying to tell you,' he shouted back. 'It's gone crazy out there... Lola. The queue for tonight's class is going round the bloody corner. That's why I've been trying to call you.'

'That's wonderful, but I don't understand how I'm even on YouTube?'

'Well, you know those students who I asked to video us? They uploaded it and we've already had 300,00 hits since it went on at lunchtime. You're being hailed as the sizzling senorita from Brum... no one can believe you're not Spanish. And the fact you're in your forties has just blown everyone's mind. You've gone viral, my love,' he squealed.

'Wow. I've never been viral before... hey, and what's the big deal that someone in their forties is dancing?'

'Well, you are very old,' he laughed, 'but it's not that you're just dancing... you're phenomenal, Lola. Anyway, stop fishing for compliments, you vain bitch, and get ready for your close-up. The local paper have called me to ask for photos and a video for the website, the *Daily Mail* want to feature you in an article about "the middle-aged Mum from the midlands", and... oh yes, "This Morning" are doing a "glamorous granny" special and want you in the studio trussed up in frills and eyeliner on Thursday at eight a.m.'

'But I'm not a granny!'

'Who cares... it's national TV coverage, I'd tell them you are a vampire if it means getting that kind of exposure. I feel like your bloody agent. Ha, and the best bit...everyone thinks I'm your young lover,' he added. 'At this rate I'll be running classes every day,' he said. 'Lola... I'm not messing about. I'm giving up the day job.'

'Wow... really?'

'You'll have to give up Bilton's too, our bloody dream of dancing for a living just came true.'

'Oh... well, it's not quite that simple... perhaps we need to see...'

And he put the phone down on me. I was a bit surprised, but then today was turning into a day of surprises. I checked the time, shit, I was late back on my checkout, so I ran down the stairs and sprinted across the shop floor.

I'd only been at my checkout for a few minutes when there was a commotion in the queue, someone was trying to push in. I looked beyond the grumpy faces, the shouts of abuse and the grappling hands (no one likes a queue jumper at the checkout) to see Tony.

'What are you doing? If Julie sees you I'll be...'

'Sacked? Good, because there's a job waiting. I have queues forming to take my dance class and I need you, now.'

'Tony I can't... perhaps in a few months when...'

'Oh here we go again. Tomorrow, next week, in a few months...' he was shouting. The queue was silent, everyone was transfixed by the drama unfolding. 'I can't do this without you... well I could, but it wouldn't be half as much fun, and besides, you're the pull. Women all want what you've got, don't you laydeez?' he addressed my stunned customers. 'You and I can make this work... we can do personal appearances, dance performances and teach classes. This is your longed-for escape from the checkout, not many people get this, it's once in a lifetime, babe.'

'Go with him, love,' someone shouted from the back of the queue, assuming it was a marriage proposal. 'Say yes!' shouted an old lady clutching a basket full of cat food.

Tony stuck his thumb up in agreement. 'You see, everyone wants to see you escape, do it. Buried alive... that's what you'll be if you stay.'

'You don't get it, Tony. Dancing is everything, but in order to dance I have to work. If I gave up my job tomorrow to help you with classes and do the odd show, I wouldn't be able to pay my mortgage. I'm not like you – I have a daughter to consider.'

He rolled his eyes. 'There you go again, putting someone else before your own needs... or using them as an excuse perhaps?' he was leaning on the checkout, one perfectly arched eyebrow raised.

'She's not "someone else", she's my child.'

'Yes a twenty-four-year-old child who is doing mighty fine standing on her own two feet. She doesn't need you at the school gate any more, Laura – so stop using her and your mother as an excuse for not taking risks. I know it's not been easy, love, but now you have a choice, because neither of them are relying on you – guess what, they got up and out and left you behind... so start moving. I want us to start our own dance school,' he said. 'I have some money and... shit, I handed my notice in about three hours ago.'

'Oh God, Tony, are you sure you did the right thing?'

'I've never been more sure. It's what I always wanted and if I don't do it now...'

'Go on, put him out of his misery...' someone piped up.

'Marry him, just say yes so we can get served,' another voice yelled.

Tony and I laughed to each other, and with that he stepped to the side of my checkout and opened it up with a bow. 'Remember that scene in an Officer and a Gentleman where Richard Gere carries Debra Winger out of that factory to a better life?'

'Yeah.'

'Watch me.' With that, he stepped behind the checkout and with a gentlemanly flourish and to the delight of the queue, he scooped me up in his arms. I tried to protest but I was laughing too much, and as he carried me through Bilton's towards the exit, I stopped trying to resist. Everyone was looking, my queue was clapping and shouting, which seemed to have a ripple effect as we walked through and the rest of the store became aware of what was happening – like a Mexican wave through Bilton's people started cheering and stamping their feet. I waved to an open-mouthed Julie as we swept past Electricals, Carole was eating doughnuts in Baked Goods and she stopped eating to shout, 'Go Lola!' And I felt my heart somewhere in my throat, I was shaking with fear and excitement about what I was about to do. And I swear somewhere I heard the sound of 'Love lift us up where we belong', as I was taken away from one life to another... the one I'd always wanted.

❄ ❄ ❄

Later that night I turned on my computer and watched the YouTube video of me that everyone was talking about. Then I saw myself, and I could almost understand what all the fuss was about – I was a good dancer, I really looked the part too in Mum's red dress.

I thought about how proud and amazed my dad would have been if he'd seen me dance. Lack of money, time, geography and freedom all pile up, burying our dreams until they die with us. But I still had Sophie's wedding money sitting in my bank... I'd wanted it for a rainy day, but who wants to stand in the rain? I had a dancing school to run and a life to live.

Okay so if I used the money to put towards opening the school, I wouldn't have any savings, no nest egg to fall back on. I'd be living like my sad – and who knows, I may die like my dad, on the dance floor, under that glitterball... but better that way than on the checkout at Bilton's.

EPILOGUE

Six Months Later

'What's the weather like outside?' I ask.

'Cold, windy,' she smiles.

'Do you have a loyalty card?'

'No... I've not been here before,' the woman says. 'My name's Tammy Lawson.'

'Well Tammy, welcome to "Tony and Lola's". Come on through, there are forms to fill in and you will be given a Tony and Lola's Dance School loyalty card. You get dance points each time you attend and when you've collected ten points we give you a free class.' My supermarket training finally came in useful for something.

'Let me show you round, our class is in the other studio,' I say, walking with her to the studio where Tony is teaching 'Basic Ballroom'. He waves and blows us both a kiss. 'I started dancing about 18 months ago,' I explain, 'it's changed my life.'

The woman looks at me a little doubtfully. 'I saw you online, I imagined you'd been dancing for years.'

'Yeah, it feels like I have,' I smile, thinking of how a throwaway comment from my daughter about my 'little life' had started all this. I'd known I had to do something, but I didn't know what it was until I found Mum's dresses and the letter from my dad. It was remembering my parents' glitter and wanting a handful of my own, then meeting Tony that had given me the direction I needed.

Tony put the fire in my belly and the sparkle in my steps...then it was Juan who finally helped me let go. And even though it was over before it started, and I'd covered him in olive oil on a pavement cafe - he would always be a warm Spanish memory on cold English days.

Since joining Tony's Dance Class, I've danced under a Spanish moon, stomped under the glitterball in Blackpool and become an overnight internet sensation (over ten million hits on my flamenco and still counting – that's viral, baby!).

'Yes a lot's happened since I started dancing,' I say, thinking how much more I still had ahead of me. Tony and Lola's opened after Christmas, we are jam-packed every lesson, and next month Tony and I enter our Argentine Tango for the first time at the big Blackpool Competition. Whoever would have thought all this was possible for a forty-something checkout girl. I didn't.

'What's your secret?' Tammy asks. I've been asked this so many times since I've become 'famous'.

'It's no secret. I just started dancing, stopped saying "no" to everything and found a "bigger" life. I've given up my day job, and now I work here at our school teaching dance, which is wonderful, my dream. I'm actually living the dream,' I laugh. 'My mum also helps out with the performance side every Monday night and my daughter Sophie who's just come back from travelling and about to get married is a student in two of our classes. And then of course there's Tony, my dance husband – the only kind a girl needs,' I laugh.

'I've always dreamed of being a dancer, but I'm forty-seven, and until I saw you I thought I was too old.'

I shake my head vigorously. 'You are never too old.'

'Sorry, I just feel so nervous,' she smiles apologetically, her shoulders slump. She's a little overweight and lacking in confidence like I used to be and I know exactly how she's feeling. Life has rubbed off her sparkle.

'I saw you and just thought "I want to be like her"... but I'll never be as good as you, I can't even dance.'

'First of all – stop saying "I can't" because, trust me, you can.'

I gesture for her to walk towards one of the studio's full-length mirrors with me where we stand side by side looking at ourselves.

'Straighten up like this... and imagine the top of your head has a thread coming from it reaching the ceiling. Now lift up your arms,' I lift my arms high with a wrist curl and she copies me uncertainly.

'Now watch yourself in the mirror,' I say. 'I bet you don't look at yourself in the mirror very often, do you?'

'Never,' she says, going slightly pink.

'I never did either – I couldn't stand the sight of myself, which is so sad isn't it? But I do now, Tony says I think I'm bloody Beyoncé. And he's right,' I laugh. 'I bloody do.'

Tammy laughs, standing awkwardly by the mirror, her arms up but not quite there yet, she just needs a little help. I position myself behind her and hold her waist, straightening her slightly, moving an arm and, voila, she is there.

'Now, just take a look and tell me that girl can't dance,' I say.

She looks up, surprised to see her own straight back and confident, flamenco stance and she gasps. 'Gosh I look better already.'

'Yes, just the very act of lifting your arms is an instant body makeover,' I say encouragingly. 'Don't be frightened to look at yourself and like what you see, it does more for your self-esteem than any man ever could.'

She rolls her eyes, I get the feeling she's not had an easy time. 'I just don't know if I'll be able to ever dance in front of anyone,' she says, almost defeated before she's begun.

I smile, and lead her confidently onto the studio floor. 'I know you think I'm full of skill and confidence and nothing scares me, but I still have days when I'm not sure of myself, no one has all the answers. But I was just like you, Tammy, terrified of dancing in front of other people, until Tony gave me some wonderful advice. He said to dance like no one's watching.'

She nods and smiles still not convinced of her potential, her strength, but I know it's there. I can see it in her eyes.

I ask her to join in as I gather everyone together to begin the class. We go through the first, basic steps and I watch discreetly as Tammy and the other ladies try to master the movements. I know they feel foolish and self-conscious and I am whisked back to that cold, November night. I see that other Laura, who had no confidence, no life, no future – wearing somebody else's leggings. And I just can't believe how far she's come.

Later, when we get into more rhythmic movements, I can see Tammy has talent. It's in the way she moves her hips, the easy control she has over her body and that determined fire in her eyes. I reckon it's only a matter of time before Tammy is dancing under that glitterball.

I have learned so much about me from dancing and I want to share this with other women. I want them to feel their strength and beauty, know they can be independent and talented, and it doesn't matter about age or shape or past or present. With a lot of work, big determination and a little help from me – they will do it.

Sometimes when I see doubt in their eyes I want to yell at them not to put their dreams on hold, shout yes to today, and don't wait until tomorrow. I learned this from my father, in a letter written many years ago telling me to shoot for the moon and dance under the stars – before they all go out.

Letter from Sue

Thank you so much for reading 'Summer Flings and Dancing Dreams,' I hope you enjoyed Laura's Spanish adventure and are perhaps inspired to put on your dancing shoes and Flamenco round the living room? I hope so.

I have yet to leave the sofa to begin my own dancing career – but it's never too late to tango, and who knows, one day any one of us could be like Laura and find ourselves wrapped round a hot Spanish dancer moving to the sound of Englebert Humperdinck!

Anyway, if you enjoyed the book I would love it if you can spare the time between tangos to write a quick review and tell your friends – it would mean such a lot to me – and Laura/Lola!

I'm now writing my next book and as always am missing the characters from this one. I envied Laura as she became firm and slim and gorgeous (something I will never do from my position on the sofa!) and I loved meeting up with Mandy, the beauty therapist from, 'Love, Lies and Lemon Cake,' again. But I particularly enjoyed spending time with Tony whose teasing humour and drama queen tendencies remind me of so many friends I've loved and laughed with over the years - there's a little bit of all of them in Tony.

Anyway, if you'd like to know when my next book is released you can sign here:

www.suewatsonbooks.com/email.

I promise I won't share your email address with anyone, and I'll only send you a message when I have a new book out.

I would love for you to follow me on Facebook and please join me for a chat on Twitter... I'd really love to know what you think about the book and if it has inspired you to start dancing.

In the meantime, thanks again for reading, and if you happen to bump into a handsome Spanish guy who offers to write a poem for you - go with it. But take Laura's advice, enjoy the now and forget the forevers...

Sue

x

www.suewatsonbooks.com

www.facebook.com/suewatsonbooks

Twitter @suewatsonwriter